A SENSUAL ENCOUNTER

Roddy leaned his head down and kissed her just below her ear. A soft whispering caress that crimped her toes into knots. His hands were still tight on her shoulders; he shifted her slightly and drifted his mouth along her cheek to her lips. His kiss was harder this time, and not so whispery. Lucy felt her stomach heel over, fought the sensation, and then was carried away by it. Roddy's arms slid to her back, tugging her up against him, while his mouth played coaxingly on hers.

Lucy had spent the last twenty-four hours trying not to think about being kissed by Roddy Kempthorne. Which was a good thing, because she'd clearly had no idea how it would really feel. And if she had, she would have found a way to make him kiss her while they were still in the tree. Or while he was carrying her off on horseback. Or while her brother was purloining her trunk at the inn. She would never have let him stop kissing her. . . .

D0019803

COMING IN APRIL

The Gold Scent Bottle by Dorothy Mack

Max Waring left London after losing his fiancee—to his father. Returning four years later, he meets the lovely Abigail Monroe. Max has something of Miss Monroe's, and to get her property back, Abigail must pose as Max's bride-to-be. But pretending to be in love soon becomes more than just a game....

0-451-20003-9/$4.99

Falling for Chloe by Diane Farr

Sylvester "Gil" Gilliland is a friend—nothing more—to his childhood chum, Chloe. But Gil's mother sees more to their bond. And in a case of mother knows best, what seems a tender trap may free two stubborn hearts.

0-451-20004-7/$4.99

Breach of Promise by Elisabeth Fairchild

The village of Chipping Campden is abuzz with gossip when the local honey merchant, Miss Susan Fairford, leases her old home to a mysterious gentleman who calls himself Philip Stone. Time will tell whether bachelor and beekeeper can overcome their fears in order to discover just how much they have in common.

0-451-20005-5/$4.99

To order call: 1-800-788-6262

The Ramshackle Suitor

Nancy Butler

A SIGNET BOOK

SIGNET
Published by New American Library, a division of
Penguin Putnam Inc., 375 Hudson Street,
New York, New York 10014, U.S.A.
Penguin Books Ltd, 27 Wrights Lane,
London W8 5TZ, England
Penguin Books Australia Ltd, Ringwood,
Victoria, Australia
Penguin Books Canada Ltd, 10 Alcorn Avenue,
Toronto, Ontario, Canada M4V 3B2
Penguin Books (N.Z.) Ltd, 182–190 Wairau Road,
Auckland 10, New Zealand

Penguin Books Ltd, Registered Offices:
Harmondsworth, Middlesex, England

First published by Signet, an imprint of New American Library,
a division of Penguin Putnam Inc.

First Printing, March 2000
10 9 8 7 6 5 4 3 2 1

Copyright © Nancy Hajeski, 2000

For Eileen V., Chris R., and Mary R.N.
Three women with attitude to spare

Oh, young Lochinvar is come out of the West—
Through all the wide Border his steed was the best.
                              "Marmion"
                              SIR WALTER SCOTT

This fellow is wise enough to play the fool;
And to do that well craves a kind of wit.
                              Twelfth Night
                              WILLIAM SHAKESPEARE

Chapter One

How Roderick Kempthorne came to be lying in a boggy ditch, dressed in the finery of a cavalier from the court of King Charles II, was something of a long story. But then there was always a story or two hanging on the rumpled coattails of Roddy Kempthorne.

Miss Lucy Parnell, who happened upon him by accident while hiking across the moor, could not know about the exuberant birthday party for the young Earl of Steyne, which had occurred the previous evening on the other side of the moor. Neither could she know that the celebrants, soon bored with billiards and brandy, and bristling over the fact that their host had neglected to import any ladybirds to enliven the festivities, had tramped into the attic to ransack the numberless trunks of clothing that had lain there untouched for decades. These goings-on would not have amused her, even if she had been aware of them. Lucy Parnell considered herself a woman of serious intent; necessity had schooled her to firmly squelch her imagination.

Which was not to say that when Roddy reared up from the ditch beside her, roused by her footfalls from his brandy-induced slumbers, she did not let out a piercing shriek that would have done Mrs. Siddons proud.

"Damn!" Roddy said with an appreciative grin as he swept off his wide-brimmed, feathered hat and bowed to her from the midst of the withered bracken. "You've a fine set of lungs, ma'am."

Lucy clasped a hand to her breast, trying to still the erratic thudding of her heart. The young man, who had surely frightened ten years off her life, was gazing up at her with a genial expression on his grimy face.

"I thought you were a ghost," she said a bit crossly, as if to explain her uncharacteristic lapse into maidenly panic.

"Not a ghost," he said with conviction. He began to thump at his chest and shoulders with one hand to demonstrate his substantiality. "See?" he said. "Solid as a rock."

She thought he appeared quite unrocklike, as a matter of fact. He was weaving unsteadily on his booted feet and looked as though he might pitch over at any moment.

"I can see that you are not a specter, but why on earth are you dressed like the lead actor in a Congreve comedy?"

"Congreve?" His eyes widened.

"He is a playwright."

"Oh, playwrights," he muttered with a frown. "Annoying fellows, if you ask me. Spend their time scribbling away, and then expect a man to waste a perfectly good evening listening to a parcel of windy speeches."

Lucy, who had an abiding love for the theater in general and William Congreve in particular, scowled. "It is clear that any words spoken in a theater would go right over your head."

"Not true," he said. "Always sit up in the boxes. If anything, the words go under my head."

She ignored this. "You still haven't told me why you are dressed in such a bizarre fashion."

"Bizarre?"

"Oh, stop parroting everything I say," she muttered. "I almost wish you were a ghost, for I believe they keep silent for the most part. But you must admit you are dressed very strangely."

He glanced down at his clothing then, taking in the heavy fall of Mechlin lace at his throat and the long, brocaded coat with its wide skirts. He raised his hand and regarded the large felt hat that dangled there. There were traces of mire from the boggy ditch everywhere he looked.

An expression of sudden recollection widened his eyes as his mouth twisted in dismay. "Sweet Jesus," he whispered hoarsely, "Nonnie will have my guts for garters . . . he told me his great, great grandfather wore this suit to Westminster to see Charles crowned."

"It's only a bit of mud," she pronounced with authority. If there was one thing she knew her way around, as governess to young, inevitably grubby children, it was the removal of mud.

A salt-laden breeze came up then, stirring the tall weeds that edged the path. She swung her head toward the distant sea and saw a thick bank of fog rolling in. Her brow lowered. She had things to accomplish this morning, and the fog was going to put a stick in the spokes for sure.

"I must be off now," she said, catching up her skirt in one gloved hand. If she walked rapidly, she could make it back to the inn before the landscape was obliterated.

"What!" he cried as she moved away from the side of the ditch. "Aren't you going to help me up?" His voice was raised in good-natured pleading.

"You got yourself down there," she said briskly. "I expect you can get yourself out."

"Indeed, I did not get myself down here. I was attacked."

"By whom?" Her tone was just short of arch. "Footpads?"

"Sheep," he replied, and then added in a musing tone, "It's all coming back to me now. Nonnie's party . . . the attic. We all dressed up like Algernon's ancestors, you see. I drank a great deal of champagne . . . and brandy. And then I couldn't remember where the privy was. Oh, sorry, probably not a proper thing to bring up. But the next thing I recall, I was wandering about outside the house. Found a nice patch of shrubbery and well, er . . ."

Miss Parnell was gritting her teeth now.

"Faith, it was a spectacular night." His voice took on a melodic lilt. "Crisp and clear, with a sky full of light. I started counting the stars, and I suppose I just kept on walking and counting and counting and walking. Until I came across the sheep. Or rather they came across me."

"So to escape this horde of murderous sheep, you ran and hid in a ditch?"

"Hid?" he echoed, and then grinned when she scowled again. "Ah, don't expect me not to bait you, not when it puts such a delightful gleam in your eyes."

"I'm leaving now," she said. "And so should you, if you don't want to be trapped out here in the fog. And if you grin up at me and say 'Fog?' I shall hit you with my umbrella."

"Oh, I know what fog is. Live in London, don't you know. Well, most of the time. Only came to this infernal island to watch Nonnie turn twenty-five." He was attempting to negotiate the steep incline of the ditch as he spoke, with little success she saw. The knee-high leather boots he wore were not made for climbing over dew-slickened weeds. With a sigh of resignation she returned to the edge of the gully and held out the end of her umbrella.

He threw his head back and smiled up at her as he reached for the malacca handle. "There's the girl," he said softly. Something inside her chest constricted then, as she got a good look at his face. In spite of the mud which freckled his cheek and chin, it was the

most arresting face she had ever seen. Lean, bony almost, but with
a patrician arch to the nose, and a wide, mobile mouth that was at
present pursed into an amused, lopsided grin. There were dimples
beside that mouth, deep and endearingly puckish. And his eyes,
which had crinkled into merry arcs, were the true blue-violet of
irises and framed with sooty, sinfully dark lashes.

He's a devil with women, she thought. He had to be with that
face and those eyes. At that thought she nearly lost hold of her end
of the umbrella.

"Steady on," he cautioned her. "Don't want to send us both
tumbling down into the pit."

He grunted softly as he came over the lip of the incline. She
stepped back, a little timid now that he was standing beside her. He
should have looked ridiculous in his tattered costume, but the plain
truth was he didn't. Not a bit. He was tall enough to carry off the
sweeping coat and high boots and the elegant spill of lace that cas-
caded down his chest. Miss Parnell had secretly dreamed of dashing cavaliers since she was twelve, when she had happened upon a
history of the Stuart kings in her papa's library. This young man
could have stepped from the pages of that book.

Until he opened his mouth. "Lord love us," he drawled, "this is
a wretched island." He was pivoting his head from side to side,
surveying the surrounding landscape with open distaste. "Can't
imagine what Nonnie's ancestors were thinking to set up housekeeping in such a place."

"I think it's a beautiful island," she said. "But then I suppose it
looks less promising from the bottom of a gully."

Undaunted by her caustic tone, he merely took the feathered hat
from beneath his arm and clapped it on his head. The broad, white
plume had seen better days, but it still looked properly jaunty angled over his shoulder. He wiped his hands on his satin breeches
and then said, "Lead on," with an expectant expression on his face.

"I am going that way," she said, pointing to the west. "Toward
the Greene Man in Peel."

"Then so am I."

She frowned. The last thing she needed was this raggedy fellow
following her into the village. They already thought she was a bit
of an oddity—a woman traveling on her own. "No, I don't believe
that is where you are going."

"Don't have a clue where I'm going," he said evenly. "Told
you, I wandered off last night; I could be miles from Nonnie's
house."

"Surely you must have some idea where you came from."

"I came from London," he said without missing a beat. "Took a boat over from Liverpool. It was a wretched crossing. Snowball and the Joker cast up their accounts at least twice."

"You brought your dogs with you?"

"Dogs?" He chuckled softly. "That's a good one, ma'am. Wait till I tell them."

Small tendrils of fog were already scudding along the ground around Lucy's skirts. She knew the moor would be covered in a matter of minutes.

"Please," she said. "We need to get away from here or we will be trapped by the fog. If you can't remember where your friend lives, then you'd best come with me to the village."

"Of course I can remember where Nonnie lives," he protested in a pained voice. "It's a huge old pile of stones . . . puts me in mind of ghosties and goblins. Nonnie swears it's not haunted, but Snowball saw a young woman walking in the hall last night, and Lord knows, Nonnie ain't got any young women in that house. Had to be a ghost."

"I meant," she said with great patience, "if you can't find your way back to your friend's house."

"Well, how could I?" he asked. "I was drunk as a lord last night. Drunk as six lords."

Miss Parnell could detect the faint traces of brandy on his person. It had blended with the earthy smell of peat and wet bracken and the sharp tang of camphor into a not unpleasant aroma. It occurred to her then that he was probably still several sheets to the wind.

"You needn't sound so proud of the fact," she muttered as she began walking. "I don't see that getting drunk is much of an accomplishment."

He was silent after that as he plodded along behind her. She heard the crunch of his boots upon the pebbled path, and the soft swish of his brocaded coat. The sky overhead, which had been a hazy blue when she'd set out on her hike, had now gone a grizzled gray, several shades darker than the fog which swirled behind them. Lucy picked up her pace, moving over the uneven ground with long, easy strides.

"Hey, now!" he called out. "I can't keep up with you if you insist on loping along like a greyhound. These blasted boots were not made for walking across country, I can tell you."

She stopped and turned around. He was hobbling along in her wake, his hat now canted over one eye.

"You *are* a sorry specimen," she said, although there was a trace of humor in her voice. He really did look rather charmingly pathetic.

He came up even with her and, with a groan, settled his backside on a convenient boulder.

"Wasn't my idea to dress up like this," he complained. "Nonnie gets the credit for that brainstorm. But you've got to humor a man on his birthday."

Something clicked inside Lucy's head. The innkeeper in Peel had been full of excited chatter over the young Earl of Steyne's birthday. His father had been one of the Lords of Man and the villagers took it as a promising omen that his son had come among them again. That very morning her host had mentioned the birthday celebration which was to be held in Peel later that week to honor his lordship, Algernon Swithins, the seventh Earl of Steyne.

It now made sense. This hapless fellow in his ancient finery was one of the society sprigs who had come to the Isle of Man to keep the young earl company.

She was just about to ask him his name, when a muffled thudding echoed out of the fog behind them. Her companion's eyes widened in something like terror.

"Crikey!" he exclaimed, tumbling off the rock. "They've come back."

He caught up her hand and propelled her rapidly along the path, mindless of his ill-fitting boots. She tried to pull away from him, but he was surprisingly powerful for such a stripling.

"Stop fighting me!" he growled softly. "Just run!"

"But—"

He tightened his hold and increased his speed, till they were flying over the rough ground. At some point they lost the path and staggered over a hillock onto the moorland. Lucy could still hear the drumming sound behind her, and then, as she and her captor leapt in tandem over a small stream she heard the first lowing *baahs*.

"Sheep!" she cried in disbelief, digging her heels into the turf and dragging him to a halt. "We are fleeing from sheep? Of all the crack-brained—"

"Keep moving," he gasped. "They'll be upon us any second."

With a forceful tug, she managed to get her hand free. "Have you lost your wits? Sheep are harm—"

Just then the fog parted and she saw the tightly knit flock moving rapidly in their direction like a great woolly juggernaut. At its head was a large ram, whose twin sets of rippled horns curled around his bony forehead.

"Oh, Lord!" she cried. She knew enough about sheep to see that the ram meant business. His head was down and his little hooves sent up clods of peat as he galloped over the moor. She dropped her umbrella, lifted her skirts with both hands and fled. The young man likewise took to his heels, and she was sure she only imagined that he was laughing as he ran.

A lone tree, withered and gnarled, appeared on the horizon to their left. She felt his fingers on her wrist, drawing her in its direction. Once they reached the trunk, he pulled her behind it.

"Give me your leg," he said.

"What?" She saw that he had meshed his hands, as a groom did to help a rider mount a horse. She set her knee into his hands and let him boost her high into the air. She clawed her way onto a branch and then watched as he shinnied up behind her. Somehow, he'd lost his jaunty hat; it now lay at the base of the trunk. He was grinning furiously at her as he settled himself on a branch just below hers, straddling the limb with his long legs and leaning back against the trunk.

"Maybe next time you'll believe a fellow when he tells you he was attacked by sheep."

Any response she might have made was obliterated by the loud, resounding crack of the ram's head butting into the base of the tree. Lucy swore the whole tree shook from the impact.

"Is he mad, do you think?" she asked, looking down at the beast who was now circling the tree at a brisk, edgy trot.

"He's dashed cranky at the very least," he responded.

"I didn't mean—"

"I know," he said, showing his dimples. "But it's jolly fun to be at cross purposes with you, ma'am."

She rolled her eyes and said nothing. It was pointless to converse with him. Much better just to look at him, for there was at least some pleasure in that pursuit. It seemed the more rumpled and ragged he became, the more attractive he grew. His face was angled up toward her, the infuriating grin still playing about his mouth and dancing in his eyes.

She thought of Sir Humphrey Dumbarton, her one and only suitor back in England, and sighed. Sir Humphrey was a good man, a fair-minded landlord and an attentive son to his ailing mother. A lady would have to look far and wide to find such a worthy spouse. It wasn't his fault that he was inclined to portliness, or that his brown hair had begun to thin noticeably. And it certainly wasn't his fault that his eyes were not a heavenly shade of blue violet, or that his face lacked so much as one dimple. He, at least, could carry on a conversation without repeating everything she said. And he never drank, not even at dinner.

"Look, he's leaving," her companion whispered.

She peered down through the cover of brown leaves and saw that the ram was indeed moving off. His ewes parted to let him pass. They appeared to be some breed of wild sheep, their fleece hanging in long, matted strands below their bellies. Most were a mealy shade of dun, though there were a few brown-and-white specimens mixed in. The ram himself was nearly all brown. She'd seen similar feral sheep in the highlands of Scotland, but those beasts had been docile, if not downright timid.

She was about to make that observation out loud, when the ram came charging out of the herd and again plowed into the tree with a fearful crash. She threw her arms around the trunk to keep from pitching off her branch.

"You didn't by any chance have mutton for dinner last night?" she asked between her teeth. "Because he certainly seems to have taken you in dislike."

He shrugged. "I could have done. There were at least eleven courses served. I lost track of what I was eating after the salmon mousse."

And after the second bottle of claret, she added silently. She knew very well how much liquor a gentleman could imbibe during the course of a long meal.

Below them, the ram had discovered the wide-brimmed hat. He nudged it with his nose and then picked it up in his mouth and began to shake it about, like a terrier with a rat.

"I hope Nonnie wasn't attached to that hat," she said.

"Serves him right," he grumbled. "He lured us here under false pretenses. It was to have been a lively house party, which in my book means there will be females present. But except for his stepmama, and a bevy of nasty-tempered housemaids, there wasn't a one. That's no kind of house party at all, when the only company is the same plaguey fellows a man rubs elbows with every day in London."

He lapsed into silence then, leaning back against the trunk and watching the fog drift around them. Soon the sheep were obscured by the thick haze. An occasional plaintive *baah*, drifting up through the billowing sea of white, was the only testament to their presence. Even the ram seemed to have gotten over his snit and was browsing among the roots of the tree.

"I say, you're not cold, are you?" he asked after several minutes had passed.

"No, not at all. I know the weather can change out here from one minute to the next, so I dressed warmly for my hike."

"I can't imagine why anyone would purposely come walking in this godforsaken place. It's nothing but scrub and gorse, and chock full of boggy patches to boot."

"Yes, but you yourself commented on how spectacular the sky looked last night. There's a beauty to such wild places, don't you think?"

He raised his eyes to her face and said in a soft whisper, "Oh, there's a beauty here, all right."

Lucy felt her head go all fuzzy. He held her eyes for a long, breathless moment, and she feared she would plummet out of the tree like a stone if he didn't lower his gaze. But then she shook off her bemused fascination; he was just a feckless young man, and if he chose to toss compliments her way, it was his business. Seeing that she didn't respond to them, or give him one iota of encouragement, was hers.

"You have mud all over your face," she said, rebuffing him gently. She hoped his own vanity would distract him from saying ridiculous things to her.

"I daresay I do," he replied with a shrug. "It's a hazard when you spend the night in a ditch."

"Here . . ." Reaching gingerly behind her, she tugged off the small rucksack that was strapped to her back and pulled a cloth napkin and a water flask from the neatly packed interior. She doused the napkin with water and passed it down to him.

He scrubbed dutifully at his face until there wasn't a trace of mud left. "Well?" He looked at her expectantly. "Do I pass muster now?"

It would have been wiser to leave him as he was, she thought wistfully. He'd been wretchedly attractive splattered with mire, but now he fairly stole her breath. There was a faint stubbly shadow on his jaw, and two bright spots of color high up on his angular cheeks. He looked, at once, charmingly boyish and dangerously seductive. Moisture had clotted on his thick eyelashes and he swiped at them with his sleeve.

"You look much better," she said primly. "Rather more civilized."

She poured some water into the top of the flask, which was fashioned to serve as a cup, and handed it to him.

"No, you first," he said.

She drank it in one swallow and then refilled the cup. He took it from her hand, letting his long fingers linger for an instant on hers. "I must say, you are a dashed fine person to get stranded up a tree with. I don't suppose you've any food in there . . ."

Lucy drew out her leather lunchbox and held it up for his approval.

They shared her luncheon of oatcakes and cheese in silence. She watched as he consumed his portion with great gusto, and when he was done, he leaned back against the trunk and sighed. "That was possibly the best thing I've ever tasted."

"Even better than salmon mousse?"

He waved the thought away. "It must be sleeping in the open. Gives a fellow an appetite. But, Lord, I'd love a nap right about now." He was eyeing her speculatively. "Is it too much to hope you might let me lean my head upon your knee?" Since he followed up this nonsensical suggestion by doing that exact thing, Lucy didn't have time to think of a scathing reply.

"Mmm," he crooned as he snuggled against her.

"Stop that!" she said sharply, trying to dislodge his head with her hands. "I never said you could—"

He propped himself upright, a hand on either side of her and gave her a lazy smile. "Ah, take care now. You'll fret yourself right off that branch. You don't want to end up down there with the demon ram now, do you?"

He crossed his arms in her lap and laid his head upon them.

"Besides," he murmured, "you rescued me, so it's your job to see I'm properly looked after."

"My job?" she sputtered.

But he wasn't listening. He seemed to have fallen into a deep sleep almost instantly. His breath whispered in the air, a quick inhale and then a long, sibilant exhale. She sat there, afraid to move lest she send them both tumbling. But she was quivering with annoyance. How could he behave with so little restraint? Even Sir Humphrey had never dared anything so intimate with her.

Soon the heat from his body had permeated her pelisse and her skirt and even her petticoats. She fancied it might have even passed beyond the layer of skin, to her very bones. In spite of what she'd said to him, she had been starting to feel the cold. But not any longer.

He shifted slightly in his sleep and, fearing that he might unbalance himself, she leaned forward and placed her hands upon his shoulders. It was the only charitable thing to do, she reasoned. Never mind that it felt strangely comforting to hold him there, warm and relaxed, against her knees.

Chapter Two

Lucy must have dozed. She was leaning against the tree trunk, her head canted onto her shoulder, when the *baahs* of the sheep awoke her. The flock was wandering around the tree, picking at the gorse and dried heather. Fog still blanketed the landscape, a soft billowing shroud that parted occasionally to reveal a tempting, distant glimpse of hillock or rock pile. Above the treetop a watery sun was trying to break free of the hazy gray clouds, but as yet with no success.

Lucy sighed and wondered how the morning had turned into such a farce. First there was her infuriating encounter with the solicitor in Peel, whose smug and blatant refusal to answer her questions had sent her hiking furiously across the moorland to work off her vexation. Then the disheveled young man had accosted her from the ditch, after which the fog rolled in and the demon ram appeared. Nothing was going her way.

And she had so little time. Somewhere here, on the Isle of Man, she hoped to find the answer to a very important question. But if her morning encounter with Mr. Plimpton was any indication, it was going to be an uphill journey. As she'd learned the day before, when she arrived in the small seaside town and began asking questions, the Manx were a taciturn people, at least to off-islanders who came poking around with vague inquiries about things that had happened years before. Though no one had actually been rude to her, they hadn't been exactly forthcoming either.

The money for this trip, which she had inherited on the death of her mother, only afforded her one week for her search. After that time she had to return to her employer in Manchester. She couldn't bear it if she was forced to leave without any answers.

Find me. The voice, a young child's voice, echoed again inside her head. It was that voice, poignant and full of pain, that spurred her on. It would make her overlook the islanders' grumbling rebuffs and keep on with her search. However, sitting on a branch in a dead tree was not aiding her cause one bit.

"Drat!" she muttered softly.

The young man still slept on her lap, his dark hair spilling over his forearm. Up close she saw that there were laugh lines radiating out from his eyes and the beginning of a crease on either side of his mouth; he was older than she'd first thought, perhaps five- or six-and-twenty. Not a youth, then, but an adult man in the early stages of a very promising prime. She longed to gaze at his fine-boned cheek and lazy, sculpted mouth awhile longer, but both her legs had developed a severe case of pins and needles.

She gently shook his shoulders. "You must wake up now."

"Mmmm . . ." He burrowed his head deeper into his crossed arms.

"Really, you must." Her voice raised a notch. "Do you hear me?"

He lifted his head and squinted. Even that unpleasant expression looked charming on his boyish face.

"You sound like a governess," he mused irritably. "I know that tone of voice. Me and m'sisters had a whole plaguey string of them. Starchy old harridans . . ." He unfolded his arms and drew back from her, shifting his weight again onto his own branch. "You'd best look out, ma'am, or you will end up just like them, in spite of having such a splendid lap."

"I *am* a governess," she retorted a little sharply. His disparaging tone had stung her more than she liked to admit. "And not at all ashamed of the fact. It is a rewarding endeavor."

His mouth twisted. "What? Looking after another woman's brats? More of a fool's errand, that."

She swung her gaze away from him. "Yes, I wonder why I chose such a course when there are so many other gratifying professions open to women."

He looked sober for a moment, like a child who had stumbled upon a difficult and perplexing puzzle. "I say . . . I mean, I am sorry. I never thought of it that way before. That it's not something a woman in her right mind would ever choose to do. Lord, when I think of the hard times I gave my governesses. I never realized they had been forced into it."

"Not forced perhaps. It's not indentured servitude, after all." Lucy smiled ruefully—her previous post had felt like just that thing. "But when women need to earn their own keep, there are not many avenues open to them."

He was gazing at her assessingly now. "Why aren't you married?" It came out almost like an accusation. "You're certainly not an antidote. And you've a dashed pretty smile, when you care to use it."

Lucy drew up her mouth into a tiny frown. "That is hardly your business, Mr.—"

"Kempthorne," he said. "Roderick Kempthorne, to be precise. Though my friends call me Roddy. Ramshackle Roddy, when they are in their cups."

"I cannot imagine why," she said dryly.

"Neither can I," he responded. Then he chuckled. "No, I've earned that name a few times over, I suppose. And do you have a name?"

"It's Parnell. Lucy Parnell."

"Parnell is an Irish name."

She nodded. "My father's family was from Ulster originally."

"My mother's family lives in Derry," he said. "And my father is from Trouro. They say in the *ton* that I'm half Irish, half Cornish and all foolish." He gave her that gaping, good-natured spaniel grin again.

"You say that as though you're proud of it. I imagine most men would prefer to be known as the best of sports or the wisest of sages."

"Well, it's better than being Lucy Parnell, known for her famous scowl. What would I have to do to get you to smile at me, I wonder?" He laid one arm across her knee and looked her straight in the eyes. His voice lowered an octave. "Maybe if I kissed you . . ."

Lucy thought the ram must have crashed into the tree again, so violent was the shiver that coursed through her at that sultry whisper.

She firmly pushed his arm from her lap. "Of all the arrant nonsense, Mr. Kempthorne. I suggest you save your foolish flirtation for ladies who are still wet behind the ears."

"Oh, and you are such a Methuselah," he shot back. "I wonder you can walk without leaning upon a stick."

Lucy wished she had a stick just then, though not for the purpose he'd stated. She wondered how long he'd manage to outrun the demon ram once she'd batted him off his perch and to the turf below.

He must have read the devilment in her eyes, since he shifted around and grabbed on to the tree trunk with both hands. "'Ware now, Miss Parnell. You wouldn't want to do any further harm to Nonnie's grandpater's fine suit."

Before she could respond, they were both distracted by the baying of a lone hound. The keening tenor yelps echoed eerily through the thinning fog.

"Ah," Roddy pronounced, "a demon hound to chase away the demon ram."

"I doubt that would improve our situation," she responded, trying to hide her nervousness. "At least rams are not known to be carnivores. I'd as lief take my chances with a sheep as a wild dog."

The baying came closer and was followed immediately by the muffled thud of galloping horses. Roddy gave a piercing whistle and cried, "Over here!" He was tugging himself upright so he could stand on the limb.

"What in blazes are you doing?" Lucy hissed. "We don't know who is out there . . . though it's probably more poor souls lost in the fog."

"Yes," Roddy said, looking down at her. "And if it is hunters, they doubtless have a flask of brandy. The one thing you neglected to pack in your trusty knapsack."

"I don't make a habit of carrying spirits," she huffed.

"More's the pity. It has lowered you several notches in my estimation, I can tell you."

A large tan-and-white hound came loping out of the fog. The sheep scurried away, blending back into the mist. Three riders came into view hard on the dog's heels. One of the men led a riderless horse on a rope lead.

Roddy Kempthorne gave a loud bellow of welcome and began to caper on his branch like a demented wood sprite. "Oh, this is rare."

Lucy rolled her eyes. "I take it you know these men."

"It's Nonnie and the Joker and Snowball. Oh, and Elizabeth."

Since it was clear there were no women in the group that now drew to a halt beneath their tree, Lucy could only assume that Elizabeth was the tan-and-white hound.

The lead rider, a strapping young man with a large nose, appeared to be wearing barrister's robes over his riding breeches. He slid from his horse and began to lavishly pet the dog. "That's my Bess, that's my good girl." He cocked an eye up at Roddy. "You gave us a devil of a chase, Ram. Good thing you left your Hessians up in the attic—Bess was able to make your trail after only a few false starts."

A fair-haired young man wearing a blazingly blue medieval surcoat and a hat that resembled a turnip tipped his head back and winked up at Roddy. "Good old Bess nearly had us digging up a badger's burrow, until Snowball convinced us that however much in your cups you might have been last night, you would never have gone to earth in such a damp, smelly place."

The third man, the only one of the three who was not dressed like a reveler from a masquerade ball, ran a hand through his already disordered black curls and drawled, "By the look of him, he didn't overnight in any civilized spot."

"Got chased into a ditch, Snow," Roddy said with a shrug. "And if any one of you makes a cutting remark, I will not hesitate to recall equally unsavory places where each of you has slept off a night on the town."

This warning set the three men to grumbling slightly. Bess, meanwhile, was trying to clamber up the tree trunk, unsatisfied until she got within licking range of her quarry.

"So, are you coming down?" Snowball said. "Or should we reconvene the party up in the branches?"

"As if any of you have a prayer of climbing a tree after last night's excesses," Roddy said with a shake of his head. "No, no, we'll come down."

Once it had filtered into their collective brains that their friend had used a plural pronoun, the three men drew closer to the trunk of the tree and peered up through the dried brown leaves.

Lucy shifted forward on her branch and offered them an anemic smile. As she met Nonnie's pale blue eyes, his mouth dropped open.

"He did it!" he proclaimed in a voice of awe.

"By all that's holy," Snowball uttered. "He actually did."

"I'll say he did!" the Joker echoed.

"What did you do?" Lucy asked Roddy under her breath.

"Nothing," he said, looking away from her. "Don't pay them any mind. Still half foxed, the lot of them."

"Well, bring her down so we can see," Nonnie crowed. "She's not any use to us up a tree."

"Oh, bother," Roddy muttered. He took up her hand and said very quickly, "I promise no harm will come to you, but let them have their May game. It's Nonnie's birthday, after all."

"But I—"

"Bring her down," the Joker echoed. "I want to see what sort of damsel Roddy managed to find in the middle of a blasted marsh."

Roddy gave her one last beseeching look and then lowered himself gingerly from his perch, dangling off the lowest branch by his two hands for several swings before he let go and landed cat-like on his feet. He turned his face up to her. "Now you . . ."

Lucy had an uncanny premonition that she should stay in the tree, a safe ten feet off the ground. The fog would be clearing soon—already the sun was breaking through the blockade of clouds and its heat would dispatch the fog. She'd see to her business and then walk back to the inn, partake of tea and Mrs. Greene's wonderful scones. Afterward she'd have a long restorative nap, and this morning's misadventure would be just a memory.

She waved them off, with a tiny motion of her hand, as though she were shooing away a persistent lapdog. "Please don't trouble yourself over me. I will be fine."

"I rather think that is for us to decide," the Joker drawled. Nonnie guffawed. Roddy's brow darkened.

The Joker urged his horse forward until it was beneath the tree. He gave her a leering smile. "You must come down, sweetheart. Roddy can't claim payment on his bet if you don't."

"His bet?" she said with terrible restraint. But her eyes flashed wickedly enough for the blond man to see.

"Nice eyes," he said with approval, turning back to Roddy. "That hazel color that changes with their moods. I recall a whore once at Sally Birch's with eyes like that. Damned if they didn't go quite golden when I—"

"Please, miss," Snowball interrupted him. "We can't just ride off and leave you alone."

He was smiling up at her. Though she knew his pale, narrow face was not a patch on Roddy's for looks, or on the odious Joker's either, for that matter, he had a charming smile. But she was not reassured.

Her years as a governess had taught her many things; paramount among them was the understanding that a woman who was not a member of society was fair game for the gentlemen who were. She'd had to fight off her share of unwanted advances in the past seven years, but had never had to contend with more than one insistent young gentleman at a time. There were at present four of that ilk beneath her tree. And at least two of them were eyeing her with open speculation, as though she were a tasty tidbit on a tea tray.

"Please," Roddy said, laying one hand on the trunk and raising

the other up to her, fingers extended. "Come down now. I know
they look a motley group, but there's absolutely no harm in them."

The Joker winked broadly at Nonnie. "No harm at all," he
whispered archly.

Roddy spun round with a hiss and to Lucy's amazement proceeded to unseat the blond man by the simple means of thrusting
one hand under his stirruped foot and tipping him out of the saddle.
The Joker hit the ground with a thud. The turnip hat went flying
and landed in a bramble bush. Bess immediately retrieved it and
went trotting off with her booty.

The Joker leapt to his feet, his fists flexing before him. "Damn
you, Roddy, that's a dirty trick."

"You'll keep your tongue between your teeth," Roddy muttered, his outthrust chin only inches away from Joker's face. "Miss
Parnell is not . . . she is not . . ."

"I think we can all see what she is not," Snowball interjected
softly. "What she is, is more to the point."

"I am a governess," Lucy said as she negotiated her way down
from her branch to the one below it.

"Oh, a governess," Nonnie said with a tiny wince. "Pardon,
ma'am. Roddy bet us he would find a ladybird somewhere on the
island. Roddy rarely loses his bets."

"Oh no," Roddy said from over his shoulder. He was at present
standing beneath the tree and making encouraging faces up at
Lucy. "I said I would find us an attractive, amusing lady to relieve
the endless tedium at Ballabragh. Having spent the better part of
the morning with Miss Parnell, I can assure you she in every way
fits that description."

"Governesses are never amusing," the Joker said under his
breath, and then, when Roddy scowled at him menacingly, he
turned away and pretended to fuss with his saddle's girth.

Once Lucy reached the lower branch, she realized that unless
she swung herself down, as Roddy had done, she would have to
jump the last eight feet. Landing on her face in the mud in front of
these four men was not to be considered. Roddy caught her eye
and smiled. "I don't suppose you trust me to catch you."

She shook her head slowly. "You're bound to muddle it," she
said. "You're still fairly bosky."

He looked around and bit his lip. Then he went striding over to
Snowball, who still held the lead line of the spare horse. He undid
the tether, coiled the rope, and handed it to his friend, and then
mounted the beast in one fluid motion.

"Here" he said, nudging his horse up again the tree trunk. "Just shinny down onto my horse's rump."

Lucy held her breath as she scraped down the face of the trunk, reaching with her toes until they came into contact with the horse's wide posterior. With a sigh, she released the thin branch she'd been clutching and lowered herself into a sitting position.

"Well done!" Nonnie proclaimed, clapping his hands slowly. "Never seen *that* performed at Astley's."

Lucy was about to scramble down from the horse's back when Roddy shifted around and slid his arm about her waist.

"What—?"

He'd scooped her off the beast's rump and swung her around him, settling her sideways on the front of the saddle before she could object. Then he slipped her rucksack from her back and tossed it to Snowball, who caught it deftly by one strap.

"Not much of a prize," Snowball said with a grin as he slung it over one shoulder. "As usual Roddy gets the best pickings."

"What do you think you're doing?" Lucy cried, drumming her feet against the horse's side. The horse took umbrage at this treatment and began to dance sideways.

"Stop squirming," Roddy cautioned as he steadied his mount. "More ill has come of women squirming than from any two countries spatting over boundaries. Now keep still."

"But you can't—"

"Of course I can." He leaned forward and whispered against her ear. "And I believe we'll leave these fellows behind to sober up a bit."

Before she could utter another word of protest, Roddy set his heels against the horse's flanks. The horse moved out from under the tree and crossed the clearing at a trot. By the time Lucy got her wits back, they were flying full tilt across the moor in the opposite direction from where the village lay. The fog parted to let them pass, as if by magic. Roddy's lean arm was hard around her middle, keeping her snug against his chest. She had no choice but to move with him, their bodies swaying in tandem, absorbing the pounding motion of the wild gallop. Her hair had come down from its demure chignon and whipped about their heads.

"I will not be the object of a bet!" she cried over the shuddering wind. "I will not!"

"Didn't take you for a spoilsport, Miss Parnell," he called out merrily. "I promised no one will harm you . . . and you will like Ballabragh. I fancy it's miles better than some shabby village inn."

Lucy made a noise that sounded suspiciously like a growl. Roddy merely chuckled and tucked her up tighter against him.

"Stop that! I cannot breathe."

"Don't want to lose you in a ditch," he said. But he did loosen his hold slightly.

They were riding along the sea cliffs now. At that higher altitude, there was no sign of the fog. The Irish Sea stretched out below them, an endless vista of blue, frosted with roiling whitecaps.

Roddy came to a high pile of stones and pulled up.

"Lost?" she said, craning around to glare at him. "Maybe you should not have abandoned your rescuers so abruptly."

"Not lost," he said. "Just wanted to admire the view." He lowered his head and held her with his eyes. "It's truly remarkable."

Lucy growled again and pointed over his right shoulder. "The view is over there."

"Depends on what a fellow finds inspiring. Now take the sea . . . some men can gaze at it and think any number of profound things. I look at the sea and wonder what sort of fish I'll be having for dinner. But when I look into a woman's eyes, Miss Parnell, when I see beyond the lashes and behind the pool of color, why, I swear I could hold my own with any philosopher on the planet."

Lucy swung her face away from his persistent stare. "If you see anything other than anger and vexation in my eyes, you are more than a philosopher, Mr. Kempthorne, you are a delusional nodcock."

He raised one hand to her chin and forced her to look at him. His eyes were no longer playfully baiting, they had gone a deep dark violet. "You are not angry," he said softly. "You are afraid. But curious. And you are confused by that curiosity." He stroked his thumb along her cheek, the faintest of caresses. "It's never wrong to be curious, Lucy. Just wrong to resist it."

Lucy feared the turf had given way beneath the fretful horse. At least that was how it felt to her . . . the world tumbling away into nothingness. His words slid past her guard and her carefully schooled dignity—his idle prattling had been replaced by something much more potent. And the touch of his finger playing over her skin was making her tremble with some unnamed emotion. She had never been this close to a man before, held so intimately, right up against his body.

She shook herself firmly. Roddy Kempthorne was speaking nonsense in that sultry lilting voice and she'd better keep her wits about her. This was no time for fanciful imaginings, for wondering what that wide, wonderful mouth would feel like pressed against her own.

"Please," she said, tugging his hand away from her chin but keeping her eyes locked on his. "Let me go back to the inn. I have done you no harm, that you should treat me with such disregard. I aided you, in fact. What sort of repayment is that?"

He shook his head. "I am repaying you. By making you a part of a capital game. But you've got to trust me."

She sighed deeply. She knew what sort of games young men of the *ton* played . . . careless, hurtful games. "Why should I trust you? You have carried me off without so much as a by-your-leave . . . and for what purpose I cannot begin to imagine."

"Oh, can't you?" he asked in a lazy whisper.

Lucy drew back her arm and boxed his ears soundly. Roddy yelped, and then began to chuckle. "Sounded like the Joker just then, didn't I? It takes a deal of practice to cultivate that oily tone. The Joker does not have much success with women, as you might guess."

Lucy gave a tiny whine. "Can you not be serious for two minutes in a row? Listen to me, Mr. Kempthorne . . . It's bad enough I spent the morning with you up a tree, but if you take me to the earl's home, my reputation will be in tatters. I . . . I have a family connection who is very much of a high stickler about such things, and were he to discover I spent even one hour in a house filled with young gentlemen, he would make my life a misery."

"Hmmph!" Roddy commented. "If he's so concerned about you, why are you working as a governess? I haven't been hanging about in the *ton* since I was breeched without knowing a lady of quality when I stumble across one. So why aren't you off in London or Dublin dancing the night away instead of slaving for some lazy matron?"

When Lucy did not answer he added, "And who is this paragon who sits in judgment on you?"

"He is a relation—though not by blood—who thinks he needs to look after my welfare. Not that it is any of your business," she added stiffly.

"A meddling busybody then," Roddy said with a sneer. "Who makes you dance to his tune, but who hasn't the decency to see to your happiness."

This salvo was so incredibly on target that Lucy had to resist the urge to cry. Roddy, who for all his apparent witlessness, had a certain insight to her inner workings, merely drew her head against his shoulder and urged the horse forward at a slow, easy lope.

"As I was saying, you will enjoy Ballabragh. Nonnie's father, the old earl, rarely came here—it's only one of his properties—but he made sure it was kept up. The drawing room is quite pleasant, if you don't mind everything looking like it was carried directly from some pharaoh's tomb. And the great hall has a rather nice bit of fan vaulting, if you care to bother with such neck-stiffening pursuits as looking at old ceilings." While he spoke, Roddy was patting her shoulder in a consoling manner. "There are about a thousand musty pictures in the portrait gallery, which prove only that Nonnie's nose is not an accident of nature, but rather something his forefathers bequeathed him . . .

Lucy gave a weak giggle and Roddy tipped her head back. "Feeling better now?"

She nodded and grinned at him and then, wondering what had come over her, shook her head emphatically. "No, I am not feeling better. You are beyond reasoning with. If I wasn't afraid of being caught in a bog, I would leap down from this horse and make my way back to the inn."

"Faint heart?" he asked, canting his head down so that his words sighed against her cheek.

"Yes," she said. "I saw a deer caught in a mire only yesterday outside of Peel. Poor thing had worn itself out struggling and was covered with froth. Now I know how the beast felt."

He ran his hand along her face and down the side of her throat. She reeled back, which only brought her up against the wall of his chest. "Stop that!"

"Just checking for froth," he said lightly. "So what happened to the deer? Sucked to its death?"

"No, a farmer came along in a wagon and I entreated him to pull it out. I fancy he thought I was mad, but he got a rope around its neck and between us we freed the poor beast. Which was a relief . . . I was afraid I would have to shoot it otherwise."

"Shoot it?" He drew up his horse again.

"To put it out of its misery, you see."

"You carry a pistol?"

"Mmm, in my rucksack."

"Lord," he said with a whistle, "I hope Snowball doesn't do himself an injury with it. He was a tad careless, slinging your pack over his shoulder."

"It's not loaded," she said. "I carry the balls and powder separately."

"Very wise," he said sagely. "That way if you are waylaid, you can ask your assailants to wait until you have loaded your pistol before they have at you."

"Don't mock me. If I had leveled it at you, you'd have no way of knowing whether it was loaded or not."

"I gather you wish you had it with you now."

"Fervently," she replied.

He laughed and ruffled her hair. "You are a bloodthirsty creature, Miss Parnell."

She pushed his hand away, and then, before he could set his heels to his mount again, she boosted herself off the horse's withers and landed lightly on the ground.

"Oh, that's no fun!" he cried as she started walking back along the cliffs at a healthy clip. "I promise you a lark, and you act as though I am luring you into a den of vice."

"Sometimes life is more than a lark, Mr. Kempthorne," she said without turning her head. "I am on this island for a reason, there is something I need to find. I do not have the leisure to play May games."

He brought his horse alongside her, keeping pace with her long strides. "Ah, I detect a mystery."

Lucy blew out a weary breath, but said nothing. She was discovering that the less one said to Roddy Kempthorne, the better.

"You might enlist us in your search," he commented. "Four idle fellows with time hanging heavy on their hands. You could do worse, you know. Snowball is clever, the Joker is a natural-born ferret, and Nonnie may not be long on brains, but there are few doors closed to him on this island."

She stopped and looked up at him. "And what will you bring to this endeavor?"

He grinned. "Why, I'll be your bodyguard, of course. I'll stick close and ward off anyone who threatens you."

"You've been reading Mrs. Radcliffe," she muttered. And started walking again.

"What was that?"

"Nothing," she huffed. "I keep forgetting that talking to you is pointless."

"Oh, now you've hurt my feelings. I am only looking for a way to be of service to you."

"Then go away. I gather you would like to think yourself

something of a Lochinvar, but I don't need looking after. And in fact, you are giving me the devil of a headache."

To Lucy's astonishment he drew up his horse. She went on another twenty paces and cast a quick look over her shoulder. He was sitting there unmoving on the rocky path, his head down, his shoulders in a pronounced droop.

Find me. The child's voice drifted into her head, sad and lost and so very plaintive. It shocked her to hear it in daylight, that which had haunted her nightly dreams for months. She started to shiver noticeably.

Roddy must have sensed something was wrong; he set his horse forward and when he reached her, slid from the saddle and put one hand out.

"Are you ill, Miss Parnell?"

She shook her head. "No . . . no, it's just a feeling I get at times. Nothing I can explain . . ." Taking several deep breaths, she at last managed a weak smile. "I am fine now."

He was still looking at her with concern.

"And I am sorry I was rude to you."

His expression of concern increased. "You must be ill, if you are apologizing to me, ma'am."

Lucy found herself grinning. "Am I such a shrew then, Mr. Kempthorne? I can only blame my temperament on the strange morning I've had." She touched the sleeve of his coat. "But I really must be going. Good day."

"You're sure you'll be all right? I feel like a beast now for carrying you so far. Let me at least take you back closer to the village."

Lucy shook her head. The last thing she needed was to be cradled again in his arms. The first time had nearly undermined her sense of propriety. "I was headed this way today. And I don't mind the walk back. Truly."

"And what of the bogs?"

"I'll take my chances. There's no danger if I keep to the path."

"Good luck with your search," he said softly. He held one hand out to her and she took it, thinking he meant to shake it. Instead he raised it to his mouth and kissed the palm, a long, slow, lingering kiss. Lucy's stomach did a tiny somersault.

She did not snatch her hand back as her conscience prompted her to. Instead she closed her eyes for an instant and let the thrilling sensation wash over her. He may have been a callow, foolish young man, easily five or six years her junior, but he had a mouth that felt like satin again her skin.

When he freed her hand at last, he was smiling. "I wish you'd let me play this Lochinvar fellow for you, ma'am, whoever he might be."

"He is a character created by Walter Scott."

"Another playwright?" he asked artlessly.

Lucy shook her head slowly, trying to keep the bemused expression from her face. Mr. Kempthorne's governesses had surely had their work cut out for them.

Roddy shrugged and remounted his horse. Lucy looked up at him with a half smile playing over her mouth. Whatever had passed between them that morning could have no lasting meaning in her life, but it would furnish a pleasing memory.

She again started along the path. This time he did not follow her and she did not turn around to give him any encouragement. When the narrow path diverted away from the cliffs, she followed it inland, toward a cluster of rough stone houses. Lucy prayed that she would find an answer here. Or that somewhere, in some hamlet on this island, she would come across the child who cried in her dreams.

As she made her way down from the high cliff to the snug valley where the houses lay, a momentary pang of regret washed over her, a longing for more than a chance acquaintance with a playful, charming young man like Roddy Kempthorne. But she had made her choice all those years ago, to forego the position she'd been born to, and to toil for her bread. Young men of the *ton* were no longer an option. Not even for her dreams.

Still, it was a pity that she would never again look upon that lean, engaging face. Or feel the whisper of his mouth against her skin.

Chapter Three

Lucy sat finishing her breakfast in the dining parlor. As the inn's sole guest, she had the room to herself except for the landlady's tailless cat, which lounged on the windowsill. It was a pleasant space to plan out her day without interruption. At present she was reviewing the notes she had written in her journal. The blacksmith at the village near the cliffs had been a garrulous man and had furnished her with several possible leads. Now it was only a matter of following up on them. She'd rent the innkeeper's dogcart and go inland this afternoon. Not a hardship, since it was a glorious day for a jaunt—the morning had dawned bright and balmy. Mr. Greene had commented yesterday that spring was taking its time appearing on the island, but the soft breeze that wafted in through the inn's open windows promised a taste of warmer weather at last.

Even after nearly fifteen years of living in England, Lucy still hadn't adjusted to the mild weather. She had been born in Ceylon, a land of violent extremes—the dry, dusty heat of summer followed by the ceaseless, driving rain of the monsoon season. There were nights when she lay in her bedroom in Manchester, listening to the rain beating on the slate roof of her employers' home. It sounded eerily like the sharp patter of monsoon rain on the baked tiles of the veranda at her father's tea plantation outside Kandy. She would feel a homesickness then that tore at her insides, for a home that no longer stood, and a fierce longing for the man who had fathered her, who had ultimately forfeited his life to the violent seasons of his adopted country.

At least the dream had not troubled her last night, which she took as a good omen. She'd awoken refreshed and hopeful. And perhaps a bit heartsore, when she recalled her encounter with Mr. Kempthorne. If she was still in Peel on Saturday, she might catch a glimpse of him at the village fete. But it was unlikely; if her search proved fruitful, she would be otherwise occupied, and if it proved unsuccessful, she would be too cast down to join in any type of celebration.

So Roddy Kempthorne would be tucked away with her other memories of the island, along with the vivid, rugged landscape, the quaint limestone houses, and the wide, blue sea. A charming recollection to amuse her in her old age, once she grew too old to be a governess. Since she was quite alone in the world, it was a bleak future she envisioned then, unenlivened by the antics of her young charges. Perhaps one or two of the children she had taught would continue to write to her, as she had done with Miss Purdy, her own beloved governess. Would those letters sustain her? Would her memories of Roddy, and the other young men who had occasionally smiled upon her, offer her some solace? Or would they become needling reminders of the barrenness of her own life?

Lucy sighed. Lord, she was becoming maudlin.

If she feared the solitude of old age, she had only to accept Sir Humphrey's repeated proposals of marriage. He had not repeated his offer after Lucy's mother died in the winter, since she was technically in mourning. However, she knew he would break with protocol if she gave him the slightest encouragement.

His courtship had begun nearly three years ago, soon after she had gone to work for the Burbridge family near Manchester. Mrs. Burbridge had been delighted by her neighbor's interest in her new governess. It was a pity Lucy wasn't equally delighted. But try as she might, she couldn't muster anything stronger than amused tolerance for the man. She doubted that emotion was the sort that forged the bonds which matrimony required.

In spite of Sir Humphrey's sometimes tiresome attentions, her time with the Burbridges had been one of contentment. Their three children were bright and curious and brimming with fun. She missed them now, dreadfully, and after only four days. Sometimes she had to pinch herself over her good fortune, especially when she recalled her first post in the Scottish Highlands with the MacTeague family. They'd been parsimonious, short with their servants, and had two hell-born children who made Lucy question her abilities as teacher. When she left them, after their daughter went off to finishing school, Lucy knew she had managed to instill some amount of learning into the children's thick heads, which was a consolation. It gave her the confidence to accept the post with the Burbridges.

Then three months ago, her mother had died. And the dreams had started, the disturbing haunting cries of a lost child that made

Lucy fearful of sleep. She grew gaunt and lost all her bloom. It was
Mrs. Burbridge who suggested she might need a holiday. Lucy
took her employer's kind offer as a sign that she should at least attempt to discover the truth behind those dreams.

So here she sat, armed only with her instincts and a very salient
piece of information she had stumbled across in December while
at her stepbrother's home for her mother's funeral. She had always
suspected, but now she knew. And knowing, she had to take action.
It was that simple.

If her stepbrother got wind of her whereabouts, he would be in-
censed. She could almost hear him ringing a peal over her, his
piercing voice rising and falling—

"Of course I don't need to be announced."

The cat sat up at once and laid its ears back.

Oh, God! Lucy's head flew up. He was here at the inn, as
though she had conjured him—like Beelzebub—just by thinking
about him. She quickly shut her journal and laid her napkin over it.

The parlor door swung open and Yardley Abbott stepped into
the room. He was a tall man, cadaverously thin, dressed in a fine
suit of black broadcloth. The stark white of his cravat reflected up
onto the sallow, stretched skin of his narrow face.

"What madness is this, Lucy?" he growled softly, without pre-
amble.

She set down her teacup and drew a long steadying breath. "I
am on holiday, Yardley. Hardly madness. You've been known to
take them yourself, as I recall."

"Holiday?" he said. "Here?" He made a disparaging gesture
with both hands, though directed at the room or toward the whole
island, she could not tell.

"This is a very restful place," she said, meeting his dark eyes.

They narrowed into deep crevices, pulling at his taut cheek-
bones. "It is totally improper that you are here. All alone." He
crossed his hands over his lean belly, looking for all the world like
a starchy schoolmaster—which was what he was.

Her eyes widened. "Oh, have the innkeeper and his wife gone
away?"

"Don't fence with me, Lucy. You know precisely what I mean.
It's not fitting for a lady to be sitting in the common parlor. Any
sort of riffraff could walk in."

It just has, she remarked wryly to herself.

Lucy could barely contain her elation. If she had gone to the
Isle of Wight or the Outer Hebrides, Yardley would still be sitting

in his manor house outside Oxford, plotting the downfall of his academic rivals with Sophia, his viper of a wife. The fact that he was here now, on this particular island, only corroborated that she was on the right track.

"As a governess, I am no longer constricted by such silly conventions. I am surprised to see you here . . . in the middle of school term."

"I told the dean my bookseller had come across a report of a rare medieval manuscript for sale in Dublin. They were all too eager for me to track it down for the Bodleian. I have some expertise in that area, you know."

She nodded; his scholarship could not be faulted, only his humanity.

"And how did you find me? Only the Burbridges knew I intended to come here."

"I spoke with Sir Humphrey while he was at my home for your mother's funeral; I asked him to keep me informed about your state of mind. He wrote to me last week, said he was worried, that you'd been ill. And that you'd gotten some harebrained notion to visit Man."

"You set Sir Humphrey to spy on me?" Her voice rose a notch. "He had no right to tell you anything."

He crossed to the table, setting his hands on its edge. "I insist you come away with me this afternoon. I am done with looking the other way while you follow your own wayward impulses. It is bad enough that you gave up your rightful position in life to work for cits . . . and now, this jaunting about on your own. It is intolerable. I have my reputation to think of, Lucy. I was able to hush up the scandal over your sister, thank God, but then I was not so highly placed at the time. I was not under such scrutiny. Now I cannot afford to watch my other sister become a byword. So you will heed me and leave this place."

Her eyes narrowed at his peremptory tone. "I will not."

"I can be reasonable, my dear. If you require a restorative rest, then you shall have one, with your caring relations."

"And which caring relations would that be?" she drawled. "Oh, do you mean you and Sophia? Pardon me for being obtuse, brother. As I recall, during my last visit to your home in December, your wife made a point to criticize my gowns, my hair, my speech, and my manners. And that was only my first day there. Then there were her thinly veiled slurs against my sister. And you, dear brother, never once did a thing to stop her."

He was unmoved by her words. "You always were an ungrateful child, Lucy. From the moment you and your sister came to live with us, I saw it. There was ingratitude in you, and wildness in Susanne. A pity my father was too besotted with your mother to see the truth about her daughters."

"My sister was merely headstrong and full of life. You tried to break her spirit, but you couldn't. I believe that has eaten at you for years now. She bested you, Yardley, in her own way."

His lean cheeks drew in. "Shamed me, is more like it, and her whole family. I knew it was only a matter of time until her wicked nature would land her in trouble."

Lucy rose slowly to her feet. "You will not slander my sister. She is dead, and if you cannot honor her with your words, you will honor her with your silence."

He leaned toward her. "I did not come here to fight with you. But you must leave this place. I will speak with your landlord and there's an end to it."

Lucy put out her chin. "And I have said I will not. You no longer have any control over what I do or where I go."

"And where will you go when your little sojourn here is ended?" he asked idly.

"Why, back to the Burbridges. They expect me home on Monday."

Yardley smiled then, and showed his teeth, which were small and slightly pointed. Lucy hated his smile. She felt the first whisper of foreboding, a tight clenching in the pit of her stomach.

"I think not," he said silkily. "I have a letter to the Burbridges here in my pocket." He tapped his somber black waistcoat. "I have told them, Lucy. About your violent, ungovernable outbursts and your melancholy tendencies. I have written that I hardly think you fit to be around children, let alone guide them or instruct them."

"You wouldn't . . ." She barely got the words out. Her heart began to pound ferociously. It had never occurred to her that he would act so vindictively toward her.

"If you do not leave this place today . . . if you are not on a boat back to England by this evening, then I will post this letter. I rather think an impressionable pair of cits like the Burbridges will take an Oxford don's opinion of you to heart, don't you?"

Lucy's eyes flashed. "They know me, Yardley. I've worked for them for three years . . . I am not afraid of your trumped-up accusations."

He sighed. "Not trumped up. They are all true. I still recall how you went after poor Squire Hodges, the time he accidentally shot at your dog. You'd have ridden right over him if I hadn't been there. As it was he broke his ankle trying to get away from your horse."

Her face darkened. "It was no accident. He'd threatened repeatedly to shoot Bodger for disturbing his pheasants."

Yardley shrugged. "And what of the time, after your sister's death, when you stopped eating and would not let a soul into your room for weeks?"

"That is called grieving, Yardley. A foreign sentiment to you, I know."

"Why grieve over such a poor creature, who was doomed from the moment she grew into womanhood? I believe she was better off—"

"No!" Lucy cried. "That is a wicked and unjust thing to say. Susanne would have none of you, and you hated her for it. Because she spurned you."

Yardley's pale face grew several shades whiter. "You are still delusional, I see."

Lucy moved away from him to the window, where a large, well-appointed coach was blocking the soothing view of the sea. She desperately needed soothing then. And the coach was as much her enemy as Yardley was—it had carried him here to this inn.

"Are you finished spewing your evil words now? You cannot make me leave—and I would sooner throw myself into the sea than spend a minute with you and that wasp you married."

"See," he purred with a smug, tight smile, "still self-destructive, Lucy. I offer you a sanctuary and you say you would rather die."

"I have made my way in the world for seven years without your aid. I will continue to do so . . . unless you intend to follow me about like some awful nemesis and poison all my employers against me."

His voice softened. "I only have ever wanted good things for you. For you to take your place in society—you were born a lady, the granddaughter of a baron. You could marry Sir Humphrey Dumbarton . . . I would approve it, for all that he's only a country farmer."

"I don't need your approval for anything, when will you comprehend that?"

"All I comprehend is that you are not fit to be on your own. Traveling here without an escort is ample proof of that. You need someone to look after you, as your mother did. And it is my Christian duty as your brother to be that person."

She felt her fingertips grinding into her palms and willed herself to relax. This was an old ruse of his, inferring that she shared her mother's mental instability. It would have been amusing if it wasn't so infuriating. And frightening.

"We both know there is nothing wrong with my mental state, Yardley, save that you irritate me beyond words. I want nothing to do with you. Now please leave."

He crossed his arms and shook his head. "I could force you, you know. I have one of my hired men with me to assure you will do as I say . . . he is waiting in the taproom. He will see that you come away quietly."

Lucy was about to tell him what he could do with his hired man, when the hall door creaked open and Roddy Kempthorne strolled in.

He gave Yardley a startled look. "Oh, sorry. Didn't realize Miss Parnell had a visitor." He bowed slightly. "Roderick Kempthorne, at your service."

Yardley ignored this overture. "This is a private conversation, sir."

Roddy's eyes lit up. "I had a feeling I'd barged in on something."

"Then I suggest you leave," Yardley said in a voice of ice.

Lucy said nothing, but her gaze darted to Roddy in a wordless plea. She was so distracted by his unexpected arrival that she was barely able to take in his appearance, to note only that the cavalier suit had been replaced by a riding coat and buckskin breeches worn with topboots. In spite of the stylish apparel, his hair was disordered and his neckcloth was drawn into a careless knot.

"I rather think I will stay." He pulled out a chair, sat himself at the table, and proceeded to butter a scone. He shot Yardley an impish grin. "Miss Parnell has been rattling on about the food at this inn. Oh look, Manx kippers!" He held up a forkful of limp fish toward the man in black. "Care to have a taste?"

Yardley swung to his stepsister. "Who in blazes is this buffoon?"

Roddy began nibbling the edge of his scone. "Been called worse," he said, gazing up at him over the edge of his treat. His eyes drifted to Lucy. "Having one of those episodes again, Miss Parnell? You look a bit peaky."

"It's nothing," she said, holding on to the back of a chair.

He grinned at her encouragingly and then winked. "I think I

know what's troubling you—hobgoblins. They rise up from these poxy marshes and won't let you be. Isn't that right, Mr.—?"

Yardley again ignored him. He went to the door and called out, "Tom! In here."

A few seconds later a brawny young man appeared in the doorway, still holding a mug of ale.

"This person"—Yardley pointed to Roddy, who was unconcernedly poking at the tray of breakfast buns with one finger—"refuses to leave. Perhaps you could encourage him."

Tom shrugged and set down his tankard on a side table. He approached Roddy. "Now, sir, don't make me riled. I'd hate to mess up your pretty face."

"Yardley," Lucy said. "This has gone far enough. There is no need for your hired thug."

"Are you a thug?" Roddy asked the burly man genially. "Don't know if I've ever met a proper thug before."

Yardley sneered down at Roddy, and then his eyes raked over Lucy. "Is this pretty boy your champion, my dear?" He gave a dry laugh. "I'd have thought even you could have found a more promising specimen."

Roddy glared up at him, his expression full of affront. "You can insult me all you like, sir, but I'd rather you left Miss Parnell out of things."

"Tom!" Yardley snarled.

The burly man set his hands on Roddy's slim shoulders and lifted him out of his chair. The next instant Tom was sprawled on his back on the planked floor, holding one hand to his bloodied nose.

Roddy sighed as he straightened his cravat. "Sorry," he said to the fallen man. "I know you were only doing what you were told."

"Gor, that's a punishing right you've got," Tom croaked, halfway between awe and resentment.

Roddy shrugged. "Had three older brothers . . . and I never could stand being manhandled." He grinned across at Yardley. "Now where were we? Ah, yes . . . you were about to introduce yourself to me. I gather you are some relation of Miss Parnell's . . . and I suspect I know exactly which one."

Yardley's scowl was monumental. He strode over to Lucy. "I am not through with you. I have allowed you to follow your foolish course for all these years, but now the time has come for me to put an end to it."

"I am nearly one-and-thirty, Yardley," Lucy said softly. She saw

Roddy's eyes widen slightly and she nearly winced. "I wish you would just accept that."

"If you refuse to leave," he added, "I can make your life a misery."

"You did that for the five years I shared your home. Wasn't that enough for you?"

Roddy sidled in between Lucy and her stepbrother. He laid an arm companionably over the man's shoulder. "What I think you should do, old fellow, is leave Miss Parnell alone."

Yardley thrust away from him. "You young upstart."

He motioned Tom out of the room, and after a swift, vengeful glare at Lucy, he stalked toward the door. The landlady's cat had a similar destination in mind, and when he neared Yardley's feet, the man kicked out at him in irritation. The cat neatly dodged his boot and went scampering out the door. Yardley followed and slammed it behind him.

Roddy turned to her. "He is a frightful old scarecrow, ain't he? Puts me in mind of a prosy classics professor I once had at Oxford. I used to attend his lectures just so I could catch up on my sleep."

Lucy nodded. "He *is* a classics professor at Oxford."

Roddy hooted, "Oh lord! Don't tell me your Yardley is Professor Abbott? I thought you said your surname was Parnell."

"He is my stepbrother," she said. "His father married Mama after she was widowed. I was forced to spend part of my youth in Yardley's company." She shuddered. "And when his father died, he took it upon himself to see to us. We lived with him for another five years."

"You and your mother?"

She turned her face away from him. "Yes . . . and my sister."

"Why has he come here?" he asked in a gentle voice.

"I don't want to discuss this," she said sharply. She sat again in her chair and fidgeted with her teacup, refusing to meet his eyes. Roddy moved from the table to the wide bow window, and leaned against the sill. Several minutes passed.

At last Lucy looked up at him. "I wish you would just go away. I fear your interference has only succeeded in making him more angry."

"I was trying to help you," he said earnestly.

"He will be even more determined to see me away from this place. He surely knows why I am here—"

"That's a deal more than I know," Roddy pronounced. "Why

won't you trust me? If there's one thing I can do, it's keep a secret."

"You are a stranger to me, Mr. Kempthorne. I see no reason why I should tell you anything."

"Because," he said, nodding in the direction of the inn's yard, where the landlord's voice could be heard raised in protest, "I suspect you are going to need an ally."

Lucy rose and hurried to the window. Tom was at that moment loading her small trunk onto the back of the ornate coach. She headed out the door with Roddy close behind her.

The landlord came huffing up to them in the front hall. "I tried to stop them, miss," he cried. "But those ruffians just tossed me aside . . . and in my own inn." Lucy wagered no one had ever called Yardley a ruffian before now. "They went up to your room and made off with everything in there."

Lucy's face paled. "He must be mad."

"He's persuasive," Roddy remarked. "I give him that."

Lucy brushed past the two men and went out onto the small porch. She watched in disbelief as Yardley disappeared inside the coach.

He leaned one arm out the window and smiled at her. His teeth would have done a cannibal proud. "We'll see how you fare without your luggage." His gaze shifted to the landlord. "And I believe Miss Parnell's purse was among the things we collected. I hope she's paid for her lodging in advance." He motioned for the driver to move off.

"Oh," he called back as the coach creaked into motion, "I am staying with the Wibberlys near Castleton. So you'll know where to find me once you've come to your senses, Lucy."

Lucy leaned back against the door frame and watched all her possessions drive off along the cobbled lane. She had about nine pence in her reticule. Perhaps enough to pay for the scones Roddy had helped himself to. Certainly not enough to pay what she owed the landlord.

Roddy stood beside her, arms crossed, one fisted hand tapping against his wide mouth. "I expect you'd like very much to get even with him at this moment."

"I would like to throttle him," she said between her teeth.

He drew her back into the inn, past the landlord, who was still muttering apologies. His wife had joined him, and, having overheard Yardley's departing shot, was obviously troubled by their lone guest's suddenly penniless state.

"Miss," she said, touching Lucy's arm, "we are sympathetic to your situation, but Mr. Greene and I run a business here. We need to know how you intend to pay for your room."

Lucy looked down at the gold and ruby brooch she wore on her bodice. It had been a gift from her father when she turned sixteen, the same year he died. It was one of the few things of value Yardley had allowed her to take when she departed his home.

She reached down to undo the clasp, and Roddy's hand shot out to stop her. His fingers closed over her own, brushing the rise of her breast and making her gasp slightly.

"No," he said. "That is not necessary."

He tugged his own purse from his coat pocket, opened it and then grimaced. Lucy could see that it was empty. He shrugged and then smiled at the landlady. "I make myself responsible for Miss Parnell's expenses . . ."

"And who might you be?" she asked sternly, hands spread on her ample hips.

"I am a guest of the Earl of Steyne," he said. "Staying at Ballabragh."

To Lucy's utter surprise, Mr. and Mrs. Greene all but genuflected. "Well then," said the landlady, "we trust you will settle things with us before the earl leaves for London."

Roddy bowed slightly. "I will return tomorrow. You have my word on it."

"No," Lucy said forcefully. "This will not do. I will not take money from you."

"I don't see that you have any choice. Unless you plan to work off your tick in the kitchen and then sleep in a hedgerow."

"I will think of something," she said determinedly. "I must."

Roddy smiled at her tolerantly and coaxed her back into the dining parlor.

"Now," he said as he again seated himself at the table and began to dismember a honey bun. "While you think, I am going to finish this excellent breakfast I have paid for."

Lucy gave a long, weary sigh and settled opposite him. She set her chin on her hands and watched him consume nearly everything that was left on the table. He motioned to the last remaining scone. "You sure you don't want this?"

"I have no appetite for food. Especially food that is not paid for."

Undismayed, he polished off the scone and then dusted the crumbs from his shirtfront with a napkin. She wondered how he managed to look so attractive in spite of his unkempt appearance. Or perhaps it added to his allure—the wind-tumbled hair and skewed neckcloth gave him a devil-may-care air that was devastating.

Then she wondered why she was musing over Roddy Kempthorne's physical appearance when she had just experienced a disaster of daunting proportions.

Roddy caught her eye and cocked his head. "Think of anything yet?"

She put her hands over her face and shook her head. "No, but I will not give in to him. Never."

He rocked his chair back and said thoughtfully as he gazed up at the cross-beamed ceiling, "I've thought of something." His eyes lowered to her face. "But I fancy you won't like it."

"Tell me," she said wearily. "I find I am open to any suggestion at this point."

He flicked a speck of powdered sugar from his lapel. "You can come with me to Ballabragh." He halted her objection with a raised hand. "Hear me out now, Miss Parnell. If you came with me, I would win my bet with my friends . . . a thousand pounds would weigh nicely against what I owe your landlord. As I promised you yesterday, no one will do you any harm while you are there. The Senora Dolorossa will see to that."

Lucy was about to ask him who on earth the Senora Dolorossa was, when he added, "And won't it put a flea in your smug stepbrother's ear when he learns you have made an ally of the Earl of Steyne. Well, even if it's just silly old Nonnie, Professor Abbott won't know that. He's bound to be intimidated."

"It's out of the question," she said, but not harshly. She had received few enough kindnesses in her recent life to take any in a poor spirit.

"Just for a few days, then, until we can wangle your trunk back from your stepbrother."

She nearly laughed. "Yardley is not fodder for wangling, I'm afraid."

Roddy accepted this judgment, but still appeared optimistic. "The thing of it is, I still haven't come up with a gift for Nonnie's birthday, turning twenty-five is a milestone . . . and I believe you might be just the ticket."

Her eyes narrowed ominously. "I think it is bad enough to be the object of a bet, but to be presented as a birthday gift . . ."

"No, no," he quickly said. "I want you there for his stepmother, the senora. He frets over her, we all do . . . and you might be just what she needs, someone bright and pretty to distract her. Nonnie's not been able to budge her out of her room since we arrived there."

"Then she won't be a very effective chaperon," Lucy pointed out.

"Ho, you don't know the countess. She knows everything that goes on at Ballabragh . . . two hundred years ago they'd have taken her for a witch. She'll watch over you, in her own way, never fear. Please say you will come, Miss Parnell."

"I can't," Lucy repeated fretfully. "For one thing, I can't go to Ballabragh with no luggage . . . I don't even have a hairbrush."

Roddy rolled his eyes. "You think the Earl of Steyne don't have a spare hairbrush? Lord, Lucy, where are your wits? And don't worry about furbelows and such—the countess has plenty to spare. I promise you will find her kindness itself . . . you might even be encouraged to stay on. And since you've likely lost your position in Manchester—"

Her head snapped up. "How do you know that?"

He had the decency to blush, though it only made his face more charmingly boyish. "I, er . . . was listening at the door of the dining parlor. I came here to see you this morning and when I realized you had another visitor . . ." He shrugged lightly.

"Why *did* you come here, Mr. Kempthorne? I mean other than to incense my stepbrother into making off with my trunk."

He disappeared from the room and returned shortly, carrying her rucksack and her lost umbrella. "I came to return your things," he said as he held them out to her. "I left them on the hall settle . . . I say"—he shook her knapsack—"at least you've still got your pistol."

Lucy looked as though she wanted to use it on someone at that moment. She took her rucksack from him, and then sat down again, clutching it to her chest. She knew there was a sovereign tucked in one of the pockets, placed there for emergencies, but she doubted she would get far on such a sum.

"I don't know what to do," she said in a throaty whisper. "I thank you for coming here this morning and for offering me a place to stay. But I think I would do better to return to England."

"You going to swim back?" he asked idly as he toyed with his watch fob.

"I bought a return passage," she said. "Thank goodness."

"Which is where at this minute?"

Her face fell. The ticket was packed in her trunk, the trunk which was now making its way to the Wibberlys' home, whoever the devil they might be.

As though he'd read her thoughts, Roddy commented, "The Wibberlys are one of the island's first families. We all attended Oxford with their son. The Swithenses and the Wibberlys never got on, as I recall. Nonnie would love to put their noses out of joint by having you come to stay."

Lucy stood up and gave him a grim smile. "It seems I have little choice. Until I get my trunk back, I am trapped on this island."

"It's not a bad place," he said teasingly. "As you yourself pointed out, there is a wild beauty here."

"There is no beauty to a place that's become a prison."

"Ah," he said, "you haven't seen Ballabragh. I expect you will like it enormously. So are we in agreement? You come with me so I can win my bet, and I will help you thwart your stepbrother."

Lucy recalled Roddy's empty purse and thought to herself that a man with no money had little business making such an extravagant bet. But she owed him something, if only for knocking Yardley's bullyboy on his posterior end. She'd never forget the expression of stupefaction on her brother's face.

"Yes," she said as evenly as she could manage. "We are in agreement."

Roddy called for his carriage then. He settled her onto the high seat before he climbed up himself. The landlady waved them off, her look of concern warming Lucy's heart until she realized the woman was likely more worried about her unpaid bill than about Lucy's uncertain future.

She was thankful Roddy didn't chatter as they drove away from the seaside village. Her head ached abominably and the bright sun was doing it no good. She didn't even have a bonnet to shade her eyes She didn't have so much as a clean handkerchief. Yardley had left her with her dignity in tatters. But once her head cleared and her shock diminished, she would be able to think of some way to get around him.

Chapter Four

Roddy kept stealing looks at her as he tooled the carriage along the cliff. She was bearing up remarkably well for a woman who had just been burgled by her own kin. He'd never liked that Professor Abbott back at Oxford, not that he'd liked many of his teachers. Always determined to fill his head with nonsense, they were. But Abbott had possessed a mean streak; he delighted in belittling the less capable students and thought nothing of making the hapless youngsters into laughingstocks. Roddy had always counted himself lucky that he'd stayed out of Abbott's range—by the simple fact that he rarely attended his classes. And when he did, he made sure to have gotten the current lessons from Snowball, who was a dab hand at anything remotely academic.

He'd take great pleasure in bringing that fellow down a peg or two.

And there was also Miss Parnell's mystery to contend with. Not just the matter of the mission she had spoken of yesterday, but the more intriguing mystery of her past. Yardley Abbott was clearly a wealthy man, well-connected in the gentry. Yet his stepsister worked for a living, and though the dress she wore was nicely tailored to her slim figure, it was old and a bit faded. How was it that Abbott looked so prosperous while his stepsister, in her dowdy gown, appeared one step away from poverty?

Ah, but there was nothing dowdy about the way the March sun gleamed off her sleek hair, he thought appreciatively. Yesterday morning, in the gloom of the fog, he'd thought her hair an indifferent shade of brown. But now he saw it was a glorious mix of rich shades—mahogany and deep gold blended with the darker coffee-colored strands.

There was also an easiness to her manner that delighted him. Here was a woman without a whisper of self-consciousness, whose beauty did not rely on artifice but rather on the character in her face. He studied the straight nose and the elegantly determined chin, framed in profile by the bright blue sky. In between those two patrician features lay the tempting mouth of a courtesan—wide, rosy and ripe. It was all Irish, that mouth, with nothing of prim England in its form.

Roddy had a feeling the lady had no notion of her own subtle beauty. No idea of how speaking her hazel eyes could be when she was amused, or how inviting that rosy mouth became when she smiled. A pity she so rarely smiled. But he'd see to that. It was his special gift, making people smile. And Lucy Parnell was in dire need of that gift.

At one point in their silent journey, he heard what sounded like a small, stifled groan. "You're not going to swoon, are you?" he asked gently. "Because if you are, I'd better stop the carriage."

She made another noise in her throat and when he craned his head to look at her, he saw that she was fighting off tears.

"Oh, blast," he muttered as he pulled up his horses. "I will have his liver out, Miss Parnell. Ah, no, please don't cry."

"I am trying very hard not to," she said thickly as he fished in his vest pocket for his handkerchief. She took it from him and blew her nose noisily. "I never cry . . . I don't know what's come over me . . . I am angry and so frustrated. He does that to me, you see. And I have so little time here . . . Oh, but that's no longer true . . . the Burbridges won't be expecting me, once Yardley posts that wicked letter."

That loss, which was just now beginning to filter into her brain, devastated her. She would never see Mandy or Todd or little James ever again. Or their kind, good-natured parents.

She began to cry full out, her shoulders shaking with each quavering sob. Roddy did what any well-brought-up young gentleman would do . . . he took her hand and began to stroke it consolingly. She pulled back at first, but then relaxed her guard and let him soothe her.

After a minute or so, she managed to control herself and turned her face away from him. He coaxed her head around with his forefinger. "You needn't be shy with me, Miss Parnell. Not ever. I have three sisters and I know about females and tears."

"I thought you had three brothers," she said with a watery hiccup.

"We Kempthornes are very prolific," he said with a smile. "There were seven of us all together. I was the youngest."

"I was the eldest," she said. "Though there were only the two of us. And Yardley, of course."

Roddy muttered, "The less said about that person, the better. Now we will sit here for a bit until you calm your nerves. I can't take you to Ballabragh looking like that. The senora will have my scalp if she thought I'd distressed you."

Lucy had little personal vanity, but the thought of Roddy Kempthorne seeing her with her face all red and swollen made her want to burst into tears all over again. "I must look dreadful," she said as she kneaded his damp handkerchief into knots.

"Yes you do, rather," he said with a chuckle. "But at least that's behind us. That I've seen you all teary-faced, I mean. Hasn't put me off you one jot, if that's any help."

Lucy was about to ask him what he meant by that cryptic revelation, but when she looked into his eyes she lost her voice. He was gazing at her with tender concern and not a little heat. No man in her recollection had ever bestowed such a potent look upon her. Especially not after she'd been crying.

He raised his hand to her face and stroked one finger over her flushed cheek. "I meant it when I said I'd have his liver, Miss Parnell. Or anyone who distresses you, for that matter. If there's one thing I know, it's how to look after my friends. Anyone can tell you that."

Lucy murmured some response that sounded like "Thank you." She wondered if he was leaning closer to her, or if it was her imagination. Or perhaps she had shifted closer to him. His eyes held hers captive, bluer than the open sea that sighed below the high cliffs where they sat.

Just then the stillness was broken by a distant bleating from somewhere behind the carriage. They both spun around in their seats. A herd of shaggy brown sheep meandered into view from around a tor, although the four-horned ram was nowhere in sight.

"I think we'd better keep moving," Roddy said, casting a nervous glance behind him. "Just in case"

"Faint heart?" Lucy chided him gently.

Roddy merely grinned and set his horses in motion.

They drove for another ten minutes along the coast and then inland for a short while. When they topped a small rise, Roddy again pulled up. "See—I told you it's an old pile of stones, but it does have a certain majesty."

She turned her head to the east and beheld Ballabragh.

Washed in sunlight, it appeared to be something out of a fairy story—a fantasy castle built of rough-hewn yellow stone, with crenellated battlements and narrow, leaded windows. All it lacked was a drawbridge and a moat.

"Thirteenth century," Roddy pronounced. "Normans built the keep and Nonnie's family kept adding to it over the years. They used the local stone, so it's all of a piece. Not like my own family's home, which looks like a magpie dropped the different bits out of the sky."

"It is rather overpowering," she said breathlessly.

He was amused by the awestruck expression on her face. He had a thought then, an instinct, that once he got her inside the castle, she would closet herself away from him. The senora would abet her in that. His plan was for Lucy to draw the countess out, not for the senora to lure her into seclusion.

He'd best remind her of the mysterious mission that had brought her to Man. That would keep her from succumbing to the countess.

He turned to her and said forthrightly, "Before we go down there, I want you to do me a favor. Not a huge favor, mind . . . but a favor nonetheless."

She cocked her head. "What can I possibly do for you, Mr. Kempthorne?"

"Tell me," he said softly, "about the child who cries in the night."

Lucy almost tumbled out of the carriage. Her hand rose to cover her open mouth.

"No," he said quickly, "I am not blessed with second sight, though they say my Cornish grandmother had some ability in that direction. It was something you kept murmuring yesterday while you were asleep in the tree. I was afraid to wake you, so I lay there listening."

She said nothing, and so he again took up her hand and stroked the palm gently. "You are not alone in this, Lucy. Not any longer. I have a notion that the child and your insufferable stepbrother are connected somehow. But that's as much as my feeble brain has allowed me."

Still she said nothing.

"So tell me why you are on this island, and why your brother has come here from Oxford to threaten you. What are you looking for that has him so riled that he had to ransack your bedroom and carry off your belongings?"

"I can't tell you," she said at last, "because I am not certain myself why I am here."

"Who is this child?"

She looked away, over the rooftops of the stone castle. "It is a very long story, Mr. Kempthorne. And even I can only guess at the details."

"I have all the time in the world, Miss Parnell. And all the curiosity of a proverbial cat."

Her eyes brightened. "Mrs. Greene told me the Manx cats lost their tails because they dawdled on the way to the Ark, too busy being curious, no doubt, and so had the door shut on them."

"Well, I can sympathize with those cats. I've been delayed going to Almack's any number of times and had the doors closed on me. It's very distressing, I can tell you."

"I've never been to Almack's, but I hear it's dreadfully dull."

"Ah, it is. But the watery punch makes up for it." He was rewarded with a barely stifled chuckle. "But you won't distract me this way, my girl. I am determined to have my curiosity satisfied."

"Do you always get your way with people, Mr. Kempthorne?"

"Generally," he said without any smugness. "I have a knack for wearing them down."

She could heartily agree with that. She felt worn down and dispirited. But strangely, for the first time in many years, she did not feel alone. This young man, who had risen up muddy and tattered from out of a gully, had for some unfathomable reason attached himself to her. Like a sticklebur. But he was right—she needed an ally right now, and one could not be too choosy when one was staring disaster in the face.

"I was born in Ceylon," she began in a low voice. "My father owned a tea plantation. My mother was never happy there, she hated the heat and the endless dust. After my sister was born, she grew increasingly restless. Eventually she returned to England with Susanne. I stayed on in Ceylon. Perhaps it is only vanity on my part, but I believe my father needed me with him."

"And the heat and dust didn't trouble you?"

She shook her head. "Ceylon was a magical place to me. A land of extremes, it's true, but also a land of beauty and history. I was very happy there."

Roddy's hold on her hand tightened. "Then what?"

"The year I turned sixteen my father was killed in a cyclone. Our part of the island was decimated and the entire plantation was destroyed. I was sent back to England with a missionary lady . . . only to find that my mother was already being courted by a gentleman she had met in London, a wealthy landowner who lived outside Oxford. They were married almost immediately after my arrival—my family's impecunious state made that a necessity.

"I hated England at first, it was so restricting. And Papa Abbott's son, who was seven years my senior, made no attempt to disguise the fact that he resented us all very much.

"Happily, I got a chance to become reacquainted with my sister. As a child, Susanne possessed an unfettered spirit. She was always up to something—fingers in the jam jar, or off roaming the plantation with the workers. As a young woman, she was still willful and independent. Yardley's father adored her, which only increased my stepbrother's dislike of her. After my stepfather died, Yardley took over the running of his estate outside Oxford. He had been a brilliant student and was then already a don."

"I thought all the dons at Oxford had to be ordained ministers."

"He is," she said.

Roddy made a face. "Never met a man of the cloth who stole from his own sister. I doubt the Bible condones such things."

"I expect there are more than a few dons who see their ordination as a mere formality. My brother's idea of practicing Christian charity is to bully people and intimidate them. But the condition of Yardley's soul is his own business," she added. "The point is, my stepbrother all but sequestered us in that house. We were no longer allowed visitors or callers, except of his choosing. We no longer attended assemblies or village fetes. I believe this was due to Susanne. He didn't want anyone to get near her."

"Why was that?"

Lucy sighed. "She was quite beautiful and Yardley seemed to think that meant she was also wicked. He used to lecture her constantly, which only made her laugh. But then, after our stepfather died, he began to make overtures toward her. Very noticeable overtures."

Roddy frowned. "Surely your mother could have put a stop to such things."

Lucy fidgeted on her seat. "My mother was not always alert to her surroundings. I'm afraid she developed a dependency on laudanum while she lived in Ceylon. Even once she was back in England, there were many things she did not, or would not, acknowledge.

"When Susanne was seventeen, she ran off. She left a note claiming she had met a man who wanted to marry her. Yardley was furious. He refused to send for the Runners—said it was good riddance."

Roddy mulled over this information. "I gather you were not close to her, that she didn't tell you of her plans. I mean, my sisters tell each other everything . . . they always have their heads together, laughing and gossiping, even now that they all have their own children."

Lucy had a momentary pang of envy for Roddy and his large, loving family.

"Susanne and I were close, but we'd had a row the week before she left home."

"Over what?"

Lucy tugged away from his hand. "It's not important." She drew a breath. "After Susanne's disappearance, my mother grew worse. Yardley hired a woman to look after her, to make sure she kept to her rooms. I offered to look after her myself, but she only wanted her lost chick at that point. I was an uncomfortable reminder of Susanne."

"I am sorry . . . I know how it is with parents. They have their favorites, even if they swear they love all their children the same."

Lucy wondered how he could shift from idle prattle to telling insight all in the space of a few minutes. It was unsettling. "I gather *you* were a favorite," she said with an attempt at lightness.

His eyes danced. "Who me?"

"Don't bother to deny it . . . as the baby in a family of seven children, I wager you were coddled and cosseted like a royal prince."

"I was wretchedly spoiled if you must know. Can't you tell?"

"No," she said softly. "I swear there is not a selfish or mean-spirited bone in your body."

Roddy gave her a close-mouthed grin that set the dimples deep in his cheeks. "That's the nicest thing anyone's ever said to me. On my honor."

Lucy felt her heart start to flutter. Something was happening to her, here on this rugged island. Feelings she had shut away for years were starting to blossom like the pink tips of the new heather on the hillsides. Feelings she had no business experiencing, she reminded herself.

"I betrayed my sister . . ." she said darkly, in an attempt to make Roddy stop twinkling at her.

"What?" His face lost all its merry gleam.

"Three years after she disappeared, she sent me a note from London. Asking me to come to her. She was carrying a child, she said, and that the father had been killed fighting in Spain."

"What did you do?"

Lucy gripped her hands against her knees. "I was still living with Yardley; I had nowhere else to go and no prospects. He was married by then, to a horrid woman. All I wanted was to get away from that house, but Yardley controlled my funds. I barely had enough pin money for hair ribbons. So I stole some sovereigns from his desk—"

"Good girl," Roddy murmured.

Lucy shot him a look of vexation. "I stole, Roddy. I broke into his desk like a thief and took what was not mine."

"Oh, piffle," he said, unrepentant. "The man just made off with everything you own, and you are crying over a few coins. So I gather you went off to find her."

"Yes, but unlike my sister, I left an easy trail to follow. I was foolish enough to ask one of Yardley's stable lads to drive me to the mail coach, you see. My brother and a groom caught up with me outside Hemptstead—and Yardley found Susanne's note in my reticule. The groom brought me back to Oxford, while Yardley continued on to London."

A dark look clouded Roddy's bright face. "I would have burned that note, you know. Or eaten it, rather than let that creature find my sister."

Lucy's voice shook. "I believed he would bring her home." She clutched at his sleeve. "I could not think he would turn her away, not when she needed her family. I had no idea of how truly monstrous he could be until then."

"So what did he do with her?"

"I don't know. He returned home several days later and told us that the man who had promised to marry her had done nothing more than fill her belly before he was killed. He said not to worry, that she had been 'taken care of.' He spoke of her as though she was a rabid dog that needed to be shot. I railed at him to tell us where she was, but he would say nothing.

"And then, only two months later, he told me she had died. As he put it, 'while giving birth to her stillborn bastard.' He wouldn't tell me where the baby or my sister were buried, only that the child was female. He did tell me that much. That was when I began to advertise for a position. I knew I would go mad if I stayed on in that house. I found a situation in Scotland . . . and I took my mother with me. I leased her an inexpensive room in the village and spent my weekends with her. Mama had always been very docile, she was hardly any trouble to look after. And the landlady was a kind soul who kept a watchful eye on her."

He appeared perplexed. "So you had no money except what you earned as a governess? I realize Yardley would have choked before he gave you a groat, but was there no money for your mother from your stepfather's estate?"

She shook her head sadly. "She had a jointure, but since my mother was not of a practical nature, my stepfather had left all her funds under Yardley's control. Needless to say, when we left his home, it was without a penny."

There was an expression of barely contained anger on his face. "Yet he wants you back there, doesn't he? So he can have you under his thumb. Even a petty king needs subjects."

"Exactly," she said, amazed that he understood Yardley's particular brand of malice so well.

"And after Scotland?"

"I found a post with the Burbridges in Manchester. Mama and I lived in the gatehouse on their estate; it was a perfect arrangement. But then this past winter my mother suffered a congestion of the lungs. She never recovered." Lucy's voice took on a strange, fey quality. "During her last week, she began to have disturbing dreams. She told me about them just before she died . . . a little child crying 'Find me.' Mama was convinced the dreams were sent by Susanne, so that we would seek after her lost child." She sighed and shifted her gaze to his face. "And now those dreams have begun to plague me."

She waited for his response with some anxiety, but he appeared untroubled by her tale. Perhaps between his Irish blood and his Cornish blood, Roddy Kempthorne was inured to such otherworldly goings on.

"Is that why you are here, Lucy . . . do you believe your sister's little girl is still alive? Is she the one crying in your dream?"

"I don't know. Susanne's child would be nearly eight years old by now. The child in my dreams sounds much younger. But those dreams break my heart, Roddy."

"So you must answer that child's cry for help."

"Yes, I must. Even if it means brooking Yardley. And the fact that he is here means I am following the right trail. While I was staying at his home for Mama's funeral, I found some papers in his desk—you recall I had no trouble breaking into it once before. For the past seven years he's been sending money to a lawyer here on Man, a Mr. Plimpton. Small sums, barely enough to keep a child in linens, but it was the only clue I was able to discover."

Roddy set his fisted hand gently against her chin. "You make a proper bloodhound, ma'am. I gather we must have a look in on this Mr. Plimpton."

"When I arrived here, he was the first person I sought out. He refused to answer any of my questions. He wouldn't even acknowledge that Yardley was his client. Which doesn't surprise me now . . . I expect my stepbrother wrote and warned him of my visit."

"I'm still not sure I understand why your brother kept the truth from you all these years . . . and why is he is now so determined to prevent you from finding the child?"

Lucy know the answer to this because she knew Yardley. "In his mind it would give me power over him. He is being considered for a post in his college, the dean, I believe. If I discover that he lied about my sister's child, I could make things very sticky for him. It wouldn't look good for a man of learning, a man whose life is supposedly dedicated to improving young minds, to have deceived his family in such a way. Or worse, to have contributed to the death of his stepsister out of pure malicious neglect."

"And," Roddy added, "if your sister was unwed, then he would also view the discovery of the child as food for scandal."

"How does that sit with *you*, Mr. Kempthorne, knowing that the child is baseborn? Does that affect your decision to help me with my search?"

"The last time I looked," he said intently, "children had little say in their own parentage. If she's here on this island, then she needs to know she has family."

"If she has been fostered with good people," Lucy continued. "I do not intend to take her away—I am hardly in a position to raise a child. I just need to see her . . ."

"To find her," Roddy amended.

He wasn't going to share his misgivings with Lucy, but he reckoned that any child whose cries traveled across the wide sea into two women's dreams was probably not living with a good family. If the child was alive, if Lucy was able to locate her, Roddy doubted she would like what she found. But he'd make sure he was at her side when that time came, to comfort her if need be.

"And you will find her," he said stoutly. "You now have influential friends who will see that you have as much assistance and money as you require to achieve your goal."

"Why?" she said wonderingly. "Why would you do this for me? I have been surly and cross with you at every turn. My brother even set his bully on you. I cannot understand why you are willing to help me."

He patted her hand. "It will come to you in time, Miss Parnell.

There is a rhyme and reason to all things, as my Cornish grand-mother used to say. You just need to trust in that."

He took up the reins and urged his horses forward. "And be-sides, I have a yen to play Lochinvar, don't you know."

"Yesterday you didn't even know who Lochinvar was."

"Ah, but this is today, and I have learned a world of new things. Now hold on, Miss Parnell, I'm going to spring the horses. Nonnie and the other fellows will be wondering where I've gotten to."

As they drove past the gatehouse, a bevy of children ran along-side the carriage, shouting and laughing. They were a mixed group of boys and girls, ranging in age from perhaps seven to ten. Coun-try children, Lucy saw from their rough, homespun clothing.

"The welcoming committee Nonnie calls them," Roddy said as he slowed the carriage. "They belong to the countess's servants. She has them for tea once a week."

Lucy was struck, not only by the countess's eccentric behavior in entertaining her servants' children, but by the fond expression in Roddy's voice whenever he spoke of her.

Roddy helped Lucy down from the carriage and whisked her into the house, right past Algernon, who was crossing the front hall. The earl tried to sputter out an introduction, but Roddy imme-diately handed her over to the housekeeper, Mrs. Granger, with in-structions to see her to a guest room and make sure she was comfortable. Her last view of him was from over the carved stone railing on the landing as he gazed up at her from the center of the baronial hall. His eyes were so blue she could make out their color even from that distance.

The room she was led to was small but elegant, the stone wall softened by tapestry hangings, the floor covered by a thick Persian carpet in hues of deep blue and rich yellow. Lucy went to the win-dow, which looked out over the wide moor. A tiny crescent of the Irish sea could be seen in the distance.

"Master Roderick said you had lost your luggage," the house-keeper said, as Lucy turned back into the room. "I will see that you have what you require, miss."

Lucy smiled weakly. "Thank you."

Master Roderick. The term tickled her, it was so apt. Though it was not encouraging to think she had placed her fate in the hands of Master Roderick. Or his equally rackety cronies. She doubted there was a one among them who had the wherewithal to stand up to Yardley. But no, that wasn't fair. Roddy might not have stood up to her stepbrother, but he had rattled him just the same. *And* bested his hired thug. It was a new perspective for her—that you could possibly defeat someone without meeting them head-on. Roddy Kempthorne seemed to excel at doing things in roundabout ways. Wearing people down, as he put it. She wondered if she could possibly wear Yardley down.

But that was not her style—she was more likely to stand toe to toe with someone and lash them with her tongue. She recalled how bitterly she had argued with Yardley over Susanne, insisting he allow her back in his home. He'd protested that his career would not withstand the scandal of a deflowered stepsister bearing her out-of-wedlock child under his roof. She'd chided him for his lack of charity, but she had to admit there were few people in her acquaintance who could weather such a thing. Propriety was paramount to most people in society.

After Yardley's callous treatment of her sister and her subsequent death, Lucy had turned her back on society and gone into service. She would no longer be taken out like a trophy and shown off to Yardley's fellow academics over tea. "This is my stepsister, the granddaughter of Baron Lansdale." They would no longer mumble platitudes over her hand and then admire Yardley for having acquired such a well-born connection.

She never knew how he explained her departure from his home to his peers. She had other worries by then. Looking after her mother, for one thing. And keeping the bloodthirsty MacTeague children from murdering each other, for another. Those were not her fondest memories.

The housekeeper knocked once, and then came in bearing a pile of linens topped by several toiletry articles. "Her ladyship would like to meet you," she said as she laid her burden down on the tooled chest at the foot of the bed. "At your convenience."

Lucy stood up and smoothed the front of her gown. It was one of her oldest dresses, the gray bombazine faded from repeated washings. She had put it on that morning, thinking she would be driving out in Mr. Greene's cart. It was the last dress she would have chosen to wear if she'd known she would be meeting a countess.

"I am ready now."

"You wouldn't like to have your luncheon first?"

"No, I am not very hungry." Her stomach was so knotted she didn't know if she would ever eat again.

The housekeeper gave her a curt nod, and then led her down the hallway, across the landing and through a narrow passage. "Her ladyship has a suite of rooms in this wing," she whispered over her shoulder. "She rarely comes downstairs."

She knocked on a richly carved oak door, and then opened it. "She's here, my lady. Miss Parnell, that young Master Roderick brought home."

There's a winning introduction, Lucy thought wryly as she stepped into the chamber.

The room was lit only by small candles in red glass containers. There were hangings layered over the walls, tapestries, and woven rugs. The windows were covered by heavy draperies in a dark-colored velvet so that not even a splinter of light filtered through. The atmosphere, heightened by the smell of incense and rich coffee, was at once barbaric and churchlike.

As Lucy's eyes grew accustomed to the semidarkness, she noticed a figure reclining at the center of a large, round divan in the far corner of the room. Brocade pillows and fur throws littered its surface.

"My lady," Lucy said as she curtsied in the direction of the woman.

The figure stirred and then sat up. "Closer." She motioned with one hand. Lucy moved forward until she was beside the opulent bed.

"You will eth-cuse me if I do not rise," the woman said in heavily accented English. She patted the edge of the divan with a beringed hand. "But you will sit, yes?"

Lucy perched there, sitting upright, her hands clasped in her lap. The woman lay back with a deep sigh. "Rodrigo has just been to see me . . . he is wearying that one, no?"

Lucy swallowed and said nothing. She was not sure she wasn't in the middle of some fantastic dream. The woman who lounged beside her was swathed in layers of gauzy material, some of it spangled with metallic lace, shimmering gold and silver. Her complexion was dark, like tea with cream and her hair was a riot of golden curls spilling down over both shoulders. Lucy guessed her age to be not much more than thirty-five, though her dark eyes were ageless. It was difficult to assess her figure, obscured as it was by the gauzy peignoir, but the white arms that were revealed where the loose sleeves fell away were round and plump.

Lucy was reminded of the portraits of Spanish nobility by Velasquez that she had seen once in Edinburgh. Though how a Spanish noblewoman came to be on the Isle of Man, she had no idea.

"You are very quiet, Miss Parnell," the woman said. "Perhaps I should introduce myself. I am Consuelo de la Pinero Swithens, Countess of Steyne." She gave a low chuckle. "Not an easy name for a woman from Castile to say."

Lucy nearly returned the chuckle. In truth the countess had stumbled over it badly.

"And this I tell the earl when he asked me to marry him. How can I go through life lisping out my own title? Ah, but then I was so in love with him . . . it was foolish to refuse for such a reason." She leaned forward and touched Lucy's sleeve. "Have you ever been in love, Miss Parnell?"

Lucy's eyes widened. "No. I am not sure such a thing even exists."

The countess made a tsking noise in her throat. "Such a pity. But that will soon be remedied."

"Whatever are you talking about?" Lucy said almost sharply.

Consuelo moved her shoulders in an indolent shrug. "I see a great deal, though I rarely leave my rooms. But I will not vex you with my own imaginings. I understand you have had some trouble with your brother this morning. For me, I would wish my brothers at the devil, but since they are still in Spain, that will suffice." She smiled. "So you see, I am on your side completely, my dear. Whatever you need, you must only ask Mrs. Granger."

Lucy thanked the countess and rose. Consuelo shifted up and held out her hand. "Come and visit me again, *cara*. And bring that tiresome boy with you next time. He makes my head ache, but he is such a . . . what do you English call it? A sight for sore eyes."

Oh, he is that, Lucy agreed silently.

She left the room and found Roddy waiting for her in the hallway. He pushed away from the wall where he had been leaning and took her arm. "So what do you think?"

Lucy tipped her head toward the countess's room. "Is she unwell?"

He shook his head. "She is not ill. Only sad and bored and in need of distraction. It's such a shame; she used to be the best hostess, when the earl was alive. She lived to entertain." He stopped to let her precede him down the narrow passage.

"What happened to her?"

"You'd best ask her that," he said cryptically.

"Oh, that's a fine thing," she said heatedly, turning to him. "I poured my tale out to you . . ."

"Yes, you did." He set his hands on her shoulders. "But Consuelo's tale is not mine to tell."

She started to move away from him and he tightened his hold. "Hey, now, I warned you about squirming, ma'am. Bide a minute, and I will tell you something."

"What?" There was impatience in her tone, but what she was feeling was a heart thudding panic. Roddy Kempthorne was nearly right up against her in the narrow passage and the space was very dark.

"If you let her, she can help you with your search, Lucy. There are few things on this island she does not hear of—no one can resist confiding in the Senora Dolorossa. That means the sad lady, you know."

"I know it now." It occurred to her that Roddy might be on to something. Idle women of wealth often spent their days gossiping with their neighbors and servants, and the countess was nothing if not idle.

She blinked up at him. "But I am still not sure how I am to help her . . . or cheer her. I am hardly a ray of sunshine these days."

"But you will be soon enough," he said softly. "You will be brimming over with happiness."

"You are demented," she said under her breath.

"And in the meantime," he went on, "they do say misery loves company. In that case, you and Consuelo should get on like a house afire. I do hope she is going to do something about your lamentable taste in clothes." He let his fingers drift to the starched collar of her gown. "Is there a law, I wonder, that declares governesses must wear the drabbest shades of gray and brown?"

"I did not tell her about my stolen luggage," she stated.

"She'll see to your wardrobe, never fear." He gave her a long, assessing look. "If it were up to me, I'd dress you in greens and golds." He dipped his head until his forelock tickled against her brow and he said in a sultry purr, "But I'd *un*dress you in crimson."

The floor beneath her feet pitched over at a crazy angle. Lucy drew a breath to steady herself against his nonsensical flirtation and narrowed her eyes.

"Are you quite finished playing with other people's lives, Mr. Kempthorne?"

"Not quite." He leaned his head down and kissed her just below her ear. A soft whispering caress that crimped her toes into knots. His hands were still tight on her shoulders; he shifted her slightly and drifted his mouth along her cheek to her lips. His kiss was harder this time, and not so whispery. Lucy felt her stomach heel over, fought the sensation, and then was carried away by it.

Roddy's arms slid to her back, tugging her up against him, while his mouth played coaxingly on hers.

Lucy had spent the last twenty-four hours trying not to think about being kissed by Roddy Kempthorne. Which was a good thing, because she'd clearly had no idea at all how it would really feel. And if she had, she would have found a way to make him kiss her while they were still in the tree. Or while he was carrying her off on horseback. Or while her brother was purloining her trunk at the inn. She would have never let him stop kissing her.

As it was, he was the one who pulled back. "Damn," he said under his breath, and she sensed it was the first time he'd been nonplussed since they'd met. His eyes glittered in the gloomy hall. "You're not going to box my ears again, are you? I've wanted to do that forever. In fact I'd like to do it again."

"Why?" she asked breathlessly. If she could have seen herself at that moment—eyes bright, cheeks flushed, mouth slightly swollen, with her bosom rising and falling in a most provocative manner—she wouldn't have asked such a silly question.

Roddy's response was to set his hands on either side of her face and look deep into her eyes. "Because," he said slowly and carefully, "it makes you happy."

"How can you tell that?" she protested.

"Because you are nearly smiling." Lucy tried to wipe the expression of idiotic joy from her face. "Ah, no, don't try to force a frown. You've been itching to be kissed . . . I can always tell."

"Of all the presumptuous—"

He took up her hand and drew her out of the passage. "And I promise that whenever you are sad or out of sorts, I will kiss you again."

She dug her heels into the hall carpet to slow him down. "And what of the other promise you made to me—that no one would harm me while I was here?"

"Harm?" He turned back to her and put his hand to her mouth, letting his fingers stroke over her lips. "Tell me the truth . . . didn't you enjoy kissing me?"

Lucy's brows lowered. "It was not what I am used to."

"Not yet," he said. "But it will be."

Chapter Five

He left her at the landing above the main hall, sending her off to her room with a genial smile. She still claimed she had no appetite and so he let her go. He knew his friends were clamoring to meet her, having sussed that his interest in her was more than passing. For himself, he hadn't a clue what his interest in Lucy Parnell was . . . only that he intended to kiss her again, and sometime soon, at that.

He was astute enough to know that she was vulnerable to those kisses, and humane enough to know that she might get very hurt if he went anywhere past kissing. Unwed ladies of quality made the very worst partners for serious sporting. But for less weighty play, Miss Lucy Parnell might prove to be a charming, challenging diversion. She was a willowy armful, with just enough soft curves to tempt a fellow and just enough bright spirit in her eyes to keep him on his mettle. And then there was that Irish mouth of hers, lush, sensual, and, he had just discovered, wonderfully matched to his own.

Still, as he made his way down the sweeping staircase, across the flagged floor of the main hall, he wondered why a passably pretty woman of thirty-odd years, and one with an uncertain temperament, to boot, had taken his fancy. If she was a horse at auction, he'd have walked on by. But there was something about her that was oddly familiar to him. As though she were a dearly loved companion returned to him after a long separation.

There was also another factor—the charms of the young ladies of London, those dewy-eyed misses that the *ton* furnished each Season with tiresome regularity, had seriously palled. He was weary of simpering chits in pastel frocks. Now it appeared he was smitten with a troubled termagant in bleak bombazine. No wonder his friends were amused.

Well, let them be, he muttered. Not a one of them had been near a respectable woman in months. Nonnie, in spite of his rank, was too shy, Snowball was too immersed in his blasted books and the Joker, who also boasted a title, was too full of himself. Roddy was the only one who possessed the least address where women were concerned. So let them rib him for being in the petticoat line . . . none of his friends were likely to have the satisfying privilege of kissing a woman anytime soon. And they certainly wouldn't be kissing Miss Parnell.

He found them in the dining parlor lounging about with half-drunk glasses of claret. He'd given Algernon a truncated version of what had transpired at the inn that morning, but as yet had said nothing of Miss Parnell's haunting dreams. He'd need her permission before he could reveal that to his friends.

"How is she faring?" Nonnie asked from across the table. "Been to see Consuelo, has she?"

"Yes, she's been to the inner sanctum. Your stepmother hasn't cheered her up any, though."

"I hear she hasn't any clothing," the Joker remarked. "That should prove interesting."

Roddy sighed. He really hated coming to blows with his friends.

"Connie will see to her," he pronounced stonily. "So you can just stop imagining whatever it is you've been imagining."

The Joker looked affronted. "I was merely making an observation."

"We've *all* made an observation," Snowball said from over his glass. When Roddy cast him a dark look, which was a rare occurrence between those particular friends, Snowball merely raised his glass and said, "Cheers."

"Come and eat, Ram," Nonnie said placatingly, as he pulled out the chair beside him and motioned Roddy to take it. "We've left you the best portion of the roast . . . seeing how you've spent the morning working up an appetite with the lady."

The other two men lapsed into baritone giggles then, and Roddy wondered what the devil had come over them. He scuffed the chair forward and picked up his knife and fork. "You may laugh all you like" he said. "But I am warning you, she is not to be touched. For your information, she is one-and-thirty years old, and not likely to be amused by anything any one of you might have to offer her. I expect she thinks of us as a lot of callow young sprats. And from the look of you, I would say she is right."

"I see you've set yourself up as her protector," Nonnie observed.

"Wonder who's going to protect her from you?" Snowball murmured just loud enough for Roddy to hear.

"The lady can look after her own virtue," Roddy said evenly. "As long as none of us loses sight of the fact that we were gentlemen born."

The Joker toyed with his immaculate neckcloth. "Then you lose your bet, old fellow."

"Joker's right," Nonnie piped in. "You bet us you could find an amusing companion. She won't be very amusing if she stays cowering in her room at every meal."

Roddy waved an unconcerned hand. "Give her time to settle in. She's had a wretched morning. And if you're in the mood for fisticuffs with someone, which I sense is the climate at present"—he cast a speaking look at Snowball—"then you can all ride over to the Wibberlys and thrash her beastly brother."

"Dash it all!" Nonnie cried. "You didn't tell me that. What the devil is he doing with those poxy toadies?"

"Fitting right in, I expect," Roddy said through a mouthful of potatoes.

Then he ground his teeth as he recalled the way Yardley Abbott had treated his sister. Roddy's mother always said it took a paltry man to browbeat a woman, and to his thinking it took a complete worm of a man to steal from one. And he, Roddy, had stood there in the dining parlor, yammering like a nodcock, while Yardley whisked off her belongings. Some Lochinvar he made, he thought ruefully.

Then his brain slipped into gear, and he was silent for a bit. He let his random thoughts spiral in his head until they gathered together into a plan.

"What are you up to?" Snowball asked intently, his elbows on the polished surface of the table.

Roddy gave him a wicked smile. "Something delicious, Snow. Something absolutely delicious."

Lucy paced fretfully in her room. This inactivity was making her decidedly cross. Roddy had promised to help her, and they could be driving over the countryside this very minute, looking for leads. But no, he was too busy having his luncheon to help her. Though maybe if she'd eaten something, her temper would be less frayed. She'd also developed a pounding headache, and so settled into a chair and closed her eyes, willing the pain to go away.

She must have fallen asleep—it was the dream of the crying

child that awoke her. She gazed in confusion around the strange room, fearing she had somehow drifted into madness. Then she remembered coming to Ballabragh with Roddy Kempthorne and the circumstances that had forced her to do such a rash thing. She made an effort to forget how he had kissed her in the passageway . . . there was no point in reliving something that was not going to be repeated. He'd said he would kiss her whenever she was sad, so she would make a decided effort to be cheerfulness itself.

She climbed off the bed and went to the mirror to arrange her hair. The afternoon light coming in from the windows was watery at best. She lit a candle and set it on the vanity table.

"Oh Lord," she murmured. Here she was in an earl's stately home, wearing a wrinkled, faded gown, her hair in drooping tendrils, and with the stain of Roddy's kiss still on her swollen mouth. She was almost tempted to flee from this place and seek out her stepbrother. Perhaps if she agreed to return to his home as a docile and cooperative social ornament, he would agree to tell her the truth about her sister's child.

Yes, she mused, *and pigs will fly.*

She took her candle to the delicate writing table that sat between the two windows and pulled a sheet of paper from the drawer. Her first order of business was to write a letter of rebuttal to the Burbridges. She would tell them that she and her stepbrother had had a falling out, and that she feared he would retaliate with some nonsensical slander against her.

Then she dipped the quill into the inkpot and made a list of what she had so far learned—which was pitiable. She had been counting on Mr. Plimpton to be her chief source of information and he had failed her. She had no choice now but to turn to Roddy. Though most of the people she had so far spoken with had been uncooperative, there was a possibility Roddy's brand of easy charm might unlock secrets the islanders had kept from her.

Once she was done with her list, she wrote out a description of Susanne for him. She assumed the child would have some of her sister's physical traits, perhaps her white-blond hair or her bright green eyes. It was a pity there was no way of knowing what the little girl's father looked like—if he was Gypsy dark, then the child might look nothing like Susanne.

From her years as a governess, of caring for her employers' children and those of their relations, Lucy knew that young children looked a great deal alike. Often their features had not yet taken on strong individual characteristics. She recalled when

Mandy, who was eight at the time, had dressed in Todd's clothing and fooled Lucy for the space of five minutes into thinking she was her seven-year-old brother.

Wretched scamps, she thought wistfully.

If there was any chance of finding the child before Yardley traced her to Ballabragh and continued with his threats, she and Roddy would have to split up. Which was a shame, because she fancied watching him work his magic on the taciturn villagers. She fancied watching him do just about anything.

Her pen splattered across the sheet and she cursed softly. It was a reminder that she would do better to attend to her mission and stop mooning over a man who was five years her junior.

As she gathered the pages together into a neat pile, she was struck by a dismaying thought. If Yardley searched her trunk, which she knew he was quite capable of doing, he would find her journal. She had recorded her mother's deathbed revelations there, as well as her own discovery of the mysterious stipend he'd been sending to Man. He would also see her scathing commentaries about himself and his unlovely wife, though that bothered her not at all.

Yardley would know then why she had come to the island. And, being Yardley, he would make haste to move the child beyond her reach. Perhaps he had already done so, when he realized she was on the island. But no, if that were the case, he wouldn't have been so determined to see her gone that morning.

Still, she had to find Roddy and tell him. They would need to scour that part of the island, which meant she would have to confide in his friends. Five people, among them an earl and a viscount, would certainly be more effective at locating the child than she and Roddy alone would be.

She walked quickly down the hallway to the main staircase. The great hall was dark, lit only by a brace of candles on a console table. Little light filtered in from the leaded window over the door. The high ceiling, with the fan vaulting Roddy had spoken of, was hidden in the gloom. If there was ever a house that beckoned lost spirits to roam its halls, it was Ballabragh. Even the eyes in the elk's head over the fireplace seemed to follow Lucy's progress down the stairs.

Mrs. Granger came out of her small sitting room beneath the hall stairs when she saw Lucy walk by. "Can I help you, miss?"

Lucy nearly gasped at the woman's sudden appearance. "I was looking for Mr. Kempthorne."

The housekeeper pursed her mouth. "The young gentlemen are in the billiard room, I believe. But I wouldn't advise you roaming about, miss. It's a rambling place. You'd do better to let one of the servants fetch him."

Lucy was determined not to be cowed by Mrs. Granger's cool manner. After all, she was a guest of the earl's. Or at least of the earl's friend.

"I don't want to trouble anyone. If you would just point me in the general direction . . ."

The woman nodded. "It is in the north wing." She pointed to her left with a narrow finger. "Follow that passage and go up the second set of stairs. The billiard room is beyond the third door." Mrs. Granger jutted her head forward. "The third door," she repeated.

Lucy thanked her and went off muttering the directions under her breath. She made her way up the shadowed second staircase, wishing she'd thought to bring a candle with her. What would she find if she ventured behind one of the other doors, she wondered. A demented Swithins relation chained to a bed, or a room full of smuggled brandy? More likely just another guest chamber or sitting parlor. She really had to start holding her imagination in check.

Even though she had visited several of England's great houses—she'd strolled the grounds of Carillon in Cornwall during her only childhood visit to England, and years later her stepfather had taken the family to visit Blenheim Palace in Oxfordshire—she had never actually stayed in such a grand place as Ballabragh. And never in one with so many twisting passages. After five minutes of walking, as she made her way along a wainscotted hallway that looked exactly like the one she had first passed through, she knew she was hopelessly lost.

A set of imposing double doors loomed on her left and she cracked them open and peered inside. It was the portrait galley. She moved inside, but left the door slightly ajar.

The gallery proved to be typical of its kind. Situated in a cavernous hall with a series of tall mullioned windows along one wall, it contained, as Roddy had promised, a great many musty portraits of indifferent quality. All the male subjects bore a pronounced similarity to Algernon—the large nose and pale blue eyes, plus his strapping, bullish physique.

As she waked along, it occurred to her that it was odd for this gallery to be here, and not at Steyne, which was the earl's seat.

"They are Gurneys," Roddy pronounced, as he came up behind her.

"What!" Lucy spun to face him, alarm coloring her face. She hadn't heard his booted tread on the carpeted runner.

"Sorry," he said. "Didn't mean to creep up on you like that." He bowed his head. "Mrs. Granger said I would find you wandering in this wing."

"Isn't this the north wing? She said that's where the billiard room was."

"This *is* the north wing, but the game room is in the south wing. You must have heard her wrong."

Lucy frowned. She distinctly recalled Mrs. Granger's instructions.

"No mind," he said with an easy smile. "Now what was it you wanted to see me about?"

"It's something I just recalled. Something rather distressing."

"We'd better sit then." He motioned to the long padded seat that ran beneath the windows. "Distressing news is always better when you're off your feet."

She moved to the windows and sat down, spreading her skirts over the velvet cushion so that he couldn't sit beside her without crushing the fabric. Roddy was not intimidated by a bit of bombazine, however. He merely plucked up a fold of cloth and sat down nearly hip to hip with her, then craned his head around in a display of intent interest. Lucy noticed he was still holding the swatch of her gown in his hand. It was disturbingly intimate. So much for her attempt at setting a boundary between them.

She quickly explained about her journal, the entries she had made concerning the lost child and her fears that after reading them, her stepbrother would move the child off the island.

"We'll never find her then," she said sadly.

Roddy was unconcerned. "I hope he does read it," he said. "We'll know where she is then."

"We'll know?"

He gave her a smug, self-satisfied grin. "Yes, my little worry-wart, because while you were sulking in your room, I was seeing to things."

She purposely did not rise to his baiting and merely echoed, "Things?"

He smiled even wider. "Do you have to parrot everything I say, Miss Parnell?" he teased her gently. "As a matter of fact, we've now got a man watching the Wibberly house. If Yardley sets one foot out of the place, we shall know of it. If he buys a haddock in the market, if he has his horse shod, if he so much as sneezes on the road to Castleton, we shall know."

Her eyes brightened. "Oh, Roddy, that is a capital plan."

He appeared a bit sheepish. "It wasn't my idea exactly. My valet, MacHeath, was involved in a bit of espionage during the war. It was his idea."

"Your valet was a spy?"

"He was a brandy smuggler who occasionally carried information back from France. Capable fellow, till he lost an arm in a skirmish with a French warship.

"So if Yardley does read your journal," he added, "it will save us a deal of work."

"In case he doesn't lead us to the child, I've written down what I've learned and also a description of my sister for you, in case her daughter resembles her. The notes are in my room."

Roddy nodded as he rose and reached for her hand. "Now, come and walk with me. I can show off Nonnie's illustrious ancestors, since I've none of my own."

"Who are these Gurneys that you spoke of?"

"They are Nonnie's mother's family, cousins to the Swithins."

"So these portraits are not the previous earls then."

"Some of them are," Roddy said. "Not enough room in the gallery at Steyne to house them all, I expect." He pointed to a painting where a man and a woman in the clothing of the previous century were gazing adoringly at a toddler in a lawn gown who held a golden rattle. "That's Nonny's grandfather, the fifth earl. And Nonnie's pater there, in the fetching white dress."

"Not a pretty baby, I'm afraid," Lucy said in honest appraisal. The child was already showing the promise of a truly remarkable nose. "But he looks happy enough."

"Well, he's got his little hands on the gilt, just like all nobs," he pronounced.

Though she could detect no resentment in his tone, she had a feeling it must be difficult at times for Roddy to be in company with wealthy noblemen like the Earl of Steyne. Roddy had no title, and, as she had seen that morning at the inn, he had no money. Yet, for some reason, he had been drawn into this group of young men. Though his clothing was of good quality, on closer examination she saw that his shirt cuffs were frayed, his cravat was badly pressed, and there was a button missing from his coat. No wonder his friends called him Ramshackle, she thought wryly.

It occurred to her then that much of Roddy's tattered appearance could be laid at the door of his one-armed valet. In Lucy's experience, ironing and mending were taxing enough with both arms intact.

He was motioning her toward a large portrait of a man in a dashing hussar's uniform. The soldier's eyes gleamed brightly over the inevitable large nose.

"This is Nonnie's Uncle Theodore," Roddy said. "Was wounded during the Peninsular campaign, poor chap, and came back here to die three years ago. I was mad to join up, you know. This picture went a long way toward inspiring me." He gave a mournful sigh. "But it wasn't to be."

"Commissions are dreadfully expensive," she said in sympathy.

"Wasn't that. The war was winding down by the time I had gotten quit of Oxford."

She stopped walking and turned to him. "I am a bit confused, Roddy. I thought you said no one ever came to Ballabragh, yet you seem so familiar with everything about the place."

"Oh, I've come here with Nonnie every few years since I was at Eton, summers mostly, when London is too beastly hot. It was always too crowded in my family's house."

Lucy pictured a small manor house overflowing with children and toys and spaniels.

"Tell me about your home," she said. "What was it like growing up in Cornwall?"

He made a face. "Just the usual thing . . . me getting into scrapes at my brothers' instigation. My sisters pleading for my hide with my father. My mother raised prizewinning tulips, and I used to help her in the garden, which made me into an object of mirth with my gentle brothers. We were never far away from a bout of fisticuffs in those days."

"Which also explains how you were able to disable Tom so easily."

"Aye. I learned to give as good as I got. But my mother used to tell me that there was more strength in resisting violence, than in submitting to it. But then, she is also the one who taught me how to land a punch."

Lucy giggled. "Truly?"

"She said that if I was going to get the stuffing beaten out of me twice a week, I'd better learn to defend myself." There it was again, that fond, husky tone of voice he'd used when speaking of Consuelo.

"She sounds delightful."

"Mmm, as mothers go, mine is a treat. Still as pretty as the day my father carried her off from her uncle's home in Derry."

"My mother managed to keep her looks," Lucy said softly. "She was something of a sensation when she made her come-out. Susanne got her coloring—white-blond hair and emerald green eyes." She made a small moue of discontent. "I was always the less flamboyant sister."

Roddy cocked his head and gazed at her assessingly.

Lucy felt the beginning of a blush and raised her hands to her cheeks. "Oh, no . . . I wasn't fishing for a compliment. Please don't think that."

"You don't need to fish with me, Lucy," he said, touching her sleeve. "I will always tell you what I think of you." His eyes told her exactly what he was thinking at that moment; there was admiration there and a sudden flaring of desire. He bit his lip as he leaned his head toward her.

Lucy felt the panic return, the faltering, ragged heartbeat of fear. He was going to kiss her again, which served her right for griping about her sister's looks. Her vow to stay chipper in his company hadn't lasted long.

"I'll let you get back to your friends now," she said as she moved rapidly away from him toward the door.

He watched her retreat with amusement. "I expect they can spare me," he said as he followed cautiously in her wake, like a man trailing a timid fawn. "I thought you might like a tour of the house . . . keep you from getting lost, at the very least."

The last thing Lucy wanted was to spend the rest of the afternoon with Roddy. Actually, it was the first and only thing she wanted, but she knew that giving in to temptation only weakened a person's character. She had been strangely and uncharacteristically compliant with him in the passage when he'd kissed her. But that aberration would never happen again.

"Thank you, but no. I will do fine on my own."

Roddy caught up with her at the doorway. She was halfway out into the hall, when his arm reached out and drew her back into the room. He gently pushed the door closed with his free hand and settled her against the wide embrasure of the doorpost.

"We might never find you," he said softly. "You'll end up wandering these halls like Snowball's ghostly maiden."

"Snowball's what?" she said, trying to sidle away from the hand that still lingered at her waist.

"I told you yesterday morning. Snowball swears he saw a ghost in the hallway—a young woman in a dark cloak with long white hair. He went after her, but she disappeared into thin air. He's taken to roaming the halls late at night now, hoping to see her again."

"That's daft," she said. "I fancy he just had too much to drink that night."

"Wouldn't surprise me," he said. "We've all been over-indulging these past nights. Only way to fight off the boredom. But that's changed now."

"And why is that?" she asked.

He tightened his hold and drew her to within an inch of his chest. "Because you're here. You'll keep us civilized, ma'am."

"Oh will I?" she asked archly. "Lesson one, then," she added as she firmly disengaged his arm with her hand. "No familiarities unless they have been requested."

His eyes darkened and his voice grew soft. "I thought I was being extremely civil, Luce."

She drew a long breath. "Roddy, you must stop this. I know it seems I was willing there in the hall outside Consuelo's room, but you merely caught me unawares."

"Oh, I see. You'll only let me kiss you if I jump out at you from a dark corner."

"No, that is not at all what I mean." She had to restrain a growl of frustration. "You dishonor me with these attentions." She wracked her brain for a stronger deterrent. "What would your mother think?"

He grinned and slid one hand along her upper arm. "She'd think I had finally come to my senses," he replied. A sudden expression of dismay narrowed his eyes. "Never say you find me repellent, Lucy . . ."

She groaned softly. He was possibly the least repellent creature on earth.

"No . . . oh no," she said, stopping herself from laying a reassuring hand upon his furrowed brow. "You are kind and amusing." And gloriously fair, she longed to add. "But, Roddy, as much as I enjoy your company, there is no place for such . . . intimacies between us. It's not . . . it's not sporting of you."

This arrow went home with a vengeance. He winced. "I didn't mean to take advantage of you," he said with a sigh. "As I said before, I just wanted to do something to make you happy."

"Happiness never comes without a price tag, Mr. Kempthorne. In this case, a very high one."

She moved past him and opened the door. This time she was fully into the hall when he caught her. He lifted her off her feet and set her against the closed half of the double doors. She felt the hard wood against her back, his body pressing her there.

"What are you doing?" she growled softly.

"Giving you a point of comparison," he said and then his mouth was on hers. He kissed her hard, his lips and teeth and tongue urgent and relentless.

Lucy's initial panic ceased immediately when she realized he was laughing under his breath as he kissed her. She struggled away from him, her eyes flashing. "What the devil was that about, Roddy?"

"I was demonstrating the sort of kiss that makes you unhappy as opposed to what I am offering you—the sort that does."

"No kisses make me happy," she cried, nearly stamping her foot. "I am a thirty-year-old spinster, for heaven's sake. Kissing is not, nor will it ever be, something that pleases me."

"Liar," he said, chucking her quickly under the chin. "You were nearly delirious after the first time."

"Shock," she said heatedly.

"Happiness," he shot back. "Ah, but I'll heed you. The next time we kiss, it will be at your instigation. You have my word on it." He bowed swiftly and went striding down the hall.

As she made her way back to her room, she tried to tamp down her simmering frustration at Roddy. She'd never met anyone who so charmed and infuriated her at the same time.

Of course she wanted him to kiss her. She'd have to be in her grave not to want that. It was a measure of his callowness that *he* could not distinguish between wanting something, and the repercussions of fulfilling that want. He was like a child who couldn't keep his fingers from the jam jar, regardless of the sticky mess that resulted. He was a lot like Susanne that way.

That sudden revelation startled her. Roddy Kempthorne was indeed very much like her sister—both of them willful and charming, adroit at getting their own way. Not brusque and direct as Lucy herself was, they used their winning natures to bend others to their will. But Lucy swore she would not be swayed. She was certainly not going to initiate any more kissing, so if Roddy kept to his promise, there was an end to the problem.

As Lucy crossed the great hall, she had a thought to look in on the countess. Roddy had said she might know something useful about the missing child, and there was no time like the present to find out. She went upstairs and made her way quickly through the narrow passage, trying not to dwell on the sublime taste of Roddy's mouth as he'd kissed her up against the wall.

The countess bid her enter after one knock. She went into the room and drifted over to the divan, which was now littered with playing cards.

Consuelo looked up at her and smiled. "So how do you find Ballabragh, Miss Parnell?"

"It's very overpowering . . . it almost makes me feel like a ghost," Lucy responded truthfully. "Transparent and ungrounded."

"Yes," the countess said, making room on the divan for Lucy. "The house does that to you at first. But that will change, *you* will change . . . once you begin to feel its warmth." She gathered up the cards, the bangles at her wrists clinking softly. "Would you like me to read your fortune in the Tarot?"

Lucy looked intrigued as she settled on the side of the bed. "What is the Tarot?"

"The wisdom of the ancients . . ." She waved her hands over the cards, looking like an Iberian sorceress with her flowing gown and glittering eyes.

"Very well," Lucy said tentatively. "If it will amuse you."

"It will amuse us both, I expect."

The Spanish woman fanned the deck, her plump fingers impatiently flicking the edge of the cards. "This one represents you," Consuelo said at last, setting down the one she had chosen. "The Queen of Swords, a hazel-eyed brunette."

"I have my own card?" Lucy squinted down at the mournful woman displayed there.

"Yes, of course you do. And now, since you are an unmarried lady, you must chose a man's card. If his card appears in my formation, it is a very good sign."

"Must I choose?"

Consuelo nodded. Lucy looked through the pack with its arcane, garish drawings and drew out the Fool.

"Ah," said Consuelo with a gleam in her eye. "Why does this not surprise me? Now you must ask a question."

Lucy worried her lip a moment, and then said, "Will I . . . find what I am seeking?"

She watched, nearly mesmerized, as Consuelo shuffled and then rapidly set the cards down in a cross-shaped pattern around the Queen of Swords. She studied the cards before her and then her mouth pursed into a frown.

"What do you see?" Lucy asked, a little breathless. She'd often had her fortune read from stones or coins in the marketplace in Kandy, but never once since she'd come to England, not even at the yearly fair in Kiddlington. Yardley frowned on such pagan practices.

"I see great unhappiness in your past." Consuelo's beringed finger touched a card with a drawing of the moon. "Loss, fear, madness . . ." She paused and added, "Betrayal."

Lucy's eyes were widening now. "What about the present?"

"Hmm . . . there is an obstacle, here—the Emperor reversed. It means your focus is too narrow, you must seek with the heart and not with the brain. And this one, the Nine of Swords, indicates your present state of mind." The card bore a picture of a distressed woman sitting up in bed, her hands over her face. "You are feeling desolation, sorrow, perhaps even guilt."

Lucy felt the air thinning out in the room. This pastime was no longer amusing, it was almost frightening.

The countess stopped the reading and studied Lucy quietly with her dark, deep eyes. When she spoke again, her voice was hushed. "This, now, is what you must face—the Tower." Lucy saw the crenellated stone tower with flames shooting from it. Hardly reassuring. "You must break free from the things that bind you, *cara*. You must knock down walls, and learn to accept change."

"And what of the future?" Lucy asked in a constricted voice.

Consuelo grinned ruefully. "There is no Fool in your future, I am afraid. He has not shown his face."

"Well that's a good thing then," Lucy said, trying to sound glib. She knew what Consuelo was telling her, though. Roddy was not going to be more than a passing acquaintance.

"You will be guided by the dark-haired Knight of Wands, however. He's a turbulent fellow, so be warned. But he generally brings about good things.

"And," Consuelo added, "there is something more." She stroked the edge of a card which displayed a man and woman walking with a child. "The Ten of Pentacles . . . it means home and family, and sometimes riches." Consuelo smiled and reached out to tug Lucy's sleeve. "That is not so bad then, eh?"

"Do the cards tell you anything else? I still don't have an answer to my question."

The countess's eyes narrowed. "You must draw your own con-
clusions, Miss Parnell. The Tarot is only a guide.

Lucy gave a little sigh. Even the wisdom of the ancients could
not reassure her.

Consuelo again scooped the cards off the coverlet, slipped them
into a small box, and then wrapped the box in a piece of violet silk.
Lucy was glad to see the last of them.

"So tell me," the countess said, as she leaned back against her
mound of pillows, "tell me about this wicked brother, and the child
who cries in the night."

Lucy opened her mouth to protest, but the countess stopped her
with a raised hand. "I do not like mysteries, Miss Parnell. Roddy
told me because I insisted he should. He asked if you could stay
here, and I needed to know why I should take a stranger into my
home. I must say, he made a good case for you."

Lucy knew when she had been beaten. She shifted onto her
side, one hand cradling the side of her head, amazed that she could
be this informal with anyone, let alone a countess. But Consuelo
seemed to invite informality, and Lucy was finding herself drawn
into the Spanish woman's indolent spell. As she told her tale, the
countess occasionally pushed a large box of sweetmeats to her side
of the divan. Lucy had rarely tasted anything so delicious, and
since she had foregone lunch, her appetite was keen.

She offered only the basic elements of the tale—Susanne's
abrupt departure, the birth of the baby, her sister's death. She purposely omitted the part she had unwittingly played, allowing Yardley to get his hands on her sister's note. The countess's mention of
betrayal during the Tarot reading continued to trouble her. Still, she
must have painted a very black picture of Yardley; when she was
through speaking, her companion had sparks of anger in her eyes.

"The injustice," she said fiercely. "That such men exist, who
dare sit in judgment on women." She looked away from Lucy for
several heartbeats. "I left my church to marry the earl," she said in
a husky whisper. "My brothers cursed me for it. As though God favors one brand of faith over another. So foolish to think that. But
they cursed me and said I would be barren for my heresy."

Lucy gasped. Even Yardley had never presumed to speak for
the deity.

"So that is why you and the earl had no children?"

A large, round tear drifted down Consuelo's cheek. "I had three
children, *cara*, All taken from me. The last only three years ago.
My Miguelito was only two months old. And the others . . . did not

live more than six months. That is why I came to this house after
the earl died. I cannot bear to be at Steyne, to see those tiny graves
beside that of my husband."

Lucy slid across the bed and touched the countess's arm. "After
my sister died," she said, settling herself beside the countess, "I
stayed in my room for nearly two months. But, dear lady, I eventually rose from my bed and took up my life again. In truth, I took it
up with a vengeance. That was when I left my brother's home and
began to make my own way in the world."

"You think I am weak for staying here," Consuelo said, putting
her chin up. "But it is not weakness, it is strength that keeps me
from returning to the world. I long for my life, for London and my
friends there. But I will not let myself have those things again.
Those pleasures are gone from me."

Lucy worried her lower lip. "I see . . . you are doing penance.
For leaving your church and bringing your brothers' curses down
upon your children. Which means you are letting them rule your
life . . . even now, years later."

The countess blinked several times. *"¿Es verdad?"* Her mouth
twisted and her eyes grew black. "Ah, but how can I live my life
without my children? With nothing of my dear husband left for me
to cherish? I must bear the burden of my loss."

Lucy had no answer for this. Her own grief now seemed so
petty compared to that of the countess. She had lost a beloved sister, it was true, and perhaps a niece, but not the child of her own
body or a beloved spouse. That would rend a woman's heart beyond anything.

"Leave me," Consuelo ordered wearily in a curt, imperious
voice.

Lucy scrambled from the divan. The countess reached out
quickly to take her hand and said in a gentler tone, "But come and
see me tomorrow. Perhaps we will walk in the garden."

"Yes," Lucy said, her eyes growing bright. "There will be new
buds and spring grass."

"New buds," Consuelo echoed with a wan smile.

As Lucy moved toward the doorway, another door to her left
opened and a tall, thin woman came into the room, bearing a pile
of clothing. Lucy paused for an instant to look at her. It was hard to
make out her features in the dimly lit room, and then Lucy realized
the woman wore a sheer, dark veil that covered her face and drifted
behind her over her severe black dress.

"Ah, Zuzu," Consuelo called softly from her bed. *"Esta es Senorita Parnell."*

The veiled woman nodded once in Lucy's direction. "How do you do?" Lucy nodded back.

"She has no English," Consuelo remarked. "But she looks after me very well. Here—" she motioned for the woman to hand the garments to Lucy—"these are for you."

"You are very kind," Lucy said just before she slipped out the door. For some reason the hair on the back of her neck was standing quite on end.

She returned to her room and laid her three new gowns on the counterpane. There were two day dresses, one lavender and one a pale russet. The dinner gown was stylishly cut and, though it was gray, it was a soft, shimmering shade that brought to mind the undersides of silvery clouds. She undid the tabs on her own faded dress and tugged the dinner gown over her head. It fit her perfectly, as if made to her form. She tried to do up the row of tiny buttons that graced the back, but after struggling fruitlessly with them for several minutes, she went to the bellpull and tugged, embarrassed to be bothering a servant over something so trivial.

Several minutes later there was a knock at the door.

"Come in," Lucy said as she turned around to allow the maid to do her up. "I can't seem to reach these buttons."

Two hands made their way up her back, fastening each closure with maddening slowness. Lucy felt herself start to tremble as the heady scent of tobacco and claret and sandalwood permeated the air around her.

She closed her eyes, and prayed she was only imagining that scent.

"There," Roddy said from behind her, setting his chin on her shoulder. "That's about the pleasantest chore I've been set to in years."

"Roddy," she said with a whine, still unable to turn and face him. Her back felt like it was dappled with heat where he had touched her. "I was expecting a housemaid."

"I came to get those notes you mentioned." He hesitated. "I did knock, you know. I should have spoken, made you turn around, but a fellow can only resist so much."

His arms slid around her waist, his hands crossing beneath the fitted bodice of the gown. She allowed herself to lean back against him for the space of a heartbeat. She heard his swiftly indrawn breath as her body nested with his.

"Lucy . . ." he crooned raggedly.

Her insides went liquid. Her only thought was to turn and find his mouth, to bury her hands in his hair, to feel the lean, graceful length of him against her. She was about to cast her scruples to the wind, when the door swung open.

"Miss?" Mrs. Granger stood there on the threshold, a dark silhouette of judgment.

Roddy stepped back from Lucy without the least show of alarm. "Miss Parnell was having trouble with her buttons," he said in an offhand manner. "Doing them up, that is," he added.

Lucy thought she was going to expire. She had a fair idea of what was going through the housekeeper's head at the moment. Nothing that was at all complimentary to Lucy.

"Thank you, Mrs. Granger," Lucy managed to choke out. "Mr. Kempthorne came to my room to get these—" She went to the desk and practically threw her notes at him. "And he noticed I had missed one or two of my buttons."

The housekeeper gave a minute curtsy. "You don't owe me any explanations, miss." She drifted away into the shadows of the hall.

"Now that," said Roddy as he sprawled back on her bed, "is the proper way to deliver a set-down. Pity Mrs. Granger ain't in the *ton*—she could give lessons to Brummel himself."

Lucy picked up the fireplace poker and brandished it at him. "Get off my bed!"

He cocked his head. "Louder, Luce. I don't think the kitchen maids heard you."

She gave him a stinging whack on the sole of his boot. "Off!"

"Oh, be that way. But you're as good as compromised now, my girl." He stood up and moved toward the door.

"I most certainly am not. It takes more than doing up buttons." Her pique heightened to resentment. She called out, "And what about your promise to leave me alone? You were the one who started this."

He turned with a grin. "I said I wouldn't kiss you, Lucy. Never said I wouldn't touch you."

"Well, promise me now . . . come on."

"Lucy—"

"Promise me, Roddy. I don't like being manhandled any more than you do. Only I don't possess a right uppercut to defend myself."

He looked thoughtful for a moment.

"If you are to help me find my niece, I can't always be wrestling with you," she added. "It's exhausting."

"Very well, I promise not to touch you." He added with devilish twinkle, "Unless you ask me to."

He was gone before she had a chance to utter the satisfyingly crude word she'd learned from the Burbridge stableboy.

Chapter Six

Lucy finished arranging her hair and left her room for dinner. Roddy was waiting on the landing; she attempted to skirt him but he fell into step beside her.

"I hear you went to visit Consuelo this afternoon. Twice in one day," he said. "That's a good start."

Lucy looked over her shoulder, toward Consuelo's suite. "Who is that woman who waits on her? The one in black?"

Roddy shrugged and reached for her hand to lead her down the staircase. Then he obviously recalled his promise and merely motioned for her to precede him. "She has any number of people who wait on her, some who came with her from Spain, when she was the Spanish ambassador's daughter in London. That wing is full of Consuelo's servants. Lady's maids, hairdressers and the like. Pity she rarely uses them anymore. I expect they are bored to flinders stuck here on this island."

He led her across the main hall, through a rabbit warren of passages until they came to a brightly lit drawing room. His three friends were standing near the fire, and after seeing the furnishings, the spindly chairs and delicate, straight-backed couches, all in the popular Egyptian style, Lucy did not wonder that they feared to sit down. Mrs. Burbridge had cajoled her husband into ordering an Egyptian settee for their drawing room, and after five minutes of sitting on it, the doughty Mr. B. had declared it was so uncomfortable he didn't wonder that the Egyptians resorted to asps.

Nonnie came across to the doorway. "Miss Parnell," he said with a deep bow. "Welcome."

"Algernon Swithens, Earl of Steyne," Roddy pronounced. The Joker and Snowball likewise bowed and Roddy said, "Gregory Asquithe, Viscount Broome. Owen Griffith—"

"Lord of the library," the Joker interjected.

"Alas, it's true. I have no title," Owen lamented with a smile. "But I've a deal more in my brainbox than these paltry fellows."

"And his father owns most of the ships in Wales," Roddy whispered over her shoulder.

Lucy curtsied to each of them in turn. The earl poured her a cordial and settled her on one of the spindly chairs. It creaked as she sat down and she prayed it would bear her weight until dinner was announced. All of the young men, with the exception of Roddy, seemed ill at ease to have her in their midst. She imagined they would be laughing and joking among themselves if they had been alone. Now they stood in a semicircle around her and twitched at their neckcloths, looking for all the world like restless schoolboys in their best Sunday suits.

"I understand you have had a birthday, my lord," she said lightly.

"Nonnie," the earl replied. "Please call me Nonnie. Whenever I am addressed as 'my lord' I keep looking over my shoulder for my pater."

"You'll grow into your title," Roddy assured him.

"Even if you never grow into your nose," Owen remarked from behind his hand.

"I heard that," Nonnie said with a scowl. 'I am proud of the Swithins nose, if you must know. If you would drag yourself from the library, Snow, and take in the portrait gallery, you would see that all the earls have possessed this nose."

"And a few of the countesses as well," the Joker added.

"And as for my birthday," Nonnie said, getting back on track, "it's not until Saturday."

Lucy looked at Roddy with some confusion. "But I thought you said you were celebrating it the other night . . . when you tried on the old clothing in the attic."

"We were looking for costumes for Saturday," Owen explained. "There is to be a fete in Peel and Nonnie thought it would be a lark if we arrived dressed like his ancestors."

"But Snowball was a killjoy," Nonnie said with a frown. "I found him a fetching gown worn by my late grandmother—she had Jacobite leanings and spent a month in the Tower before my grandfather whisked her off and married her."

"That would rather startle the villagers in Peel, don't you think?" Lucy responded, trying to suppress her amusement.

"Roddy's the pretty one," Owen grumbled. "Let him wear the dress."

"Oh no," Roddy said, "I have my costume all picked out."

"If Mrs. Granger can get the mud off it," the Joker reminded him.

"Still," Nonnie said, it's a pity about that dress. It's a corker. Miles of lace and yards of brocade. With panniers out to here—" He spread his arms out from his sides. "A shame to keep it hidden away in that attic. But dash it all, Miss Parnell is right. A woman ought to wear it."

Lucy watched as, one by one, all four young men turned their eyes on her.

"I say," Nonnie crowed. "*you* must wear it, Miss Parnell."

"I . . . I am not going to the fete. That is . . . I was not invited."

"You are now."

"And I am trying to avoid my stepbrother. It would not be wise to attend a public party."

"Well, the Wibberlys and their guests ain't invited," Nonnie assured her. "What's more, you will be in disguise. I doubt anyone would recognize you once Consuelo's dresser got through with you. She's a dab hand with hair and such."

Roddy had latched on to this idea with glee. "We will have such fun, Miss Parnell. The mayor is to give a speech and there will be dancing and street performers." He was looking at her with open expectation, but then his face fell. "Oh, sorry, I forgot." He turned to his friends. "Miss Parnell suffered the loss of her mother this winter. She can't attend a party so soon after."

The other three men mumbled their condolences. All the bonhomie in the room seemed to have vanished.

"I would like to go," Lucy said, trying to resuscitate the cheerful mood. "In fact I will go. My mother never held with long periods of mourning. I don't think she would mind."

"Good girl," Nonnie said, rubbing his hands together. "We shall have a splendid time. And now there is my butler hovering in the doorway. Yes, Travis, we see you. Come, Miss Parnell, let me take you in to supper." He held out his arm and Lucy rose and laid her hand over his sleeve.

Roddy followed behind them. Owen and the Joker both noted the expression in his eyes when they rested on her. The two exchanged wry looks as they made their way into the dining parlor. There was a standing wager in the betting book at White's that Roddy Kempthorne would be the last of them to succumb to a woman. Not because he disliked women, mind, but because he had proven particularly adept at avoiding lasting entanglements.

"She's hobbled him," the Joker said under his breath. "For all her one-and-thirty years."

"I'm not sure," Owen said with a skeptical frown. "I think it's just Roddy doing what he always does, bringing home the wounded birds and lame horses."

"Hardly flattering to Miss Parnell," his companion remarked. "And in spite of her age, she does have something in the way of beauty." His gaze shifted to Lucy, who walked several steps ahead of him. "Graceful carriage, proud tilt to her head . . ."

"You're still making her sound like a horse," Owen drawled, cuffing him on the arm. "Why not just say, good strong teeth and a knowing look in her eyes, and be done with it."

"I'd bid on her," the Joker said softly. "And take her for a good run afterward."

"Oh, Lord," Owen muttered. "Don't let Roddy hear you say that. He'll have you by the throat, the mood he's in lately."

"Well, that's my point. He's never been 'in a mood' before over any of his amours. That's what is different about Miss Parnell."

Lucy did her best to be amusing and entertaining to Roddy's friends. It was difficult though. Her social life in Yardley's home had been restricted to dry academic teas. She had little small talk and though she could have spoken of her life in Ceylon, it was still a painful topic, even all these years later. Aside from Delhi and a brief stay in London, Edinburgh was the largest city she had ever visited, and that trip hardly warranted a mention. The city had been cold, smoky, and full of disagreeable people, paramount among them the MacTeagues, with whom she had traveled.

Though in fairness to Edinburgh, she might have had a better time if she'd been with better companions. She had managed to slip away from the family for one evening to see a production of *Twelfth Night,* and when she mentioned this, Nonnie, Owen, and the Joker perked up.

"Never say you are a devotee of the Bard," Nonnie exclaimed. "You can't get Roddy into a theater on a bet, but the rest of us relish a good play."

Lucy soon found herself chattering away, all her self-consciousness fled. She discovered that Nonnie's library contained at least two Shakespeare folios, and that Owen had himself written for the stage while at Oxford. The Joker, meanwhile, claimed to have acted the role of Romeo in his uncle's yearly theatrical production at Levelands in Hampshire.

"Fell off the balcony during rehearsals, as I recall," Roddy drawled. "Took Juliet with him, too. Good thing they were performing in a hayloft."

Lucy hid her laughter behind her napkin. She gave the Joker a consoling grin. "I adore rustic productions."

"Oh, it was rustic," Roddy assured her.

By the time dinner was over, Lucy felt in great charity with Roddy's friends. Even the Joker had left off his ogling behavior and contrived to converse with her as though she were a lady and not a lightskirt.

She excused herself, intending to leave the men to their port, but Roddy rose and followed her out into the hall.

"We won't be joining you in the drawing room," he said a bit hesitantly. "We've got plans to, um, visit a neighbor after dinner." Lucy wondered why he was being so mysterious. "But before you go, I want your permission to tell my friends about your sister's child. They need to know the particulars if they are going to help you. I went over your notes—you are not a don's sister for nothing—they were very thorough. But we both know it will be more expedient if they aid us."

"They won't mind looking for Susanne's bastard daughter?" she asked forthrightly.

"My friends may be many things, but they are not sticklers. Snowball grew up with one of his father's byblows, as a matter of fact. Daffyd is now his father's bailiff. You won't find them cutting up stiff over this."

She mulled this over. For so many years Susanne's scandal had been a closely guarded secret. Then she realized it no longer mattered. She had no prospects for marriage who would be put off by her sister's fall from grace. She wagered Sir Humphrey would take her on any terms, even if she were the one who had fallen.

"Tell them," she said. "And make sure you thank them, Roddy. For their kindness to me."

As she made her way upstairs, she realized their kind offer had been directed not at her, but at Roddy himself. Because, she suspected, there was little his friends would not do for him.

All through dinner, in spite of their playful teasing behavior toward him, each one of them had followed Roddy with their eyes. They sought his approval of their jests and were gratified when he was amused. Roddy was not their fool, as she'd first thought, he was their leader. Not Nonnie, the earl, or the Joker with his supercilious airs. Not Owen Griffith, the clever one. No, it was

Ramshackle Roddy, the charmer, who set the tone. It was an unsettling discovery.

She had to rethink her opinion of him. It was easy to dismiss a
man who was a pretty fool. Not so easy to dismiss him when he
showed sudden depth of understanding and bursts of insight.
Roddy had been keeping her off balance since he'd showed up in
the parlor of the Greene Man and enraged Yardley. He had further
confounded her when he'd told her about the man they'd set to
watch the Wibberlys' house. Although it had been his valet's idea,
she had to applaud Roddy for thinking to ask him. Even very wise
men didn't always know enough to ask others for help.

Lucy was sound asleep, wrapped in a borrowed nightgown which
must have belonged to the countess, since it was a confection of
creamy lace and bronze-colored tissue, and several sizes too large,
when Roddy roused her. She grumbled and pushed his insistent
hand away, thinking only that she was having a vexing dream.

"I say, Luce, you've got to wake up."

When she realized she wasn't dreaming and that Roddy
Kempthorne was sitting on the edge of her bed, she sat up with a
start. The neckline of her gown slid down off one shoulder.

He had carried in a candle; it wavered in his hand as he watched
her tug the lace back over her bared skin. He was dressed in a loose
coat of dark canvas and black breeches.

"What on earth are you doing in my bedroom in the middle of
the night?" she croaked irritably. "And why is there burnt cork all
over your face?"

He brushed a hand across his cheeks. "I thought I'd gotten most
of it off at the pump."

She pointed to his brow. "You missed several spots."

"Never mind that," he said impatiently. "I've brought you
something." He pointed to the side of the bed, where her small
traveling trunk now sat.

She looked from the trunk to Roddy, and then back again to the
trunk.

"Did Yardley return it?" She couldn't keep the disbelief from
her voice.

"Don't be a nitwit, Lucy. Of course he didn't. We went and got
it. Burgled it back, in fact. I told you the Swithens hate the Wibberlys. Nonnie was only too happy to be my accomplice. We gave
the groundskeeper's mastiff the roast left over from lunch to keep
him distracted, and then climbed in through the library window.

The Joker kept watch and Snowball minded the carriage, which we'd left in the lane behind the house. It was rare fun, I can tell you."

"I had a feeling you were off getting into mischief," she said dolefully.

"Not mischief . . . we were righting an injustice."

Lucy gritted her teeth. "And making Yardley even more furious. He'll know who was behind this."

"How will he know?"

"Because the only person who has any interest in my trunk is me. It will make him even more determined to harass me. And if he suspects you aided me, he will surely learn from his host that you are at Ballabragh. It won't take him more than a minute to deduce that I am here too."

"You think he'll come here then?"

She nodded slowly.

Roddy uttered, "I hope he does. Nonnie will pour boiling oil on him from the battlements."

She sank back onto the bed and pulled the covers over her head. "You are still beyond reasoning with, aren't you, Roddy? Still behaving as though this is a game. If you'd really wanted to be a help to me, you wouldn't have gone haring off with your friends. You'd have stayed here and planned a strategy for finding Susanne's child."

"I can do that tomorrow," he said. He tugged the covers down and glared at her. "And a 'thank you' would be nice, right about now. We risked our skins to bring you that trunk. That mastiff has jaws like a steel trap. Good thing he liked rib roast, or we'd all be torn to shreds."

"Such melodrama," she said with a sniff. "But I am not impressed. It wasn't dangerous and you know it. Just another lark. But you've made it dangerous for me now. Yardley will be keeping watch on this house, and I wouldn't put it past him to set his bullies on me next time."

Roddy gnawed his lip. "I don't understand. I heard him threaten you at the inn, but didn't think he would really take you against your will. This is a civilized place, there are laws against abduction."

She sat up again and crossed her arms over her chest. "I am mad, you see. Addled. Unbalanced. He has medical documents attesting to that. Written by more than one physician. He could have me placed in Bedlam if I really infuriated him. And I don't want to go to Bedlam."

"Of course you don't. That is all nonsense. What sort of doctor would sign such papers?"

"The sort who owe Yardley favors. He has any number of doctors and lawyers in his pocket. It's what he does, finds people who can be of use to him and then figures out ways that they can be made to dance to his tune. He discovers their weaknesses and . . ."

"Blackmails them." He finished the thought for her.

She nodded. "One doctor had gambling debts that Yardley paid off. The man was all too eager to sign those papers. The other one actually treated me after my sister died. Yardley convinced him that it was only a matter of time before I became as unstable as my mother."

Roddy slipped his hand into hers. "It's what you fear too, isn't it? That you will fall prey to the same ailment? It's why those strange dreams trouble you so much."

"Of course I fear it," she said intently. "Even though I remind myself that my mother was high-strung and nervy from her childhood on. And that I am neither of those things, nor ever have been. Susanne was more likely to have followed my mother into madness than I was."

Roddy slid from the bed and knelt on the floor, his face canted over her. "Listen to me, Luce. No one will ever put you in that horrid place. Not while I have breath in my body. And bear this in mind—if Yardley fears a scandal if you discover your sister's baseborn child, what then of the scandal of having a stepsister in Bedlam? How can he hush that up with his precious peers at Oxford?"

"I don't think he would really do it, Roddy. It's just such a fearful thing to even consider."

"Then don't consider it," he said simply. He was watching her expectantly, and she tried to muster a smile. But none was forthcoming.

"I was going to work on being more cheerful today," she said. "Not a very good beginning."

"No, and you are frowning again and you know what that means . . ."

"Oh, no," she said, pushing him back. "You promised, remember?"

His eyes shone so blue, his dimples carved so deeply into his lean cheeks as he nodded. "I also remember what it felt like to kiss you, sweetheart. Every minute since then, I've relived that feeling.

Of holding you, of tasting you . . . your mouth tastes like sweet wine, do you know that? Better than claret, hotter than brandy . . ."

His voice was a low, hoarse whisper, melting her resistance. She raised herself from the bed, lured by that voice. "Roddy . . ." she murmured softly.

"Yes?" he crooned. His eyes gleamed in the candlelight, expectant, bemused.

Her choice, she knew. Her decision. To flirt with the danger or to push it firmly away. He'd said he wouldn't coerce her and she believed him. The only problem was resisting her own insistent desire to touch him.

"I can't . . ." she murmured.

"Can't what?" he asked as softly.

"Do this," she said in a throaty whisper.

He set his mouth a millimeter from hers. "Yes," he said.

"I can't."

"Ask me," he coaxed, drawing even closer. Lord, she could feel his soft breath against her lips.

"I dare not . . ."

"Ask me." He wasn't touching her anywhere, but her body was tingling all over.

"Please," she moaned. She wasn't sure how she'd meant the word, but he took it as assent. He caught her head between his hands, and lowered his mouth that infinitesimal distance to hers, stealing her breath with the gentleness of his kiss. His tongue danced against her lips and coaxed her mouth open a hair's breadth. Her lips parted as she sighed. It was all the license he needed.

She felt him invade her, slick and hot. His murmuring groans increased in urgency as he forced her down against her pillow. This was no kind of kissing she had ever envisioned, with his mouth open and hungry, and his tongue lashing against hers, filling her with trembling heat.

Her hands tangled in his dark hair, drawing him into even closer contact. He slid onto the bed, one long leg angled over both of hers, holding her, trapping her from squirming away. Though that was the last thing she wanted to do.

Roddy's hand traced down her side, clasping her hip beneath the thin coverlet. At that intimate contact, she arched against him, her body willful and eager.

He reared his head back from her, his eyes wild and darker than indigo. "I . . . need"— he panted— "I . . . I want to . . . to go slow for you, Jenny. Don't do anything just now. Please . . ."

Her eyes clouded with uncertainty. He set his mouth against each eyelid. "Ah, don't look at me that way. You've done nothing wrong. But I am on a hair trigger with you, my girl. Now let me find my own pace."

Lucy drew her hands away from his hair, mourning the loss of its silky texture. Roddy shifted off the bed, but kept his hands on her shoulders.

"What should I do?" she asked in a husky voice.

"You should send me off to my own bed," he said a bit sharply. "I wonder that you don't."

"And I wonder you would remind me of that. It's clear you stole back my trunk so you could come here tonight and compromise me. Who am I to begrudge such a gallant act?"

"I don't want to talk about that festering trunk, Jenny. I just want to kiss you."

He was making inroads on that very thing, when she opened her eyes and said, "Why do you keep calling me Jenny? Are you foxed?"

"You *are* Jenny." He sighed against her cheek. "You've always been Jenny, I just never realized it."

Lucy had a sudden fear that he'd been in love with another woman, one who had spurned him. And that he was merely smitten with her because she reminded him of that lost love. That would be a pretty comedown.

"Who is Jenny?" she demanded, shaking him by the shoulders.

He rose up on his elbows, his chest hovering above the bodice of her nightgown. "Jenny," he said with great forbearance, "is my youngest sister's favorite doll. I used to hide all her other dolls to tease her, and sometimes we'd pretend to behead them when my brothers and I played at King Louis and the guillotine. But I never touched Jenny . . . there was a look in her eyes, you see. She was . . . unapproachable, almost stern, as she sat there on her shelf. But beautiful and graceful. Like you, Miss Parnell."

He set a kiss upon her shoulder and murmured, "I fell in love with that doll when I was five . . . but I didn't know the real Jenny existed till I was twenty-five."

"You *are* foxed," she said, still a little dazed by his confession. And by his lovely, lilting words.

" 'Pon my honor I am not."

"Fanciful then . . ."

"Yes, very, very fanciful when it comes to you."

He lowered his face to the neckline of her nightgown and let his tongue trace over the soft skin that peeked above it. Lucy could not prevent herself from drifting one hand through his disordered hair. He smelled of night air and burnt cork and there was the faint lingering scent of roast beef. She swore she could have devoured him.

Instead she lay back and watched him lace kisses along her collarbone. His dark hair was tumbled over his brow, and when he looked up at her through that shaggy forelock, she was reminded of the demon ram. Only this ram was no demon, not unless demons kissed like angels, which she doubted. She giggled softly at her own nonsense, and he raised his head.

"Ticklish?"

"Not a bit," she assured him. "Are you?"

He shook his head soberly and then his mouth twisted to one side. "Well, only in one place. But you'll never find it, so there's no point—"

But she was already reaching out, digging her fingers into his ribs with a determined grin.

"Ah, no . . ." As he scuttled back from her, she lost her balance and tumbled onto the floor. She lay there laughing up at him, the gown's neckline now fallen off both shoulders. He sat back and looked at her for the space of a heartbeat and then laid one hand over her breast. Lucy felt the heat careen through her, from breast to spine and from the depths of her belly up to her throat. Roddy's eyes were shadowed as he leaned forward and slid his arm beneath her shoulders. He raised her up, again surprising her with his strength, and caught her mouth in a long, suffocating kiss.

Between the sweet fire of his mouth and the piercing pressure of his hand on her breast, Lucy thought she might indeed swoon. Only who wanted to be insensible when there was so much new sensation to experience? Unfortunately, along with the heady rapture that swirled inside her, there was a healthy measure of maidenly guilt. She'd end up paying the piper for allowing Roddy such familiarities, as much as she craved them.

"No." She sighed as he tugged the lacy collar of her nightgown lower. Her hand caught at the fabric, halting its downward progress.

His eyes were narrowed when he pulled back from her. "No?" He read the answer in her face.

She shifted onto the bed and boosted herself up until her back was against the headboard. He sat there unmoving beside her, still on his knees, his hands curled in his lap, his head lowered. She reached out to smooth his hair with her hand, setting the disordered locks into a sleek cap.

"I'm sorry. I don't know what else to say . . ." she said in a shaky voice. "When you kiss me like that, I have no defenses. But it is wrong . . . you must know it is wrong."

He still said nothing.

She hugged her arms around her, suddenly chilled. She had a distressing insight of how ridiculous this situation was. Like something from a theatrical farce—the parched spinster hungry for the caresses of the virile young hero.

"You truly don't understand," he said at last as he got to his feet. There was not a shred of the usual playfulness in his face.

"It doesn't matter, Roddy" she said softly. "Now that I have my purse back, I can return to the Greene Man in the morning. I'm sorry if you lose your bet over that, but maybe this will be a lesson to you not to wager money you don't possess."

Roddy went to the door without another word.

"Roddy, thank you for everything. I . . . I won't ever forget you."

He turned and shrugged carelessly. "You barely know me, Miss Parnell. And I am hardly the stuff of memories."

He went into the hall and shut the door behind him.

Lucy sat there and wondered why her heart felt like a lump of coal.

Chapter Seven

Roddy made his way down to the main floor, whistling a tuneless series of notes. Snowball would be poking around in the library, and Roddy needed his counsel. Not that Snow had much useful knowledge regarding the pursuit of women, but he did have a dashed fine brain.

Owen looked up from his volume of Viking lore when Roddy came into the room. He closed the ponderous book and set it aside. "Was she pleased to get her trunk back?"

Roddy shook his head as he poured himself a healthy measure of brandy. Miss Parnell had accused him of being foxed, and he now fully intended to achieve that state in short order. "She parted my skull with her tongue for being so . . . rash. She thinks her brother will be able to find her now . . . through me."

"That's not what's troubling you though, is it?"

"No," he said as he sat down opposite his friend. Bess moved from the hearth where she'd been drowsing and came to lie at his feet. He poked at her gently with his toe and she sighed in pleasure.

"Let's have it then," Owen said.

"Now that she has her purse back, she wants to return to Peel," Roddy told him sourly. "I never foresaw that outcome when I stole her trunk. Never thought she'd take it into her head to run off."

"Maybe it's for the best," Owen said. "That she leaves here before either of you tumble into something awkward." Roddy's eyes were narrowing. "She's prime grist for you, Roddy. Lonely, mistreated . . . badly in need of looking after. You always manage to find the helpless ones, the strays. So it is natural she feels beholden to you for your intervention. But I doubt if her feelings go much beyond that."

Roddy growled over the edge of his glass. "Are you implying that my feelings do?"

Owen shrugged. "I wouldn't presume to guess. Still, you have made yourself her protector. If she forms a *tendre* for you, things could get sticky. Not to impugn your charms with the fair sex, but you're probably the first personable man she's been near in years. She's easy prey."

"Stop making me sound like some wretched libertine. I don't want to seduce her, I just like being with her."

"Then why didn't you wait till daylight to deliver her trunk, if you're not bent on seduction? Why go to her bedroom? You'd best be careful or you'll end up compromising her, and Connie will see that you make an honest woman of her."

"Trust me, it won't come to that. And as for Miss Parnell being needy, that may be true, but she is also steady and resourceful and determined. Hardly such a victim as you seem to think."

"She is hearing voices . . ." Owen remarked dryly. "That hardly qualifies her as steady."

His companion frowned as he rose from his chair. "At least she ain't off chasing ghosts till all hours of the morning like some I could mention."

Owen watched his friend stalk out of the library. *A bit prickly are we?* he mused. He'd baited Roddy just enough to get a reading on his friend's state of mind, or rather the state of his heart. Maybe the Joker was right, maybe Roddy was truly smitten. That was something Owen could understand, having recently suffered a similar blow himself.

He chuckled. Who was he to cast aspersions on Miss Parnell's otherworldly dreams, when he himself had fallen in love with a ghost? He glanced up at the mantel clock. Nearly three. It was too late for her to be about. It was closer to midnight when he'd first seen her—tall and willowy, with the face of an angel reflected in the light of the candle she'd carried. Funny though, that a ghost would need a candle. He'd not thought of that before. But she'd disappeared from his view like a specter, vanished into the darkness along the hall where she was walking. She'd turned to him with a look of alarm on her lovely face and then she was gone. Surely only a ghost could perform such a feat.

He lowered his head and tried to read. But that face haunted him as surely as the cries of a lost child haunted Miss Parnell.

Lucy cursed softly as she riffled through her trunk for the fifth time. Her purse and her return ticket to Liverpool were gone, and her journal was missing. Her dresses and underthings were here, her comb and brush and her bottle of jasmine scent. But her three most critical possessions were gone. She sat back on her heels and sighed in frustration. Yardley must have taken them, that was the only explanation. But why would he? The trunk had been firmly out of her reach, so why would he remove anything from it? Well, taking the journal made sense, since he would want to know everything about her reasons for being on the island. But her money? And her ticket?

She lifted one of her faded gowns from the interior, and then laid it down again. No, she would wear one of the pastel gowns the countess had given her. No more bleak grays and browns for her, not while she was here at Ballabragh. Even if it did give Roddy Kempthorne the wrong idea, she couldn't resist wearing something light and pretty.

After dressing in the lavender gown and twisting her hair up into a soft knot, she went in search of the countess. If she was to remain at Ballabragh, at least she could keep to her part of the bargain and coax Consuelo from her self-imposed seclusion.

The countess was still abed, which did not surprise Lucy. She offered her visitor a cup of tea, but Lucy shook her head . . . she had breakfasted in her room.

"We are walking in the garden this morning," Lucy reminded her.

The countess made a moue of distaste. "Not today, *cara*. My head aches."

Lucy "Hmmphed," as she went to the large wardrobe and threw the doors open. If there was one thing she excelled at, it was getting slugabeds going in the morning.

She drew out a walking dress in pale green and a chemise of fine lawn.

"Here," she said, laying them on the divan. "Shall I ring for your dresser?"

The countess's mouth puckered. "I have said that I will not—"

"Oh bosh!" Lucy snapped. "It is about time someone with a little sense took charge here. I can see that they all indulge you because they care for you, but it is not true caring to allow someone to fester."

"Fester?"

Lucy knelt on the round bed. "Yes, fester. You see, I know all about festering. I festered for years in my brother's home. Simmered and fretted and wore myself out with regret."

Consuelo set her teacup down on a book. "What has happened to that quiet lady I met yesterday?"

Lucy shrugged. "Maybe it's this house—you warned me that it changes people. I seem to have no patience with anything this morning." She slid closer to the countess. "Anyway, you have a job to do."

"I do?" Consuelo said with some amusement. "And pray what is that?"

"It's a fine old Spanish tradition," Lucy pronounced. "I need you to play duenna."

The woman's eyes lit up in comprehension. "Rodrigo has been forcing his attentions on you then . . . this does not surprise me."

"Not forcing, exactly. But he is very persistent."

"He is that. And persuasive," she added with a chuckle.

"And though he is only a boy, well, compared to me, I still need someone to play chaperone."

"Ah, *cara*," Consuelo said as she shifted off the bed. "You don't require a duenna with Rodrigo. I can assure you of this. His is not an intemperate nature. And you must not call him a boy, not in such a disparaging tone." She moved away from the bed and stretched unself-consciously. Lucy saw that her figure was lush and rounded beneath the layers of gauze.

"He is headstrong and self-indulgent," Lucy grumbled. "Hardly a pattern card of maturity."

The countess's brows rose a millimeter. "And you know so much of these things."

Lucy blushed, then said in her own defense, "I teach children . . . I surely recognize childish behavior."

Consuelo dismissed this notion with a flick of her fingers. "If you understood anything about their sex, you would know that boys become men, and rapidly once their hearts are engaged."

"His heart?" Lucy echoed and then gave a little laugh. "I doubt Roddy's *heart* is the issue here."

Consuelo's eyes widened. "Miss Parnell, I am shocked. Proper English ladies should know nothing of those other things that prompt men." She drifted over to Lucy and touched her arm. "But I will tell you something. If you get those other parts interested in you, it is not long before men's stubborn hearts follow along. Especially if you allow them some occasional contact." She winked at Lucy. "I see I must aid you, and at least make an appearance downstairs. For propriety's sake. I will get dressed and walk in the garden, and perhaps we will have lunch on the terrace. So wearying, but necessary."

She shooed Lucy from the room. Half an hour later she appeared on the landing gowned and bonneted, with the woman in black in tow. Lucy watched from the lower hall as they came down the staircase and stifled her gasp of surprise—she could have sworn the woman she'd met yesterday in Consuelo's room had been taller and slimmer than the apparition who now walked behind the countess.

"You have met Zuzu," the countess said, pulling on her gloves. The woman nodded to Lucy.

They strolled through the extensive gardens for half an hour, finally coming to rest in a small arbor. The countess sent her maid to fetch lemonade from the kitchen, and then turned to Lucy.

"We have not yet spoken of your search for your sister's child. I have asked all my servants if they have heard of a child fostered near Peel and I am afraid I have nothing to report. Many of these people have lived on the estate for years, so they would know."

Lucy gazed out over the sparse blossoms of the garden, the few tulips and daffodils that were doggedly flowering, and tried not to sigh. "I was afraid of that," she said in a low voice. "Thank you for asking. If only that lawyer in Peel were not so closemouthed, I would have more information to go on."

Consuelo made a face. "Lawyers—bah! My husband had an army of them, and not a decent specimen in the lot."

The woman in black returned with a tray of lemonade, and Consuelo changed the subject to more mundane matters. The earl came upon them some minutes later, clearly overjoyed to see his stepmother up and around. It was evident that Nonnie was deeply attached to her, perhaps more as an older sister, since only ten years separated them, than as a surrogate mother. He sat beside her and held her hand, chattering about his horses and his dogs, while the ubiquitous Elizabeth sat basking at her feet with a silly expression of delight on her canine face.

Lucy excused herself—wanting to give the earl some time alone with Consuelo in this new setting—and returned to the house. She had to find Roddy and begin planning their assault on the local villages. Mrs. Granger, whom she had not seen since the unfortunate scene in her bedroom with Roddy, sniffed when Lucy asked her where he was. Her tone all but shouted *hussy,* as she replied. "He has gone into Peel this morning, ma'am. Shall I tell him you were looking for him when he returns?"

Lucy winced. "No," she said, tamping down her frustration. "It's not important."

She went along into the library, thinking she might find a map of the immediate area to aid her search. Owen looked up and smiled when she came into the room.

"I don't mean to bother you," she said. "I'm just looking for a map."

"It's no bother," he said, rising from his chair. "In fact I'd been hoping to talk to you alone."

"You have?" she asked as she perched on the arm of the sofa.

He nodded and smiled. "Don't look so alarmed."

She was again struck by how attractive he was, in spite of his thin face and lack of patrician features. *He has wise eyes*, she thought to herself. *That's what makes him so appealing.*

"It's about Roddy," he said. "Something you ought to know."

Here it comes. She winced at the notion. Here comes the friendly warning that Roddy was just toying with her, that she should not take anything he said or did seriously.

"If you are going to tell me to take him with a grain of salt, Mr. Griffith, that is not necessary. I am not a schoolgirl to fall for a young man's flattery, you know." She thought she sounded properly composed and sophisticated.

He nodded. "I am sure you are beyond cozening, Miss Parnell. I only wanted to enlighten you a bit about Roddy. He . . . er, likes to play at rescuing things the way some fellows play at cards or dice. Broken-down cart horses, stray dogs, the odd servant cast off without a reference. His home in Cornwall is filled with the objects of Roddy's charity. Even that valet of his was one of his strays."

"As I am," she said softly.

Owen blew out a breath. "You are not a stray, certainly. More of a cause in search of a champion. He's taken up this quest of yours now, like some Galahad."

No, Lochinvar, Lucy amended silently, and then said aloud, "I'm not sure I see your point."

"It's just that Roddy's been behaving oddly since he met you." Owen rose. "Maybe this will explain it." He went to the stacks of books behind him, drew out a slim volume and carried it over to her. It was a leatherbound copy of Walter Scott's "Marmion."

"He came in here the day he met you on the moor, ranting about some Scot who'd written a book called *Lochinvar,* so I showed him where he could find the poem. I've known Roddy since we were breeched, and let me tell you, the only time he comes into a library is when he needs a fat book to prop a door open."

"He's not that much of a heathen," Lucy said, rising to his defense.

"The point is, you'd mentioned the poem to him and he was determined to read it. For four years the best professors in the land were unable to accomplish what you did in one day. He finished the poem, read all of 'Marmion,' actually, and now he's on to *Waverly*. 'A topping story,' he told me at breakfast."

Lucy was laughing in spite of herself. "And you are blaming me because he's discovered this latent taste for literature?"

Owen shook his head. "He used to say that books were for the timid, that it was far better to be living your own life than reading about someone else's imaginary life."

"From what he's told me, he's had a very pleasant life. A large family who dote on him. I don't wonder he finds books a bit flat." She eyed him speculatively. "Not like you and me, Mr. Griffith. We are the ones who dream in our books, aren't we? Who find our excitement between the covers. Roddy apparently doesn't require that."

He pondered this a moment. "I am not always comfortable with people, I see you've gleaned that. Not the way Roddy is. Everyone flocks to him and he basks in it. And do you know why they all like him? Because he is the best-hearted person you will ever meet."

"I know that," she said. "I've told him so. But I'm still not sure I understand."

"Just try not to encourage him excessively," Owen said gently. "He throws himself into things without thinking them through. Goes off half-cocked and usually ends up creating more problems than he solves."

The Knight of Wands . . . he's a turbulent fellow. She heard Consuelo's voice intoning the words.

"He follows his heart, you mean, rather than his brain." When he nodded, she added intently, "Well, perhaps that's something we could *both* learn from him."

Owen twisted his hands in his lap and looked away from her. "It's his heart that worries me, Miss Parnell. You are a woman of good sense, you must know that young men often form inappropriate attachments, to married women . . ." He hesitated and then said, "To older women."

"You mean calf love?" she asked with a frown.

"Whatever you choose to call it, I fear that's what Roddy is suffering. It's the only explanation I can think of for this strange, impetuous behavior. That it's a sort of temporary madness, which you have induced in him. He's willing to burgle for you, willing to drag his friends on a quest for you, good Lord, he's even reading books for you."

"I never asked for your help, sir," she said stiffly. "I never asked for Roddy's, if the truth be told. As for his strange behavior, as you call it, his brash enthusiasm, I thought that was his normal manner."

"Only with his friends," he said, looking at her at last. "He's never behaved like this before over a woman, not in my recollection. It baffles me."

"I have no explanation for you, Mr. Griffith. If you are baffled, I am equally bewildered."

"Just let him down gently when the time comes," he said. "You see, no one Roddy cares about has ever hurt him."

Lucy rose to her feet. Her tone was incredulous. "You think I have the power to hurt him?"

"Yes, I do. Even calf love breeds real feelings. However fleeting."

Lucy nibbled at one raised knuckle. She didn't know what to say. Owen was assuming she was a woman of the world, one who would know how to keep Roddy at bay. But she hadn't a clue of how to discourage his attentions to her; she'd have better luck holding off a charging bull than subduing Roddy Kempthorne.

"I think it would be best if you went back to the Greene Man," he said. "He told me last night that that was your plan."

"It was, but my stepbrother seems to have taken my purse from my trunk. And my ticket for the ferry. I am stranded here until my money is returned to me."

Owen did not look happy with this development. "Then avoid him as much as you can. And please don't enlist him in this search for your niece. Anything that throws the two of you together is bound to increase his feelings for you."

"I have given him no encouragement," she protested. "You must know that. But he is like a puppy, trailing about after me."

He grinned at her, his face at last relaxing. "Then tell him no and scowl. It works with Bess."

"Roddy has trouble with the word no," she drawled. "Still, I will try to keep my distance. I certainly don't want to cause him any pain." As she moved toward the door, anxious to end this awkward interview, he said something under his breath. "What was that?"

"I said, I was glad we got this sorted out. It was for your benefit as well, ma'am. Now you will know to guard your own feelings—Roddy can be dashed persuasive when he sets his mind to something. I wouldn't want you forming a *tendre* for him, when he's merely infatuated."

Lucy had no intention of discussing her feelings for Roddy with his friend. Mainly because she had no idea what they might be. He was charming, amusing, and pleasing to look at, and he knew how to kiss her dizzy, but beyond that she refused to probe.

"Anyway," Owen was saying, "I would suppose that the differences in your ages and stations in life would keep you from considering Roddy's suit, even if he were to press it."

Lucy felt her dander come up. "My age I can do nothing about, Mr. Griffith. As for my station, as you call it . . . Well, governessing is a respectable profession. And my grandfather was a baron, so I am at least on a par socially with a penniless young sprig."

Oh, Lord, she thought, *I am starting to sound like Yardley.*

"Penniless?" he repeated blankly.

"I saw his purse at the inn yesterday—it was quite empty."

"Yes, well he is careless about money. But that hardly means he is—"

"You have issued your warning," she said hotly. "All I can do is promise not to intentionally hurt him. Does that satisfy you?"

He nodded. "And the search for your niece?"

"That is rather his decision, Mr. Griffith. One thing I've learned in my short acquaintance with the man is that you can't keep Roddy Kempthorne from his own path."

"Amen to that," he said as she closed the door.

Owen was waiting for Roddy in the stable when he returned from Peel.

"Give them back to her," he said from the feed bin where he was perched.

Roddy led his horse into its stall and then turned to his friend. "I haven't a clue what you are talking about."

"Miss Parnell's purse and her ticket. It's no use playing innocent, Roddy. I know you have them."

Roddy shrugged. "What if I do? It's none of your concern."

"What did you do, creep back into her room last night and take them from her trunk? Lord, you're as bad as her stepbrother."

Roddy grumbled, "And when did you turn into a prosy old meddler?"

"You know it's going to end badly if she stays on here. Let her go back to the inn before she tumbles into love with you."

Roddy's eyes brightened as he crouched before his friend. "I say, do you think she could? It's hard to know how she feels, you see, because she is most always cross with me."

Owen uttered a weary sigh. "If I have to tell *you* what a woman acts like when she's fixed her interest with a man, then the world has taken a pretty turn."

Roddy hiked himself up onto the bin and leaned back against the stable wall. "It's the damnedest thing. I don't know how I feel, let alone trying to guess how she feels. I just want to be with her . . . for a time, at least. If I return her purse, she'll go off to Peel or worse yet, go back to England. Back to her suitor, Sir Humpty Dumpty, in Manchester."

Owen restrained a grin. "Is that such a bad thing? For her to marry someone who will look after her? Who is fond of her?"

"Fond be damned," Roddy said through his teeth. "He'd never get past that wall she's erected to hold the world away. But I have and it's worth the effort. She's worth it, Snow."

Owen leaned forward and craned his head around to look at Roddy's face. "Let her go," he said again. "Dash it all, Roddy, she's five years older than you."

Roddy slipped off the bin and smiled wickedly. "My mother is four years older than my father. She'd kill me for telling anyone, but it's true. Happiest couple in the kingdom, I might add. So there."

Roddy found Lucy walking off her pique at Owen in the large conservatory at the rear of the east wing. She looked up in surprise when he hailed her from the open doorway.

"Glad to see you've changed your mind about leaving," he said glibly.

"I didn't," she said, moving to keep a large palm tree between them. Consuelo had abandoned her role as duenna once she learned that Roddy was away from the house. "My money was missing from my trunk. Yardley was quite thorough. He also took my ticket and my journal."

"A total cad," Roddy pronounced, skirting the palm and stalking her into a cul-de-sac formed by two large tropical ferns. He slid his hands into his coat pockets. The left pocket was empty, the right one held her journal, which he had received from Mr. Greene after he'd paid for her lodging. He didn't intend to read all of it, but there was one entry made the night after he'd met her that he wanted to study. He'd seen his own name mentioned there twice.

"I've squared everything with the innkeeper . . . I borrowed the money from the Joker."

"Oh, Roddy, no. Now you've placed me in his debt as well as yours and Nonnie's."

"No mind. He's rich as Croesus—and he's heir to the Marquess of Mitford, who could probably buy and sell the Prince Regent."

"That is not the point. Just because a man has money, doesn't mean you have the right to help yourself to it. I thought you were going to pay the landlord out of your winnings."

"Wager ain't won yet," he said slyly "You have to stay on here and be entertaining. That was the bargain."

She blew out a breath. "Cheer up the countess, cajole your friends . . . anything else this bargain requires?" That was a mistake. He had her cornered in an instant, up against the cool stucco wall.

"One more thing," he said as her hands instantly splayed on his chest to hold him back. He leaned down and whispered, "We need to find your niece."

He stepped away from her then, and she was barely able to cloak her disappointment. She didn't want him to kiss her, certainly, but how vexing that he didn't even try.

"I've done some background work this morning to good purpose. Talked to that lawyer fellow, Plimpton, while I was in Peel. Made him think I was there as Nonnie's agent, looking into some lucrative contracts. The fellow was all but drooling by the time I left."

Lucy trailed after him through the garden room. "What has that to do with my niece?"

"Plenty," he said, and then briefly explained his plan to her, all the while admiring the soft blush of her cheeks and the bright swirl of green and gold in her eyes.

She looked dubious when he had finished, but he merely smiled. "Don't fret, it's all been worked out. Besides, it's time you had a lark, Miss Parnell. It seems I've been keeping all the fun to myself so far."

"If you mean burgling the Wibberlys' house, I am glad you left me out of that one."

He touched the tip of her nose. "I would never make you do anything that required putting burnt cork on your face, sweetheart. Now come have some lunch and then we're off to Peel."

Nonnie was absent from the dining parlor, and Owen barely said a word while he ate, so Lucy spent the meal talking with the

Joker about his family's estate outside London. When he mentioned that his friends often stayed there, she remarked to Roddy that it must be pleasant to have such grand homes to visit. The three men began to guffaw and then looked contrite at her puzzled expression.

"She doesn't know, Roddy," Owen said under his breath as they walked from the room. "She thinks you a pauper."

"Let her then," he replied. "Half the chits in the *ton* are after me for that damned house. Not that it's got a prayer of coming to me with three older brothers. It's a drafty old pile, at any rate."

Owen dug him in the ribs. "It's the most wonderful house in Cornwall, old fellow."

Roddy just grinned.

Chapter Eight

Roddy and Lucy set out in the curricle he had been driving the previous day. She had managed to borrow a bonnet from Consuelo, though it had been difficult to find one that wasn't embellished with two-foot plumes or large sprays of fruit. The countess was nothing if not flamboyant. Lucy settled for a chip straw leghorn with violet ribbons that obscured her view on either side. This pleased Roddy enormously, since it allowed him to gaze at her profile the whole way to Peel.

During the early part of their journey he went over the role she was to play once they got to Peel.

"I understand what it requires, but I fear I am no actress."

He gave her a long look. "My dear girl, you were polite to Yardley Abbott for five years when the whole time you wanted to clout him on the head. If that ain't acting, I don't know what is."

"That was endurance," she stated. "But I will try my best with Mr. Plimpton."

They drove on in silence for a while, and then Lucy said in an airy voice, "You know, I've been thinking. If I don't find Susanne's daughter, it would make sense for me to marry my beau in Manchester."

There, she'd done what Owen asked, given Roddy a gentle hint that she was not fodder for calf love.

"You mean Sir Humpty Dumpty?" he muttered.

"His name is Humphrey Dumbarton, as you very well know from having eavesdropped on a private conversation," she said coolly.

"And how long has this worthy been courting you?"

"We met three years ago when I first went to work for the Burbridges."

He whistled softly. "A very patient man, this Sir Humpty."

"Sir Humphrey."

"Um, sorry."

"He is a gentleman farmer who lives with his mother. A good landlord, very well-respected in the community . . ."

"And a pillar of the church?" he drawled.

"Oh, stop it, Roddy. Don't make light of him. If I have to go back to England without discovering that I have at least one blood relation left alive, I am going to marry him. Yes, I am."

She knew there was no profit in wishing for marriage with a man like Roddy Kempthorne. He was the stuff of dreams, not reality. If what Owen said was true, Roddy was merely suffering an infatuation. It was flattering, certainly, but not anything she could build a future on. Whereas, Sir Humphrey was prepared to give her a home and security, perhaps children of her own. With him she'd have a safe haven in which to grow old. Roddy had no money or prospects, he possessed little of value except for his devoted friends. And, furthermore, he led an idle, wastrelly life.

"Is that true?" he asked her after a long pause. "That you have no other relations?"

"Only a very distant cousin who inherited my grandfather's title. He had us all to tea once, and he was smug and supercilious to my mother, whose childhood home he had usurped. It didn't leave me in any charity with him."

"And beyond him, no one?"

"Only this child . . . she is the only blood kin I have left."

Roddy was silent for a few minutes and then said, "Lucy, please don't be too downhearted if we don't discover anything. I mean, don't feel you have to rush into marriage with Sir Humphrey."

"Rush?" she said with a dry laugh. "The poor man has grown gray waiting for my answer. No, I see now that it's the best solution. He has proven his merit to me. Surely a man who remains steadfast for three years deserves a reward."

If Roddy was growling during the remainder of the journey, Lucy did not remark on it. When they reached Peel, Roddy stabled the carriage and walked her to the lane beside the building where the lawyer's office was situated. She had been there two days earlier and still recalled the layout. Two small rooms on the upper floor, the outer one where a law clerk sat on a high stool and the inner one where the odious Mr. Plimpton conducted his business.

"Now, Luce," Roddy said, "remember what I told you. You must keep him occupied for no less than twenty minutes. Cry, plead, swoon if you must . . . but keep him away from this place."

"I will cast Mrs. Siddons in the shade," she promised. She watched while he scribbled a note to the solicitor, and then sent a young urchin into the building to deliver it. A few minutes later the lawyer himself came hurrying out. He was short and plump; below his low-crowned beaver hat, his sparse hair had been combed over a shiny pink scalp. She and Roddy backed against the side of the shadowed building as he hurried past.

"Now, you're sure you will be all right? I picked a rather tame-looking coffeehouse, so you should be quite safe."

"Don't fret," she said, grinning up at him. "This is my lark, remember? And Roddy, if this works, I will be very much in your debt."

"It will work; MacHeath assured me it's foolproof. Now off you go . . . and good luck." He leaned down, kissed her swiftly on one cheek, and then sent her scudding from the lane.

Lucy followed cautiously behind Mr. Plimpton; she recalled the coffeehouse where Roddy's note had lured him, she'd passed it several times during her first day in Peel.

The lawyer was standing inside the doorway looking around anxiously when she came up behind him. "Mr. Plimpton?"

He turned and his face fell. "Madam, I told you on Saturday, I can do nothing for you. Now, please, I have an appointment with an important client." He sidled away from her but she followed him into the interior of the room. Several patrons looked up from their tables. She had never played to an audience before, it should be interesting.

"You must listen to me," she said urgently. "There are lives at stake here."

He shook her off again and motioned to a waiter. "Was there a young gentleman here recently? Dark-haired, tall . . . he sent me a note to meet him here."

The waiter shrugged. Mr. Plimpton made a noise of impatience. "Tall, well-favored," the lawyer continued. "Hard to miss in a motley crowd like this."

Several of the patrons began to grumble. Lucy clutched at his sleeve.

"You hold my fate in your hands, Mr. Plimpton. My whole future rests with you."

"Damned bloodsucker," one of the men in the bow window muttered. "Hear the poor woman out," he said in a louder voice.

"Please," Mr. Plimpton hissed, again plucking Lucy's hand from his arm. "You are causing a scene. If you need to speak with me, make an appointment with my clerk."

"Don't waste your time," another of the patrons called to Lucy.

"He had my sister put out of her holding when her man died. You won't get any sympathy from that one."

"Oh, *please*," Lucy moaned. "Don't turn me away again. What sort of unfeeling man are you?"

People were getting to their feet. Men and women were catcalling to Lucy not to let the lawyer weasel out of his obligation to her. Plimpton's round face grew oily with sweat and his cheeks turned a mottled red.

"It is not as it appears," he whined to the room. "She has clearly lost her wits."

"Don't let him turn you away, ma'am," one of the women caroled. "He refused to represent my cousin over a rent claim and the poor man was transported to Australia." The crowd gasped.

Mr. Plimpton turned to flee and Lucy wailed, "Stop him! Someone stop him."

The patrons surged around Mr. Plimpton, bearing him back to where she stood, trembling and pale. "Hear her out," the waiter said, as he forced the lawyer down into a chair. "Now."

Mr. Plimpton swiped at his forehead with a napkin and took a deep breath. "There was no need for this, Miss Parnell. I repeatedly told you during our first encounter that I cannot reveal the particulars of a client's case, or even if that man of whom you spoke even is a client. There is a confidentiality which I cannot in good conscience breech."

"Lot of mumbo jumbo," a leathery older man said from the chair behind the lawyer.

Mr. Plimpton turned and glared at him. "At least allow the lady and me to confer in private." The remainder of the crowd moved away and returned to their tables. To Lucy's relief, the lawyer ordered tea. That meant he was not going to run off. She had done her job; Roddy would have his twenty minutes.

"Oh, I say . . . is old Plimpton in?"

The law clerk, a spindly fellow with bad skin and a long, narrow chin, looked up from his ledger as Roddy came in through the front door. "He's gone out, sir,"

"I was expecting to meet him here this afternoon. Got some wonderful news for him from the earl." Roddy looked at his watch and frowned. "Haven't much time though. Don't suppose you could run off and fetch him for me . . ."

"I'm not sure where he's gone. He received a note and went off directly."

Roddy paced and looked anxious. "Tell you what, when your master returns and finds he missed me, he will be vexed. And it won't be me he'll be vexed with."

The clerk nodded soberly.

"I spoke with him this morning, as you will recall."

"Yes, sir, I do. He was quite excited at the prospect of representing the earl."

"Now, the earl don't want to be represented by someone who can't be found at a moment's notice. Earls are like that, they have high expectations. So why don't you nip along now and find him for me."

The young man climbed down from his perch with a resigned sigh.

Roddy settled himself on the hard wooden bench that ran along one wall. "I'll wait here . . . occupy myself with the news from Dublin." He lifted the Irish newspaper that a client had left folded on the bench. The clerk nodded once, and then went pounding down the stairs. Roddy waited for a count of twenty and then tiptoed past the clerk's high desk and entered Mr. Plimpton's inner office. He prayed Lucy was enough of an actress to keep the man out of his hair. Nothing was as annoying as getting interrupted in the middle of a good burgle.

"Well?" Lucy said as she walked beside Roddy along the waterfront of the town. In the distance Peel Castle shone a rugged gold in the late afternoon light.

"Piece of cake," he said gleefully.

"Tell me," she said with a catch in her voice.

"You tell me first . . . how did you fare?"

She waved one hand in the air. "It was so easy; Plimpton is apparently not well liked in the town, and the patrons in the coffeehouse wouldn't let him leave before he heard me out. He just sat there and drank his tea and pretended to consult with me, to satisfy them. All he really did was whine to me how much he hates this island and how he should have been a barrister in London. Once he got started on that theme, he talked for nearly half an hour."

"Good girl. You exceeded my expectations. I was able to have a nice leisurely search." She clutched at his sleeve, but unlike Plimpton he did not shake her off, but instead laid his hand over hers. "She's here, Lucy. Your dream was true."

"Oh, Roddy." She gave a little skip of joy.

"Plimpton had the papers conveniently filed under Abbott. Your stepbrother has been sending money—'in support of an indigent child,' as the legal papers said." His voice lowered. "There was also money sent for a headstone on a grave. He at least kept your sister from potter's field."

Lucy knuckled a tear from her eye. "She should never have died . . . alone in a strange place."

"Focus on the child, sweetheart. She is alive."

"Where is she? Tell me please."

"We need to do a bit more investigating. The money your brother sends is forwarded to a church in a village called St. Margaret on Meade. Plimpton is only the go-between. Perhaps there is a priest or vicar in that place who gives the money to the foster parents. We'll have to go to the village and talk with him."

"Today? Can we go today?"

He studied the sky. "Not if we plan to do it in daylight."

She looked quite downcast and he raised her chin with one long finger.

"Lucy, you've waited seven years to find her. Surely one more day won't matter."

"I know. But I have this terrible fear that she will disappear just before I find her . . . that she will vanish as I am coming toward her."

"Merely hobgoblins," Roddy said soothingly. "Now let me buy you a scone at the Greene Man. I had two there this morning and they are quite habit-forming."

Lucy was exultant for the rest of the day. She floated on air all through dinner, after which she'd regaled the countess with her news. She now sat in the library sipping brandy with Roddy and his friends, too excited to sleep. When Snowball disappeared just before midnight, the other men exchanged sly glances.

"Ghost-hunting," said the Joker.

"His ghostly maiden?" Lucy asked as she shifted forward in her chair to refill her glass.

Roddy leaned from the chair beside hers and took the bottle from her hand. "Steady on, Luce. You're not used to strong spirits."

"I like it," she said. "It's very comforting, brandy,"

Nonnie grinned at her from across the room, where he was kneeling on the floor, scratching Bess's ears. "Let her alone, Roddy. She's got something to celebrate. It's not every day we find we have a long-lost sibling."

"Not sibling," the Joker corrected him. "Niece. I'll never have any of those . . . got no sisters or brothers. Nor cousins either. M'uncle ain't in the petticoat line. More in the meddling line."

"Well, I had three brothers and lost 'em," Nonnie said forlornly. "Poor little mites."

It struck Lucy then that Consuelo's lost children had been Nonnie's half-siblings. The countess was not the only one who still grieved over them.

"Always wanted a brother my whole life," Nonnie continued. His face brightened slightly. "Maybe that's why I keep you fellows about."

Roddy and the Joker both chuckled. "Not to mention we let you win at whist," the viscount said with a wink at Lucy.

"Oh, not fair," the earl countered. He shook his head at Lucy. "See how they treat me?"

Lucy smiled at him and then leaned back in her chair, stretching deliciously. The brandy was drifting through her blood, heating it and making her feel distinctly languid. And so very happy. Soon, quite soon, she would be face-to-face with Susanne's daughter, a deeply satisfying notion.

She gave a huge, audible yawn and then said, "Excuse me," with a giggle.

Roddy's mouth twisted into a crooked smile. "Time to take you up, Luce. Before I have to carry you." He rose and held out his hand.

She said good night to the other two men and allowed Roddy to lead her from the room.

He did not speak as they made their way through the house. Somewhere in the darkness above them, Owen was stalking the halls, hoping for a glimpse of his spectral lady. Lucy realized she was not the only one who was following an otherworldly quest. She hoped he was as successful as she had been. Even though he had lectured her in the library, she bore him no ill will—he had been motivated by his concern for Roddy,

Roddy. What on earth was she going to do with Roddy? He had stumbled into her life without warning, rescued her, befriended her, and now had brought her quest to fruition. In less than two days. No wonder his friends claimed he rarely lost a bet. She wondered if there was anything he couldn't accomplish, and then felt dispirited that there was so little he attempted by way of serious endeavor. Put the man in Parliament, put him in the diplomatic service, put him anywhere where charm and human insight were at a premium.

"You're very quiet all of a sudden," he said as they approached the staircase.

"I was going to say the same thing about you," she responded.

"What happens now?" he asked, stopping her at the base of the stairs. "After you find the little girl. You're not still going to marry Sir Humphrey, are you?"

She set one hand on the acorn-carved newel post and frowned. The image of Sir Humphrey and the consumption of euphoria-inducing brandy did not blend well.

"I don't know what I will do. Just finding her was my only focus. Now . . . I don't know. I would hesitate to take her from the people who raised her for eight years—even if I could afford to keep her with me. If the Burbridges still want me, perhaps she can visit with me there for a time. If not, I might be able to find work here on Man so I can be near her."

"Consuelo could always use a companion," he suggested.

"Roddy, the Swithens have exceeded themselves. I couldn't ask for more."

"You got Connie out into the garden, Luce. I wager she hasn't seen the sun in months. You are good for her, just as I'd hoped you would be."

"Let me meet the girl first before I make any plans." She reached up and laid her hand against his cheek. "But thank you for your help, more than I can say."

He leaned into her hand. "A little burglary goes a long way, sweetheart."

"At least you kept me from the larcenous part of our plan."

"Kept the best part for myself, you mean."

"Pity the war is over, you know. You'd have made a superb spy."

He actually blushed. "Me? I am the worst sort of bumbler. It's all to MacHeath's credit."

"Ah, your mysterious one-armed valet. But he wasn't the one who managed to get at Plimpton's files. He wasn't the one who braved the fierce mastiff to return my trunk."

He was grinning now. "Thought you were mad at me last night over that."

"That was last night, and this is now," she pronounced.

He followed her up the stairs and saw her to the door of her room. He lingered there, one arm braced against the door frame, while she fidgeted with the folds of her gown. "Roddy . . ."

"Yes?"

"I am so very, very happy."

"I know. I told you you would be, remember?"

"I . . . I just can't seem to think of a way to thank you properly."

His free arm slid around her waist. "Then do it improperly," he said gruffly.

It was the first time she'd initiated a kiss. She was tentative at first, her mouth questing and unsure. But then he tightened his hold on her, tugged her up against him, and as her body arched into him, her mouth opened in pliant invitation.

"Jenny, my sweet Jenny," he murmured as he bent her back.

"So I'm back to being a doll," she drawled against his mouth.

"Not a doll, *the* doll. The best of dolls. But I must say, you kiss much better than any doll I've ever encountered."

She laughed into his mouth and then gasped as he deepened their kiss, taking her with hard, driving hunger until they were both breathless.

"I'm going now," he said raggedly, tugging himself back from her. "We've got a busy day tomorrow."

He set one more long, drifting kiss on her cheek and turned away. She watched him recede along the passage, her back braced against the door, her knees barely holding her upright.

Somehow she had forgotten all her intentions of holding him at bay.

Chapter Nine

The low clouds had returned during the night and set a sheen of moisture on every surface. Roddy called for the closed carriage, knowing Lucy would be undeterred by the weather. He was still conferring with the head groom in the stable yard when a large black coach came sweeping up the drive. The welcoming committee was out that morning, in spite of the threat of rain, but the coachman disregarded the children who ran beside the coach and did not slow down.

Roddy watched its progress up the drive with misgiving. He knew exactly who had come to call. He excused himself to the groom and hurried into the house through the kitchen entrance. He raced up the stairs to find Lucy, but she was not in her room. Consuelo likewise had not seen her.

"It's her festering brother," Roddy announced to the countess. "Here to make mischief, no doubt."

Consuelo shifted off the divan and motioned Roddy to ring for a servant. "Then he shall find the lady of the castle at home." She gave him a catlike smile. "I have been perishing to meet him."

Roddy left her then, and as he headed back to the landing he heard Yardley Abbott in the hall below, speaking to Mrs. Granger. That lady was doing her best to deflect him, but even her icy manner was no match for his brand of arrogance.

"Of course she is staying here," he said between his teeth. "And if you value your position in this house, you will see that she is found and brought to me."

Roddy came slowly down the stairs. Yardley glanced up at him without interest, but then, when he'd recalled where he'd seen that angular face before, his eyes narrowed into deep slits.

"Mr. Kempthorne," he said in terse acknowledgement. "It would be best if you kept out of this."

"Best for whom?" Roddy said. He stopped midway down the

staircase and leaned over the banister, moving his head from side to side. "Where are they?"

"Who?"

"Your bullyboys. Or have you left them on the porch like a pack of unruly hounds?"

Yardley's jaw twitched. "I have come here alone. I intend to speak with my sister."

Roddy continued his slow progress down the stairs, never taking his eyes from Yardley. "I have a feeling she don't want to see you. Ever."

There was a deepening scowl on Yardley's face. "I know about your little foray last night," he said in a low voice. "Such behavior is reprehensible in a gentleman."

Roddy smirked at him."Oh, you mean taking something that doesn't belong to you?"

The arrow went home. Yardley drew himself up to his full height, which placed him an inch or two above Roddy. Roddy, however, chose to remain on the first step, which gave him several inches over the professor. They glared at each other wordlessly for a time, and then the strained silence was broken by Lucy's voice.

"I have no idea where he disappeared to." She and Nonnie were emerging from the north wing. "The last I heard he was out at the stable—" Her voice drifted off the instant she saw who was standing in the hall.

"Lucy. Lord Steyne." Yardley bowed to Nonnie. "You see, I have not forgotten you from your Oxford days."

Nonnie, who had been a less-than-stellar student, blanched noticeably.

Yardley smiled. "Now, sir, I wish to be private with my sister."

Nonnie recovered his poise and came toward him, a glower similar to Roddy's narrowing his face. "And I wish I could find a horse that don't balk at a brush fence, but that ain't going to happen either."

Yardley appeared unfazed by the earl's mocking tone. "Lucy, I insist that I be allowed to speak with you." He hesitated and then said with some difficulty, "It's about the child."

"So it's out in the open now," Roddy muttered under his breath. "And about time."

Yardley's eyes flashed at him. "I will brook no impertinence, sir."

"You ain't in the classroom now," Roddy said as he came down off the last step. "Miss Parnell can speak to you if she chooses, but we will not allow her to be alone with you."

Yardley turned back to Lucy, who was trying to resist hiding behind Nonnie's broad back. "You surprise me, my dear. I never knew you had this capacity for inspiring loyalty in young men." He considered both Roddy and Nonnie with a jaundiced expression. "Such very young men. It makes me wonder what you have done to earn their regard."

"No, Roddy!" Lucy cried as he took a step toward her brother, his hands knotted into fists. "Remember what your mother told you . . . about resisting."

She flew across the hall and took Yardley by the arm. "I'll speak with you. Alone, if that's what you prefer." She turned to Roddy. "It's all right. He can do nothing to me. I don't need you for this."

"But—"

"Please, Roddy. Don't make things more difficult."

She watched the anger leech out of Roddy's face. It was replaced by an expression of sullen resignation. He nodded to her once, and then spun around and went stalking off. Nonnie followed him but kept looking over his shoulder with an expression of concern.

"Go," she mouthed to him.

She led Yardley to the drawing room. Served him right if he had to perch on a hard-bottomed, spindly chair for the course of their interview. He seated himself and waited while she poured herself a small cordial. She made a point of not offering him a drink, but he didn't seem to notice.

"You have certainly landed on your feet, my dear."

"I am not without friends, Yardley."

He sniffed. "I believe there is a more apt word for men who take advantage of a woman's virtue."

Lucy shook her head slowly. "You can believe whatever you choose about me. I am indifferent to your slurs. Now please tell me why you have come here."

"There is a lawyer in Peel, a Mr. Plimpton. He came to see me late yesterday afternoon . . . most upset. He claims you accosted him in a public coffeehouse and nearly started a riot."

"And how would this Mr. Plimpton know to complain to you? How would he know we are even related?"

Yardley waved one hand. "He has done some legal work for me over the years . . . Sophia came into some property on the island

and he looks after things for her. He recognized your name, I suppose. The point is, you claim that you are not suffering your mother's ailment, but I now have Mr. Plimpton's sworn testimony that you are, as he put it, 'a very unbalanced woman.' He told me you had some deranged notion that your sister's child was still alive and living on this island."

Lucy willed her hands to stop trembling and offered him a serene smile. "Mr. Plimpton, it seems, has forgotten all about client confidentiality. I spoke to him in confidence and now he has clearly violated my trust. I wonder you would choose such a shabby man for your business dealings, Yardley. I believe lawyers can lose their credibility over such things."

She watched with satisfaction as Yardley squirmed in his chair, though that might only have been due to the hardness of the seat.

"You did not hire him," Yardley reminded her. "You were not his client."

Lucy hadn't spent her youth in Ceylon, where every village had its population of enterprising Hindu lawyers, without gleaning some knowledge of the law.

"Ah, but I was there for a consultation, Yardley. Surely a good lawyer, a sound lawyer, respects the private revelations of a potential client."

"This is all nonsense," he snarled. "You made a scene in a coffee shop, embarrassed a man of standing in Peel, and now expect me to overlook your behavior." His face grew grave. "It saddens me to see this deterioration in you, sister—your lack of moral judgment, exhibited by your presence here, in a house full of libertines. And your lack of mental stability, as witnessed by Mr. Plimpton only yesterday. I shudder to think what aberrant behavior you will next exhibit."

"Then don't," she said waspishly. "Don't think. And they are not libertines, just idle young men."

His eyes narrowed speculatively as he murmured, "Setting your cap at a wealthy young sprig, is that your game, Lucy? You think one of those tulips will offer for you? Mr. Kempthorne, for instance? He appears to have appointed himself your watchdog."

Lucy was pleased that she did not blush. "Mr. Kempthorne happens to be penniless. I know this for a fact." She rose and went to the door. "I believe this interview is concluded. You've had your say, made your usual threats, but I now have more important matters to attend to."

He came to her side and took her by the wrist, his fingers biting into the skin. This surprised her; Yardley's cruelty had never been of the physical variety.

"Listen to me," he said in a gravelly voice. "I will not allow you to sully my name across this whole island. I want you gone from here, and I will tell you what you need to know if you promise to leave."

She drew back from him. "I will make no promises. You cannot tell me anything I don't already know. I have uncovered the truth at last, you see. Without your assistance, brother."

"You don't know the truth," he bit out. "You haven't a prayer of discovering the truth without my help. And I will give it to you, but only if you leave here."

Lucy weighed this in her heart. What if the lawyer's papers led her nowhere? What if the parish church in St. Margaret on Meade proved a dead end? What if the vicar there refused to reveal who the money went to each month? Last night she'd thought herself so close to finding the lost child, but now, with Yardley's grim presence unsettling her, she was no longer sure.

"If you tell me what I need to know," she began cautiously, "if I get a satisfactory answer to my question, then, yes, I will return to England."

"And you will return to my house?"

"No!" The word was out before she had even totally processed the question.

He cocked his head. "Then you will at least marry Sir Humphrey. I can accept that. He will look after you, control you, and keep you from hurling yourself into scandal."

Her stomach knotted at the thought of a lifetime with the worthy gentleman who bored her to tears. Yesterday, he had seemed like a wise choice. Today, she was no longer sure. Anyway, she wanted it to be her decision, ultimately, not something forced on her by Yardley.

"I . . . I don't believe I care for Sir Humphrey," she said slowly.

Yardley scoffed. "No, you'd rather sport with a houseful of profligates. Well, if that is your answer, I leave you to your own devices. Much good they will do you."

He was heading for the door when she called out, "Wait, please. You must let me think."

He turned back to her and she read smug satisfaction on his long, sallow face.

"If you can furnish the information I need, I will return to Manchester. And if Sir Humphrey asks me, I shall marry him." She knew another proposal from her persistent suitor was inevitable unless she sequestered herself in her room for all time.

He smiled and displayed his sharp, vulpine teeth. "There is a church, in a small village—"

"I know about the village . . . St. Margaret on Meade."

He shook his head. "No, Lucy, that is not where you are to look. This village is north of Castleton, it's called Parapet. Look for the Church of All Saints and you will have your answer."

"I don't understand . . ."

"You will once you've been there."

He opened the door and gave a small yelp of surprise. The countess stood in the doorway. She was dressed for receiving royalty, arrayed in satin and lace and wearing a headdress that towered over Yardley by at least a foot.

"Mr. Abbott," she said, holding out one hand. "I am sorry I was unable to receive you when you first arrived."

Yardley took her hand and bowed. "My lady, I was just on my way out."

She gave him a small pout of dismay. "But surely you will stay and have tea. It is rare that I have an opportunity to entertain such a distinguished guest."

Yardley preened visibly. Lucy saw this and wondered what the devil Consuelo was up to. She knew the countess had no love for meddling brothers in general and for Yardley in particular ever since Lucy had shared her tale with her. She watched as Consuelo led him to one of the settees and sat down, motioning him to sit beside her. A moment later one of the footmen came in with a tea cart. Lucy drifted over to the window and tried to listen to the throaty, half-whispered words that the countess was pouring out to her stepbrother.

"It is not such a lot of money" she was saying. "A few thousand pounds each year. Just a small token for the university . . . my husband and stepson both attended there, you know. The late earl was close friends with Sir Emerson Cheever . . . I believe he is some sort of important person at Oxford."

Lucy saw Yardley's face grow pale. He was fidgeting with his cravat, and the hand that held his teacup was trembling.

"He and I have kept up a correspondence," she was saying in her lisping, but fluent English. "He will be quite interested to know you have been visiting our little island. Though why you would want to come here, when there are so many more convenient places to visit, I do not understand. But of course dear Emerson will know why you are here. Ah, have you caught a crumb in your throat, Professor Abbott?"

Yardley really was choking. His face grew red and then progressed to purple. Without turning a hair, Consuelo leaned forward and gave him a resounding whack between his shoulder blades.

"There now," she said with a pleased smile. "That helped, yes?"

Yardley nodded and took a quick drink from his teacup. He then thanked the countess for her hospitality and rose abruptly. "I really must be going," he said. "The Wibberlys are expecting me for luncheon."

"I'm sure you can find your way out," she said pleasantly.

Yardley bowed and then made a hasty retreat.

Consuelo shifted around to face Lucy, who was still standing by the window with an expression of bewilderment on her face.

"He is a dreadful man, isn't he?" the countess said.

"Oh, yes. Which makes me wonder why you were so cordial to him."

The countess gave a trilling laugh. "Cordial? Me? *Cara,* I just took ten years off that wretched man's life."

Lucy moved to the settee and sat down. "I saw how he reacted, but I have no idea what you said to have such an effect on him. Who is this Emerson Cheever?"

"He is the head of the university, I believe. Your stepbrother's ultimate superior, as it were."

"And you know this man? You write to him?"

She laughed again. "Of course not. But your Professor Abbott doesn't know that. My late husband did know him many years ago, so that was not such an untruth."

"You lied for me, my lady?" Lucy was amazed.

The countess was unrepentant. "What does it matter? The man is a toadying upstart . . . and I saw at once that he had upset you. That I will not countenance in my home."

"He did tell me where to find the child."

"I thought you already knew that . . . that it was only a matter of going to the village where the money was sent."

"He claims there is a different village, one called Parapet," Lucy explained. "So Roddy and I were not as close to finding the girl as we thought."

Consuelo mulled over this new bit of information. "I know that village. There was a terrible fire there about five years ago during a windstorm—the church and several of the houses nearby burned."

"He said to look for the church," Lucy told her. "Though that makes no sense now."

"Roddy can take you there this afternoon, and we will have an end to this mystery."

"And then I can get on with my life," Lucy added wearily. "Yardley made me promise to leave here once I had my questions answered."

"Surely you can stay until Saturday, for Nonnie's fete."

"I have a feeling that whatever happens, I won't be in the mood for a party. No, he made me promise to leave."

Consuelo watched Lucy twisting the skirt of her gown. "What else did he make you promise?"

Lucy grimaced. "I have to marry my suitor back in Manchester."

Consuelo laughed softly as she set down her teacup. "*Querida,* it is obvious no one has ever taught you how to bargain. You got very little information in exchange for making such a monumental promise."

There was color in Lucy's cheeks as she responded. "I had made up my mind to marry Sir Humphrey anyway, if I didn't find the child. He has been so patient, you see. And he is a very amiable man."

"Bah to amiable," Consuelo muttered. "That is a sure recipe for boredom. And what of Roddy? When will you tell him of this promise you made?"

"It has nothing to do with Roddy," Lucy said sharply. "Please say nothing to him. I'll likely be gone by tomorrow."

Consuelo clucked to herself, but said nothing more.

Unlike the other villages Lucy had seen on Man, which were tucked neatly into valleys or set snug between rocky outcroppings, the village of Parapet lay sprawled on the side of a verdant hill. Which explained why a fire during a windstorm had proved fatal to at least a half-dozen buildings. The trees and turf had recovered somewhat, but the empty husks of five blackened stone houses still stood as testimonials to the disaster. The stone church appeared sound from a distance, until their carriage drew closer, then Lucy and Roddy saw that there was no roof and that the windows were gaping holes where rock doves flitted in and out.

Roddy had barely spoken to her since Yardley's departure. Though his manner to her was polite, there was a restraint he had never before exhibited. He refused to meet her eyes when they spoke, which was not like Roddy at all. He had not asked her about her interview with her stepbrother, and had merely nodded stiffly when she told him about their new destination. It was as though a wall had grown up between them, and she hadn't a clue how to breach it. Not that it mattered so much; she would be away from the island, away from him, in a matter of days at most.

The carriage drew up at the flagged path that led to the church, and they climbed out. Behind them, in what remained of the village, a few women stood gossiping in a doorway. Beyond them, to the left of the church, lay a small graveyard. Ivy had twined over most of the weathered headstones.

"What now?" Roddy asked as he tilted his head back to take in the gaunt facade of the burned-out church. "Looks to me like your brother was having you on." He met her eyes for the first time in an hour. "I hope you didn't end up on the losing end of your bargain with him."

"Bargain?" she said evasively. "Why would you think I had made a bargain with him?"

He gave a small, tight laugh. "You told me yourself—he specializes in manipulating people. I can't imagine that Yardley Abbott waltzed into Ballabragh and handed over this new information without getting his pound of flesh first."

Lucy overlooked her surprise at his use of a Shakespearean allusion and said, "Perhaps it was guilt that motivated him to tell me."

"Yes, and I am the bloody king of France," he muttered before he went striding off toward the church, the skirts of his greatcoat whipping behind him. The anger fairly sizzled off him, like the summer heat radiating up from a sunbaked tile roof.

Oh dear, she thought. *He knows.* Even if Consuelo had kept her promise not to tell him, somehow Roddy had gotten wind of Yardley's terms.

She followed in his wake, fighting off her feelings of abandonment. Yesterday, with Roddy at her side, she fancied there was no mystery they could not unravel, no problem they could not solve if they put their heads together. Now he had shut himself off from her and the ache inside her was surprisingly sharp.

Still, she had no one to blame but herself. He had pledged himself to aid her and she had turned him away that morning, dismissed him in front of her brother and the earl.

"Roddy—" she called out to his retreating back. He was already beyond the church, heading with purpose toward the low stone wall that enclosed the graveyard.

"Go back to the carriage," he said over his shoulder. "Wait there until I come for you."

There was something in his tone that sent a chill rippling along her spine.

"What is it?" she called out.

He swung himself over the stone wall and when he turned to her, his blue eyes were blazing. "Will you heed me for once in your life, Lucy. Go back to the carriage."

She stood rooted to the ground. He had never spoken to her in such a manner. All his mellow playfulness was gone, replaced by stern authority. When she didn't move toward the carriage, he shrugged and then frowned. He mumbled something she suspected was an oath before he began to walk among the haphazardly placed headstones.

He bypassed the ones that were obscured by thick veils of ivy. Once or twice he knelt and brushed a bit of lichen from a stone. Lucy's heart began to thud audibly in her chest. She knew then why Yardley had sent her to this place. It wasn't to this church where no vicar had presided for five years. It wasn't to the decimated village. It was here, to this unkempt little graveyard that he had guided her. To look upon the dead,

Her head was spinning. She turned, but the carriage seemed miles away, too far for her trembling limbs to carry her.

Ah, Lucy where is your spirit? She had pursued this goal regardless of the ultimate outcome, heedless of the great potential for disappointment. And now it was within her grasp. She would not swoon and weep like some simpering child.

With determination she crossed the churchyard and scrambled over the uneven wall. Roddy was at the far end of the graveyard now, still turned away from her. Most of the inscriptions on the headstones near her were obscured by wind and weather. The surface of a few along the front wall had crumbled completely away, the passage of time wiping clean each chiseled tribute. She made her way along the crooked rows, noting dates that went back over two hundred years. As she neared Roddy, she saw that the dates were more recent.

He heard her approaching and turned. She expected him to be scowling, but the expression on his face was wiped clean, like the time-washed headstones in the first row.

"Lucy," he said in a low voice. "I would have spared you this."

She went to stand beside him, her concern all for him, for the pain in his voice. And then she looked down, at the small brown slab that stood upright before him. Her eyes scanned the words that were inscribed there. Once, twice, three times she read them.

"Oh," she said in a tiny, lost voice.

Her knees gave out and she sank to the grassy turf. He laid one hand on her shoulder as he crouched beside her. "It's over now, Luce. This is where it ends."

She reached out and traced the name on the stone with one finger.

Susanne Lansdale Parnell.

The stone was cold, the letters smooth at the edges where time had begun its inevitable erosion. Below her name were the dates that had bracketed Susanne's short life. And between her name and the dates were two words, inscribed in appropriately small letters.

And child.

Lucy felt the tears well up in her throat, a torrent that would not be stemmed. She gave a shuddering sob and collapsed in a heap on the grass. Roddy scooped her up into his arms and held her against his chest. He undid the ribbons of her bonnet, plucked it off, and stroked his hand over her hair while she cried out her bitter anger and her pain.

"It's the knowing that hurts now," he crooned against her cheek. "But it's the knowing that will help you heal, sweetheart."

"But the dream . . ." she cried softly. "What about the dream?" She pushed away from him, swiping her hair back from her face. "I must be mad, that's what it is. I *am* mad. Just like my mother. Only mad women dream such things."

He tugged her back against him. "Not mad, Lucy. You are the sanest woman I've ever met. Unfortunately also the saddest. Though maybe now the sadness will go away. Your sister chose her own road, you had nothing to do with that. It was not your fault she ran away—"

"It was," Lucy sobbed. "It *was* my fault."

Roddy slid his hands up her arms and squeezed her shoulders. "How, Lucy? Tell me how."

She hiccuped out another sob or two before she was able to speak. He had drawn his handkerchief from his pocket and was gently wiping the wetness from her cheeks.

"I told you, we'd had a row the week before she ran off. It was horrid . . . we said unspeakable things to each other."

"Siblings do fight, you know. If you recall, my brothers and I brangled incessantly."

"This was no mere brangle," Lucy said intently. "There was a man, you see. A brilliant young professor who was teaching at Oxford. Yardley decided to take the man under his wing. He often came to tea at our home. I was twenty at the time but had not been exposed to many eligible young men. Remember, Yardley kept watch over us like a mastiff. Anyway, we fancied ourselves in love, this young man and I."

Roddy's hold on her shoulders tightened slightly.

"Yardley got wind of this and was not pleased. He saw to it that my young professor was sent off to another university, in Cardiff. Susanne watched this happen, saw that her own hopes of a husband and children would never come to pass while she lived in our stepbrother's home."

"I still don't see how this is your fault."

Lucy shook her head wildly. "He came to me, my young man, and pleaded with me to leave with him. To make a life with him. But I was afraid. I'd known him such a short time, I knew so little about him."

Roddy was scowling now. "Then you don't know about love, Lucy. You don't stop to ask such foolish questions when you really love someone."

"That's what Susanne said. She accused me of being a coward. For choosing Yardley's path over my own. I couldn't know it, but she'd met a man who was staying at an inn near our home. She'd been sneaking out at night to see him. I never suspected that my own failed romance would send her running off from her family into the arms of this man, a man who sullied her."

"She stayed with him for three years," Roddy pointed out gently. "Even if they never wed, it sounds like they made a life together."

"That is a cavalier attitude," she muttered crossly.

"Don't start talking like Yardley, sweetheart, or I will lose all my patience with you."

When she looked up at him he was grinning. She gave a wet chuckle. "Sorry, I did sound like him, didn't I?"

"Listen to me. It was only circumstance, only the timing of things, that made you believe your sister's running away was a reaction to your own situation. But think, Lucy, she had met this man before you refused your professor; she was following her own course. Even if Yardley had not scotched your romance, he would have surely put a stop to Susanne's once he found out. The two things are unrelated, though I know you see them as entwined."

"I have always blamed myself that she ran off. I . . . I turned away from her after the fight, so she had no one to counsel her when she made her decision to leave."

Roddy sighed and laid his hand on her cheek. "I wager she knew what your answer would be, Lucy. You would have advised prudence, and though she'd have heard it as Yardley's voice, it would have been the voice of reason."

She blinked several times as she gazed up at him. The concern and caring on his face were like the blessing of sweet rain after the bitter dust of the Ceylonese summer.

He lowered his head till they were brow to brow. "Let it go now . . . please. You loved her, you wanted life and happiness for her. But you didn't mold her, you didn't raise her, and you certainly didn't make her run away, She was headstrong and, I suspect, a bit spoiled. Used to getting her way with your mother and your stepfather. Yardley's insufferable posturing and his need for iron control over his family are to blame here. Not you, Lucy."

He raised her to her feet and turned her from the grave. She swung away from him for an instant and ran her fingers over the second set of chiseled words. *And child.*

"Good-bye," she whispered. "Be at peace now. I have found you."

Roddy kept his arm around her while they walked back to the carriage. He lifted her easily over the stone wall and tucked her again under his arm as they made their way along the flagged path.

Lucy never looked back as the carriage drove away from the village. She sat with her hands limp in her lap, palms facing up. Roddy, who had seated himself beside her, raised each of her hands in turn and used his much-abused handkerchief to wipe away the traces of moss from the tombstone that had rubbed off on her palms.

"Hmmm . . ." He made a noise of uncertainty deep in his throat.

Lucy looked up. He was tucking the folded square of linen back in his pocket.

"Nothing," he said lightly. "Try to sleep, Lucy. It's a ways back to Ballabragh." He drew his arm around her and coaxed her head onto his shoulder.

She relaxed against him, letting her mind drift away from the sadness and loss she was feeling. It was much better not to think of anything at all. Better to just savor the warmth and strength of the

shoulder beneath her head, and the comfort of the constant, unfal-
tering heartbeat of the man who held her so tenderly at his side.

"Stop! Oh, please, please stop!"

Lucy came full awake as the carriage creaked to a jarring halt.
Roddy had already shifted away from her and was leaning out the
window calling up to the coachman.

"There's a boy in the road, sir."

"Well, let's see what's toward." He turned to her. "Stay here. I
won't be a minute."

She laid her head back against the squabs and closed her eyes.
She was still feeling distressed, but the ache inside her had less-
ened considerably.

Oh, but what a miserable bargain she had made with Yardley.
She had to leave Ballabragh, leave the people who had been so
kind to her, Consuelo, and Nonnie. Even Owen and the Joker had
become a part of her life in the short time she had known them.
Worst of all, she had to leave Roddy, he who had come to be her
truest friend. That he was more than friend she refused to grapple
with. There would be time and plenty to mull over her feelings for
him once she was back in Manchester.

She heard voices in the road ahead of the carriage, Roddy's
clear tenor and the voice of a young child. Her curiosity got the
better of her and she slid to the window and leaned out.

Roddy was conversing with a dark-haired boy. The child was
slim, dressed in homespun breeches and a linsey woolsey shirt
worn under a woven vest. He was at present dancing in impatience
in his thick brogues.

"You must come, sir. I cannot do it myself."

Roddy scratched his head and appeared confounded.

Lucy swung open the door and stepped down to the rutted road.
The boy saw her and came toward her at a clomping run. "Please,
ma'am. Tell the gentleman to help me. It's Samson—he's got himself caught in a bramble patch." The child held up his hands; they
were covered with scratches. "He's near worn out from trying to
escape," the boy continued breathlessly.

Roddy was shaking his head as he came up beside them.

"I don't know what to do, Luce. I want to get you home, but this
rascal clearly has a problem on his hands."

"We must help his friend," she said without hesitation.

The boy grinned, a wide, winning smile that was made even
more endearing by the loss of two of his top baby teeth. His eyes

were dark and framed by thick lashes and his short nose was sprinkled with freckles. Lucy thought he had the look of a very promising young sprat.

"Where is he?" Roddy asked, as he reached into the pocket of
his greatcoat and drew on his leather driving gloves.

"Beyond there." The boy pointed to a series of low hillocks
which were covered with gorse.

Roddy instructed the coachman to wait. He set off with the boy,
trying to keep up with the child's urgent pace. Lucy stood at the
edge of the road, and then, with a muffled curse, started after them.
Rescuing this unknown Samson, whoever he might be, would
surely prove more diverting than standing in a rut of dried mud.

Lucy came up even with Roddy and the boy as they were gazing down at a large, wicked-looking patch of thorny bushes set in a
deep declivity.

"I don't see him," Roddy said. "Perhaps he managed to get
himself out."

"Oh, he's there all right. It's just hard to see him because he's
mostly brown."

With this cryptic utterance the boy began a controlled slide
down the edge of the hill. Roddy took Lucy's hand to steady her
and together they followed the youngster.

"There," the boy said once they were in the shadow of the tow-
ering brambles. "In there."

Roddy squinted through the gloom. "Hello!" he called out.
"Are you in there?"

The boy was giggling now. "He can't answer you."

Roddy was about to ask him whether his friend was deaf or
mute, when a long, plaintive *baah* came rising out of the bramble
patch.

Roddy's face fell. "I say, this Samson ain't a sheep by any
chance?"

"Not a sheep, a loaghtan ram. The best ram on the whole island." The boy put his chin up. "And I am his shepherd. Except
that I fell asleep and Samson's ewes wandered into the brambles.
He got them all out, clever fellow that he is. But now he's the one
who is trapped."

Lucy was just able to make out the form of the ram, two or
three feet in from the outer edge of the patch.

"Sheep," Roddy muttered under his breath. He turned to Lucy.
"I believe this is more your area of expertise. You were the one
who got that deer out of the mire."

Lucy shook her head. "I have no experience in rescuing sheep. More's the pity."

Roddy swung off his greatcoat, peeled himself out of his form-fitting jacket, and handed them both to Lucy. He then found a stout branch lying at the bottom of the gully.

"Here," he said to the boy. "You hold the thorns away from me with this while I cut him lose." He reached into his waistcoat pocket and produced a small penknife. It seemed insignificant in the face of what Roddy needed to accomplish.

"Be careful you don't hurt him," the boy cautioned as Roddy opened the knife. Roddy rolled his eyes at Lucy who was trying not to laugh.

"I will do my best," he grunted as he crouched down and began to inch his way toward the dark shadow of the trapped ram. The boy, meanwhile, lifted away the brambles that intersected over Roddy's head. There were a few muffled curses, several strangled *baahs*, and then the ram erupted out of the thicket, charging wild-eyed across the rocky ground. Once he saw the boy, he came trotting back and began to lip at his sleeve.

"He's just like a dog," he said with a smug grin.

Roddy dragged himself out of the brambles, looking much worse for wear than the ram. Once he was clear, he sat up and rubbed at his head, where a dozen bloodied scratches marred his brow. Lucy knelt down beside him and began fishing through his coat pockets for his handkerchief.

He caught her wrist in a hard grip. "No, leave it. You can see to me when we get home."

The boy, however, had produced his own surprisingly clean bit of linen and passed it over to Lucy. "He is a corker, isn't he?"

"Yes," Lucy breathed as she dabbed tenderly at Roddy's brow. "I don't think there is anyone quite like him."

"I think he's talking about the ram," Roddy drawled, and then winced as she touched on a particularly deep scratch.

The boy crouched before Roddy. "You were capital too, sir, just capital."

"Thank you," Roddy murmured. His gaze swept to the ram, who was now browsing along the edge of the incline. Though his head was down, all four elaborately curled horns could be clearly seen. Roddy's eyes widened. "Luce . . ."

"Yes, Roddy," she said in a whisper. "I do believe it's the same ram. It's clear he's gotten over his snit with you now. Maybe it's like Androcles and the lion . . . because you aided him, you see."

"Androcles and *who*?"

She smiled fondly. "Never mind, dearest. It doesn't matter."

He cocked his head and looked at her with astonishment. "You called me dearest."

She rocked back on her heels. "I did?" She gnawed her lip. "I'm sure I didn't mean to."

His eyes brightened. "I bet you did. Ah, you're blushing now."

"And you've gone back to talking nonsense." She handed him the boy's handkerchief and got to her feet. "I think you can look after yourself now."

The boy was beside the ram, picking the remains of the brambles from the beast's tattered coat.

"Do you live near here?" Lucy asked him.

"Aye. In Dorne Valley."

"That's not far from Ballabragh," Roddy said as he climbed to his feet and dusted off his breeches.

The boy nodded. "My mother works at the big house some days. She sews and weaves. But we have our own cottage. My mother says its important to have a house of your own."

Amen to that, Lucy mused. A lesson she'd learned far too late in life.

"Are you staying at Ballabragh?" the boy asked, his open face now tinged with some caution.

"I am a friend of the earl's," Roddy said. "And Miss Parnell is his guest."

The boy looked uncertain. "I am not supposed to speak with anyone from Ballabragh," he muttered. "My mother warned me not to."

"We don't mean you any harm," Lucy said.

"I know all about you," he muttered. "You're the one who is looking for the lost baby."

Lucy's face tightened. "Not any longer," she said softly. "And it wasn't a lost baby, it was a little girl, about your age, in fact."

"Well, I'm not lost," he said stoutly "It's only that Samson wandered off today, which is why I am so far from home. But it's a pity you don't want a baby."

"Why is that?" Roddy asked.

"Because there is a baby who needs looking after at the end of Dorne Valley. He cries and cries, but the woman who is supposed to care for him is jugbit most of the time."

"That's very sad," Lucy said. "Why doesn't your mother do something?"

He shook his head. "My mother tried. Everyone in the valley has tried." The boy shrugged. "He will die, I suppose. My lambs die sometimes. Last year a wild dog got a few of them. Mother says it is something I should accept, but I still cried over them."

Lucy reached out and laid her hand on the boy's cap of dark hair. "That's because you're a good shepherd."

His face lit up. "I think I am. I helped Samson today, instead of running home and hiding under the bed, which is what I did when the lambs died."

"You're very young though, to be a shepherd."

He digested this. "Do you think so? I've only been doing it for a few years. The sheep were wild and I made friends with them. Now they let me trim their fleece and my mother uses the wool for her weaving." He tugged at the loose vest he wore, which was woven in a Celtic pattern of browns and golds. "She made this."

"It's beautiful," Lucy said. "She is quite skillful."

He touched the sleeve of the cream-colored pelisse she wore. "She altered this for you yesterday. I saw her working on it. It's very pretty, isn't it?"

Since Roddy heartily concurred with this sentiment, having been admiring it on Lucy all afternoon, he didn't think it odd that a stripling boy should express such a thought. But Lucy was looking at the child oddly. "What is your name?"

"Charlie," he said. "Charlie Pace."

"Well, Charlie Pace," Roddy said, "it's time I got Miss Parnell home. Will you be able to get back to your cottage?"

The boy grinned. "I know every inch of these moors. And Samson will be with me; he won't let me come to any harm."

"A fearful adversary," Roddy said intently, without a shred of sarcasm.

Chapter Ten

"Well, what do you think?"

Owen looked again at the tiny fragments that were strewn over a cloth on the library table. Two minutes before Roddy had burst into the room, insisting that there had to be a magnifying glass somewhere in the dashed place. Owen had calmly produced one from the drawer in the table and watched as Roddy opened his handkerchief and began to poke at the tiny bits with one finger.

He'd then demanded that Owen take a look.

"Stone fragments," Owen said after a second perusal with the glass. "Brown stone, and a bit of stone dust, as well. And some moss."

Roddy was pacing impatiently behind him. "Where the devil is that fellow we set to watching Yardley yesterday? I told Mrs. Granger I needed to speak to him immediately."

"What's this about, Roddy?"

"It's about humdudgeon," Roddy growled. "Or I'm Jack's cat."

He quickly explained about Yardley's visit that had led them to the burned-out church. He saw his friend's face fall when he told him about the double grave in the churchyard.

"She must be heartbroken," Owen said in a low voice. "She was so happy yesterday."

"She'll be happy again," Roddy declared. "And sooner than she thinks if I am right in my suspicions. Ah, here's that fellow now."

Roddy ran to the door and swung it open before the man on the other side could knock a second time. He came into the room and touched his forelock to Roddy. "Sir?"

He was a diminutive man with long side whiskers and grizzled hair. His moleskin breeches were permeated with the odor of horses.

"You were set to watch the Wibberlys' house yesterday."

"Aye, that I was."

"And you reported that Mr. Abbott did nothing out of the ordinary during the day."

"He never left the house. I watched and waited on the hill behind the main house. Mr. MacHeath loaned me his spyglass, and I was able to keep a pretty sharp eye on things."

"And no one visited the house?"

The man hitched his shoulders. "The usual tradesmen and such. Late in the afternoon that scabby lawyer from Peel arrived. He stayed nor more than an hour."

"And that was it?"

The man put his head to one side and then chuckled. "I was there past dark, having the dinner shift, as it were. There was one more fellow came along after dusk, a fellow a mortal man hopes to have little truck with. It was Solly Capers, the stonemason from Castleton."

Roddy nearly crowed with delight. "You recognized him then?"

"A'course I did. He rides a big gray mare. Hard to miss, even in the dark."

"Are the Wibberlys having some work done on their home then?" Owen asked.

Roddy turned to him with thinly veiled impatience. "Tell him," he said to the little man. "Tell my clever friend what Solly Capers does that a mortal man fears him."

The little man grinned. "Why, he carves gravestones, that's what."

Roddy found Lucy in her room, not wilting on the bed as he'd feared, but at the writing desk, furiously composing a letter.

"I couldn't rest," she said as he crossed the room. "I've been writing to Miss Purdy, who was my governess in Ceylon. She lives in Dorset now, and she was waiting to hear what I discovered." She sighed. "It helps to write things out, Roddy. It makes them clearer in your head."

Roddy went past her, swept the pages of her letter onto the floor, and plunked his bundled handkerchief onto the desktop. She started back at his abrupt behavior.

"Look there, Lucy. You will find perfidy and misdirection. And a heartless, wicked lie."

She sat unmoving until he opened the cloth and set her fingers upon the tiny bits of stone.

"There is no child in your sister's grave, Lucy," he said as he knelt before her. "Yesterday your brother ordered a stonemason to carve the new inscription. These bits of stone were still clinging to the engraving when you brushed your fingers over it."

She looked blank for a few seconds and then her mouth fell open. "The edges *were* sharp," she said. "Not like the inscription of Susanne's name, which was already becoming rounded. The baby's words were still sharp under my fingers." Then she shook her head. "But no, there was moss too . . . that wouldn't have grown over night."

"It wasn't growing there, it was rubbed on. To make the new words blend in with the old. But Yardley's mason was careless, he left some fragments and dust behind. Which you obligingly carried away on your hand."

"This might be fancy on your part, Roddy."

"It makes too much sense. He realized the only way he could make you stop looking for the girl, was by convincing you that she had died. So he doctored the tombstone."

She leaned down and picked up the pages of her letter and began ripping them into tiny shreds, venting all her anger and frustration on the bits of paper. "What he put me through today, Roddy, was worse than five years of living in his house. He took all my hope away, all my light."

Gently, he removed the shredded pages from her hands. "He also cozened you into making promises to him, which I would like to point out are no longer binding."

"No," she said. "I don't suppose they are."

"They never were, you silly girl. Since when do we have to honor our word to blackmailers and rogues?"

She tipped her head back and drew a long breath. "Since we were raised with them and can never believe that they are as evil as they seem."

She looked down at him, still kneeling at her feet. Sir Humphrey used to kneel like that during his repeated offers of marriage. It got to the point that whenever he twitched at the knees of his breeches she got a pain in her stomach for fear it would be the precursor to another unwanted proposal. She wondered if Roddy would kneel when he asked her to marry him and then immediately squelched such a nonsensical notion.

"What do we do now?" she asked.

"We still have Mr. Plimpton's information to check on. We will go to St. Margaret on Meade and question the vicar."

*   *   *

That night Consuelo appeared at dinner, full of bright conversation and charming anecdotes. She insisted that they make it a musical evening, and even played her guitar for Nonnie, something Roddy later told Lucy she hadn't done since the earl died. Lucy thought she must have been practicing in her chambers, though, since she played exquisitely.

"It's very sad," she said when she finished a Castilian love song. "But love is incomplete without its darker side. And I will tell you something I have observed—when men go to war, they take up the pen, when they turn to religion, they take up the paint brush, but when they fall in love, it is music that moves them."

She then looked across the room directly at Roddy, who was standing behind Lucy's chair. "Sing for me, Rodrigo."

He grinned. "Ah, Connie, it's been years."

"So you've lost your voice then?"

"No," he said. "But these fellows will never let me live it down if I muddle things."

He moved around Lucy, who was sitting in the shadow of a large pillar and let his hand drift over her collarbone as he went past. It was secret and intimate, and she felt the lingering thrill long after he had moved to the front of the room.

He sang another Spanish love song with Consuelo, his voice strong and sweet. Then they coaxed the Joker to join them in a popular ballad. Owen shifted back so that his chair was closer to Lucy's.

"I owe you an apology," he whispered. "I said some wrong-headed things to you in the library yesterday. Roddy will go his own way, as you said. As for Connie, I think you've done her a world of good."

"I haven't done anything, Mr. Griffith," she protested. "Except embroil everyone in my own troubles."

"Maybe that's the secret," he said with a smile. "We forget our own troubles when someone else's seem more pressing."

At this point Nonnie hissed at them good-naturedly to keep quiet and pay attention.

It was gray again the next day, though the rain held off. Lucy and Roddy headed across the Dorne Valley, past a stretch of marshland until they came to St. Margaret. The village appeared more prosperous than Parapet and, for its size, it possessed an impressive Norman church. The vicar was in his garden tending his early buds as their carriage drew up. He crossed over to meet Lucy and Roddy at the picket fence.

"Reverend MacTell," he said as he held out his hand to Roddy. "How may I help you?"

Lucy stepped forward. "We understand you have been receiving sums of money each month from an anonymous benefactor." It rankled her to use the word benefactor in relation to Yardley, but she couldn't very well call him a slithering serpent.

"For over seven years," Roddy added.

To their amazement the clergyman blushed, right up to the roots of his thick, snowy hair.

"This is a bit awkward," he said as he laid his secateurs on a nearby bench. "Perhaps you'd best come inside."

They went through the lych-gate, along a hedged path to the man's rectory. It was a trim house, whitewashed and rose-trellised, with the words HIS EYE IS ON THE SPARROW painted over the threshold. Once inside, the vicar hastily moved a week's worth of newspapers and a tailless brindle cat from his sofa and motioned them to be seated.

"I am not up on my housekeeping since my wife died," he said with a rueful smile.

"Oh," said Lucy. "Was it a recent loss?"

Mr. MacTell shook his head. "Ten years it's been. And to tell the truth, she would have been better able to advise me what to do with the money that comes in each month."

"I don't understand . . ." Lucy had unconsciously clutched Roddy's hand.

"As I said, it is difficult for me to explain this. When the money started coming, I directed it, as instructed, to a woman in the village, a midwife who lived here. Then four years ago she died, and I thought, if I write to the lawyer in Peel, the money will stop coming. But if I say nothing, then the people of my parish will benefit. It is not a large sum of money, mind, but every farthing counts during the lean times."

"Do you know who the midwife was giving the money to?" Roddy asked.

The clergyman looked blank. "I assumed she kept it. She was often called to assist the gentry . . . I guessed it came from a grateful patient. An annuity for her in her old age. She was at least eighty when she died."

Lucy hung her head. Another dead end.

"Where does the money go now?" Roddy inquired.

"Mostly to buy food for an elderly woman in the Dorne Valley, who was left with her daughter's baby to raise. Sadly, she has an affinity for the bottle. I used to give her the money directly, but I feared she was not spending a penny of it on the child."

Lucy perked up slightly. This must be the baby Charlie Pace had spoken of.

The cleric folded his hands over his snug black nest. "I do what I can to help the boy. So I hope you won't tell that lawyer in Peel. I must say it breaks my heart," Mr. MacTell added. "I swear there are nights when I hear that little chap crying in my dreams."

Lucy rose to her feet "Tell me," she said in a ragged whisper, "where we can find this child?"

Mr. MacTell appeared surprised. "There is nothing you can do for him, dear lady. The old woman who has him is his rightful guardian, being his grandmother."

"Tell me," she repeated. "I just want to see him."

"It's called Dorne Farm, though the family that owned the place were the McFallons. It's just old Mrs. McFallon now. Her daughter died in childbed over two years ago. She was a beauty, that one, and clever, too. Had every man in the parish courting her. But no one ever knew who the baby's father was."

"Thank you," Roddy said. "We promise that Mr. Plimpton shall hear none of this." He was at the door of the disordered rectory when he said, "And if a sallow-faced, scarecrow of a man comes nosing around here asking questions, I'd advise you to put your shutters up."

"Why?" the clergyman asked.

"Because he's the devil himself, good sir."

"It's too late," Mr. MacTell said with a wry smile. "We've already had a visit from Beelzebub—two or three days ago, it was. He wanted to know where the midwife lived. I was about to tell him what I knew, but then my cat got under his feet." He reached down and plucked the brindle cat from the floor, holding her under his chin. "Poor Tammy . . . he kicked her out of his way. Needless to say, I had a convenient case of memory loss then, and sent him away fuming. I understand he annoyed most of the village before he left."

"Why would Yardley come here to St. Margaret and bother Mr. MacTell?" Lucy asked once they were out of earshot of the rectory.

He stopped and tapped her on the chin gently. "Don't you get it yet, Lucy? Yardley doesn't know where the child is either. He's never bothered to come here to see to her well-being and now that he needs to get her out of your way, he hasn't a clue where to begin

looking. He had the same lead as we did—the dead midwife. I
wager the woman delivered your sister's daughter and then passed
the money from Yardley along to whomever had fostered her.
Yardley, being Yardley, never bothered to discover the names of
those people."

"But why wouldn't the foster parents come here looking for the
money once the midwife died? I think we need to ask the villagers
some questions."

He held her back a moment. "No, I don't think they would be in
the mood so soon after Yardley stalked through here. Let's leave
that for another day . . . besides, I suspect you have another mission right now."

"You don't mind?"

He gave her a lopsided grin. "Since when does Lochinvar have
a choice when his lady is bent on a quest."

She patted his hand. "You might make a Lochinvar yet."

Dorne Valley was composed mostly of rocks—tumbled rocks,
thrusting rocks, great hulking outcroppings of rocks that refused to
offer purchase to even the hardiest grass. It was a grim, gloomy
place at its far end, where Dorne Farm lay.

When the road grew too rutted for the carriage to pass, Roddy
and Lucy climbed out and proceeded on foot. Beside the lane ran a
fence of raw planking, which was rotted in many places. A few
emaciated sheep grazed along the stony ground, on weeds and
wildflowers. The barn lay before the house, and it was home to
several families of rooks, but looked to be unoccupied by any cat-
tle. As they moved past the barn, and the house came into view,
Lucy grabbed on to Roddy's sleeve.

"What is it?"

"This place . . . I know this place."

"Dear Lord, I hope not, Lucy. This is not the sort of place one
wants to know."

"From my dream. I never realized it before, but I think I've
glimpsed this farmhouse more than once."

He covered her hand and together they moved forward. They
came to the gate, which hung by one hinge, and already Roddy
could hear the crying. It rose and then fell like a tocsin, first loud
and piercing, and then softer but no less urgent.

"I don't know if I can do this," she said. "This child is no kin of
mine . . . why should it be haunting my dreams?"

"You don't know that this is the same child, Lucy. You don't know that Reverend MacTell was having the same dream you were. But we're here now, we might as well see how things stand."

They went up onto the porch, a rickety affair with most of the boards loose, and Roddy knocked at the door. "Mrs. McFallon," he called out.

"Eh?" a voice responded after a few seconds had passed. "Now just get yoursel' away from here and don't you be troublin' me."

The baby's cries were even louder now. "Hush!" the voice cried. "Hush now, I say."

"Please," Lucy said up against the door. "We don't want to trouble you. We just want to talk to you."

The door opened a crack and a grizzled head poked out. The woman's thin face was raddled with red patches beneath her mass of wiry gray hair. Gin fumes rose up from her whole body. "Eh? You're not from that infernal church league, are you?"

"We're from Ballabragh," Roddy said. "We just wanted to look in on you. Charlie Pace said you would let us see the baby."

"Charlie Pace, eh? That one's a rascal born, sure enough. Throws feed to my sheep, the instant my back is turned."

"A rascal indeed," Roddy concurred.

The woman shut the door.

Lucy smacked him on the arm and whispered, "She doesn't like Charlie or his mother, have you forgotten?"

He winced. "It was all I could think of to say." He squared his shoulders and knocked again. "Mrs. McFallon, please listen to me. We only want to see the baby. My friend, Miss Parnell, is writing a book about the children here on the island and we have heard that he is a splendid baby."

The door opened again. "He is a squalling little toad," she said with venom. Her eyes fell on Lucy and she squinted. "Will you pay to see him, then? If he is so splendid."

"I will give you a sovereign," Lucy said. Roddy was about to protest that he hadn't that much money on him, when Lucy dug her emergency coin from her reticule.

"Here." She displayed it for the old woman, who licked her lips and nodded.

The door swung wide and they stepped inside. The child's cries emanated from a room at the rear of the house.

"I'll fetch the little bugger," the woman said.

Lucy caught her by the shoulders. Mrs. McFallon felt as though she weighed less than a boy of ten. "No, we'll find him."

She and Roddy followed the sounds of tearful wailing until

they came to a small, dark room. It smelled worse than an out-house.

"Lucy," Roddy said from the threshold, "you are not going to be able to do this. It was a mistake."

"Get a candle . . ." she said forcefully. "Set that horrid old woman on fire if you have to, but bring me some light." She then moved past him and entered the dark room.

When Roddy returned, carrying a tallow taper set on a cracked saucer, she was already seated on the floor holding the baby.

"Look at him," she said as he set the candle down and crouched beside her. "No diaper, no bottle, not even a wooden spoon to play with . . . nothing but that disgusting cot he sleeps on."

"He's a bit old for a diaper, don't you think?"

The child was wearing what appeared to be a feed sack, with holes cut into it for his arms. Not that the holes needed to be very large, since his arms were pitifully thin. There was excrement dried on its hem and the sour odor of urine had permeated the whole room.

"Maybe you shouldn't be touching him, Lucy. Maybe he's ill."

Her face darkened. "He's not ill, he's underfed and neglected. No wonder he cries so that the whole valley can hear him." She lifted him high in her arms and he grinned, showing off his small white teeth. "He has wonderful lungs, though. Sick babies don't have such a lusty cry."

"Baby . . ." he said. "Babeee . . ."

"He talks," Roddy said with some wonder.

"Of course he does. Don't you have nieces and nephews? You must have been around babies before now."

Roddy made a face. "I generally stay clear of them till they are breeched. I say, is he a pretty baby, do you think?"

She looked at the toddler assessingly. "It's hard to say, he looks more like a wizened old man right now. There's no telling how he'll look with some flesh on him."

"Is he the one, Luce? The one from your dream?"

She tucked the child under her chin and rocked him slowly back and forth. He began a contented gurgling. "What does it matter whether he is or not?"

"I was just wondering, that's all. Whether you're going to make me spend the rest of my life looking for lost babies."

She gasped slightly and looked at him, kneeling upright beside her. The softness in his eyes and the tender expression on his face stole her breath.

"Because I would, you know. All you need do is ask . . ."

"No, Roddy," she said in a low voice, "all *you* need do is ask."

"You've had your sovereign's worth." The old woman's harsh, croaking voice broke the spell. She stood hunched in the doorway like some evil crone. "Give him over to me now."

Lucy tried to hold the child back, but Roddy took him from her gently and handed him to Mrs. McFallon. The baby instantly started to wail.

"No!" Lucy cried.

"Come away, Lucy," he said.

"Yes, away with you . . . go write your fairy story about my grandson," the woman jeered. " 'Tis the only memorial he will have once he's gone." She jiggled the child and he cried even louder.

"He needs to be clean," Lucy said over her shoulder as Roddy drew her from the room. "And he needs some toys."

"Away with you," the woman said again. "He won't live out the year, I expect. No toys for them that's bound for the boneyard."

Roddy practically had to wrestle Lucy out of the house. "You can't do anything . . . you heard what the reverend said. That woman is his rightful kin—"

"She's an old sot!" Lucy spat out.

"I know. It's disgraceful for a woman like that to be rearing a child."

"She isn't rearing him," Lucy said as he hustled her down the lane. "She's killing him."

Roddy stopped prodding her forward and spun her to face him. "Well, what did you expect? You knew from Charlie that the baby was not being treated well. What the devil did you expect to accomplish by this? Except to tear yourself up inside, which, let me tell you, is something you seem to excel at. This isn't Susanne's child, Lucy, and you must stop behaving as though it is. Stop trying to find something you lost . . . or you will lose everything."

Her face went pale, and she twisted away from his hold and made her way alone to the carriage. When he climbed in behind her, she shifted on the seat to be as far away from him as possible. She remained silent during the short trip back to Ballabragh and left him without a word the instant the carriage drew up in front of the house.

Roddy stood looking up at the staircase where she had disappeared in her silent huff and cursed himself for a bird-witted fool. There had been such warm accord between them there in the baby's room. Lord, she had looked so perfect with a child held to her breast. He'd known at that moment that he would never want another woman, that no one would ever stir him in his soul as she did. She was his Jenny, his stern, graceful doll come miraculously to life.

He had hurt her, though he wasn't sure how. What he'd said to her by the farm was true—she had been acting as though she had to rescue every child that came her way. To make up for her imagined abandonment of her sister. And it was all nonsense.

Certainly the little boy at the Dorne Farm was in a bad way, but how was that Lucy's responsibility? Mr. MacTell himself had made the pronouncement—the child was with his rightful guardian.

It will most likely die. Those were Charlie Pace's words. Charlie, who cried under his bed when his lambs died.

His eye is on the sparrow. Those words, Roddy knew, came from the Bible. He wasn't much on reading, but his good mother had seen to it that he wasn't raised a heathen. It occurred to him then that he needed a woman's advice and since Lucy was not an option, he made his way to Consuelo's rooms.

Mrs. Granger met him at the door. "She is not up to visitors today," she explained. "All this commotion over Miss Parnell and her missing niece has upset her, started her thinking on her own lost babies." She snorted like a dragon at the gate. "I knew that one would bring no good to this house."

She shut the door in Roddy's face and he wondered if that was going to become a regular happenstance. First, the old woman at Dorne Farm and now Mrs. Granger. He was clearly losing his charms with the fair sex.

He wandered downstairs, aimless, restless and trying to fight off the sense of guilt that was making inroads on his heart. Nonnie and the Joker were laughing over the billiard table. "You were right about the stonemason," Nonnie called out to him. "We tracked him down this morning in Castleton. That dog Abbott paid him to change the inscription."

Roddy thanked them both for their help, but shook off their invitation to play. He further refused to respond when they asked after Lucy's mission that afternoon.

Owen was closeted in the library, sitting in his favorite armchair and deeply immersed in some gargantuan book on the

Greeks or the Romans. Roddy selected a book at random from the shelves and sat down near the window, where the watery light trickled in.

"Oh, bother," he thought as he opened the cover. It was a book of prosy essays by someone named John Donne. Damn Nonnie for having such tiresome things in his library. Roddy was still working his way through *Waverly*, but it was up in his bedroom and as much as he longed for the rollicking words of Walter Scott, he hadn't the energy to go up there. Not to the same wing where Lucy was sequestered.

"Snow . . ." he said softly. "I need to talk to someone."

He waited, but there was no response. He muttered crossly, "Snowball, if you are no longer speaking to me, I wish you'd tell me."

Still there was silence from the other end of the room. Roddy set down his book and tiptoed to his friend's chair. Snowball was fast asleep, nodding over his tome.

"These late nights of ghost hunting have caught up with you," he said softly as he settled Owen's head against the padded chair back. He returned to his own chair and opened the book of essays at random.

The first words he read sent a shiver through him. . . . *"No man is an island."*

His eyes continued down the page. . . . *"I am involved in mankind . . . never send to know for whom the bell tolls, it tolls for thee."*

He read the essay through one more time and then leaned forward, his head in his hands. He knew he was a good person, everyone told him how kindhearted he was and how generous. But what was going through his head at that moment could not in any way be construed a good thought. The act he was contemplating went against all the laws of man and nature. At least by his reckoning.

He knew that he alone, among his friends, had stepped out of his own narrow circle to involve himself in the plight of others. He alone paid heed to the beggars that haunted the streets of London or the legless veterans who asked for alms in Trouro. He had hired MacHeath, not out of caprice as his fiends thought—because it amused him—but out of compassion for a brave man who had been facing starvation.

It was one of the chief things that had attracted him to Lucy, her compassion and her sense of justice. It was what made him believe that she was the right person to draw Consuelo from her seclusion.

He pictured Lucy's early life in Ceylon. Even though she'd lived among wealthy planters, he wagered she noticed the unfortunates—the beggars and the ailing. Only a woman who had seen that side of life and not been repelled by it could have given up her place at the high table as she had.

Sometimes life is more than a lark. She had said that to him that first morning. He'd seen the bitter reality behind that reprimand this afternoon—in the squalid back room of a tumbledown farmhouse. Life would never be a lark for young Master McFallon. Life might not even be an option.

And yet he had chided Lucy for her charity and her concern. Accused her of seeking the pain, when all she ever sought was the truth. That there could be pain in discovering the truth, he knew. But with that discovery there also came the option to right things. That was what being her Lochinvar meant, ultimately, not that he protected her or defended her, but that he made things right in her world. At this moment, he suspected, everything had gone wrong for her. There were no further clues to her niece's whereabouts. Yardley Abbott was stalking the island, scheming to remove the child from her reach. And now there was the realization that the baby who cried in her dreams was indeed a baseborn child, but one she had no right to rescue. Nothing had gone Lucy's way today.

But the day wasn't over yet.

Chapter Eleven

About midnight the sky opened up, and the rain that had been threatening for two days began to fall with a vengeance. Thunder rocked the hills and lightning crackled bright against the leaden sky.

Owen Griffith was ready to give up his nighttime vigil and admit that the woman he'd seen was nothing more than a brandy-induced phantasm. He'd stop roaming the upper reaches of the house where he'd caught that one tantalizing glimpse of her. He'd sleep in his bed like a normal person, and get back to work on the paper he was researching on the Roman settlements in Britain.

He found a convenient window seat and curled up on it to watch the storm track across the island, tucking his feet beneath him like a child. There was nothing he liked so much as a good downpour, only he wished he didn't feel so dashed lonely. It was all Roddy's fault. His one-time best friend had now turned his interest to the troubled Miss Parnell. Not that he could blame him, she was pretty and clever, even if she did have strange dreams and a very unfortunate stepbrother. It was just that Owen knew how these things transpired. First one fellow in the group lost his heart to a woman, and before long, all one's cronies were well along toward parson's mousetrap. It was as inevitable as the tides. And there he was, the least likely of the four of them to find a mate. He was too bookish for one thing. Had no title, for another. And compared to Roddy and the Joker, he fell far short in the looks department. Though he thought he could still best Nonnie . . . but Nonnie was an earl, which made looks quite immaterial.

He knew he was as prone to maudlin self-pity as any Welshman born, and now fought off the familiar sensation of bleak defeat. He had money, there was some consolation in that. Pots of money, if the truth be told. And he had brains. Not a sterling catalog of attributes, but it was a start. He'd just have to hone his skills where women were concerned.

Roddy had spent his whole academic career feeding off Owen's brilliance. Maybe it was time for Roddy to lend his friend a hand in the petticoat line. Give him a pointer or two. Push him in the direction of some eligible females.

Owen was lost in this hopeful reverie when the woman went past him. She whooshed by, her cloak flying out behind her like a dark cloud. He knew immediately it was her, even though her flaxen hair was obscured by the hood of her cloak.

He jumped up to chase after her, forgetting that his feet were tucked under him. He tumbled onto the carpet, tangled in his own legs. He lay there in the dark, cursing his clumsiness, his face pressed to the woolen runner. It was funny, he thought, as he chuckled mournfully. The one woman he wanted to impress, and here he lay like a beached halibut.

Something soft brushed against his hair, and a voice said, "Have you hurt yourself?"

He propped himself up onto his elbows and looked up. She was crouched above him, the hood now pushed back from those glorious pale waves of hair.

"No," he said. "You just startled me."

She smile. "You thought I was a ghost, didn't you?"

He nodded. "That first night I did. You disappeared when I called after you."

"It was you who startled me then. And I didn't disappear—there is a servant's passage there that leads down to the kitchen. It's made to blend in with the wainscotting."

"Are you one of the servants?"

She shook her head. "I am a seamstress and a weaver. I work for Lady Steyne, but I am no one's servant."

"That's nice," he said idiotically. "I've waited for you nearly every night, you know."

Her face broadened into a smile. "You have? I haven't been back here at night since then."

"Tonight was the last night I was going to wait. Because I realized you were a figment of my imagination . . ."

She giggled softly. "I am not a figment. But I'd better be going. I have mending to fetch."

"Why do you come at night?"

"Because that's the time when my neighbor is able to look after my daughter."

Owen's eyes grew dull. "You are married then?"

"I was once," she said. "I am a widow."

"Oh, that is wonderful. I mean, that is very sad."

She got to her feet and waited until he untangled his legs and rose beside her. "I know what you meant."

"How will you get home? It's raining blazes out there."

"I have a dogcart."

"Let me drive you," he asked earnestly. "The earl has a closed carriage . . . we'll tie your dogcart behind."

"Thank you," she said, "but I've lived on this island for years. A little storm is no trouble. And I like the rain."

"I do too," he said softly. He couldn't seem to take his eyes off her.

"Well, good-bye, then."

"Yes," he murmured. "Good-bye."

As she moved off, something inside him began punching him in the gut and bellowing words he couldn't quite comprehend. *She's leaving, you lackwit. Find out where she lives, find out her name.*

"Excuse me," he called out. "May I know your name?"

"Mrs. Pace," she said with laughter in her voice. "I live in the Dorne Valley."

"Thank you," he breathed. *Thank you, my dearest, most wonderful Mrs. Pace.*

Lucy heard the fierce hammering of the rain upon the battlements, but in her dream she was in Ceylon, where that noise was a familiar part of the monsoon season. In her dream she still rode over the plantation with her father, still held court with the neighbors' callow sons, still was lost in the belief that the world as she knew it would go on unchanged, that life with her father would remain a constant. In her dream there were no headstrong sisters, no unstable mothers, no scheming stepbrothers or lost, crying children. There was only the bliss of youth and as-yet-unfulfilled expectation.

But the thunder roused her at last from that welcome dream, and for an hour she tossed and turned, reminded that her life had not taken on a rosy aspect. She saw over and over the image of the McFallon baby, heard his cries of distress.

Roddy was right, of course. There was nothing one could do, except feel pity and chagrin that such situations existed. There were no practical solutions. Throughout the realm there were parish poorhouses and workhouses, orphanages and ladies' charitable leagues, but no institutions made provision for a child who was neglected by his own kin. And surely Britain was a better place for such children than India or Ceylon, where beggars maimed their own children to more effectively strike pity in a passerby.

She had been acting like a fool, she saw. Hoping that after her encounter with the dream-child everything would come right. But the encounter had left her feeling even more bleak.

Not every realized dream brought resolution or peace. They often brought disillusionment. Her father's dream of paradise in Ceylon had ended with the cyclone. Her sister's dream of husband and child had ended in disgrace and death. Her own dreams, when she dared to dream them, of finding someone in the breadth of the land who would love her enough to wipe away the stain of her guilt over Susanne, would never come to pass. Like Consuelo, she had been doing penance, in her own case for seven years, and for a sin that Roddy finally made her see had never been committed. Her only sin had been indecision and a natural fear of the unknown. Hardly worth fretting her life away.

She climbed from her bed and wrapped herself in the comforter before she went to the window to watch the last violent throes of the storm. It would be calm in the morning, a spectacular day . . . a good day to begin her life over, without the cobwebs of regret and sadness that had clung to it for so long.

There was the dark-haired man Consuelo had seen in her Tarot . . . the man who had looked at her with worshipful longing in a farmhouse bedroom. He was no longer the fool, he was the knight now. He'd proven himself to her and she would have him if he asked her. She was not sure she loved him, she had put love away from her when Susanne was lost, but she knew she held him in the greatest affection.

"Roddy," she whispered, leaning her head upon one cold damp pane of the window. "Forgive me for my temper and my anger. Who am I to rail against the workings of the world when I have taken so little control over my own life?"

She sighed and returned to her bed and slept at last.

It was still raining when she awoke again, but it was now a gentle spring rain, good for the gardens and the new crops in the fields. Roddy was calling her name softly.

"Lucy . . . Lucy . . ."

She sat up and saw him standing at the foot of her bed, a dark silhouette wearing a long cloak that was slick with rain. He was holding his arms crossed on his chest, as a man does who is mortally wounded. She had a sudden, irrational fear that he was dying. His voice had been so shaken.

"Roddy," she cried, springing up from under the covers. "Are you hurt?" She ran her hands along his chest, and felt him trembling.

"Lucy," he said again in that ragged voice, "you must not hate me for what I have done. You must understand, you who value kin over everything. But you saw today that kin is not equal to kind . . . you saw."

He fell to his knees and laid his head against her hip.

Her hand traced over his wet hair. "Oh, Roddy, you must tell me what you have done." She ran to the dresser and searched in the darkness for her tinderbox.

"Don't light a candle," he cautioned. "He is sleeping now and I don't want to wake him. I think the motion of my horse soothed him."

Lucy returned to him and drew him up onto the bed. She gently pulled his arms away from the blanket-wrapped bundle that slept against his chest beneath the wet folds of his cloak. The baby groaned softly in his sleep and rubbed a fist over his eyes.

Lucy's heart was beating so fast and so fiercely she wondered it didn't explode from her chest. "Roddy," she said close against his ear, "this is all that is wonderful. But you can't burgle a baby."

"Didn't burgle him, Luce," he replied.

Her heart stopped. "Oh, never say that you have killed that old woman."

He gave a dry laugh. "Would have done the world a favor, but you know I am not the bloodthirsty type." He shifted the baby onto the bed, straightening the hem of the soiled feed sack before he replaced the tattered blanket.

He drew Lucy to the window and took her face between his hands. "I did it for you, sweetheart. And for the child. And for every child who lives in squalor and neglect. I was reading John Donne, you see."

"Oh, Lord," she said under her breath. "I wanted to become a missionary nun in Calcutta when I'd finished reading him. And my family were not even Catholic." She laid her hands over his and her eyes gleamed at him. "So tell me, if you didn't burgle him, and you didn't kill his grandmother and carry him off, how did you come to have him?"

Roddy swallowed audibly and said, "I bought him."

She nearly laughed. The old witch had charged her a sovereign to hold him for the space of five minutes; she doubted there was enough gold in the kingdom to pay for a transfer of ownership, let alone in Roddy's perpetually empty pockets.

"With what?" she asked, trying not to sound too skeptical.

"With good English gold. Two thousand pounds to be exact. It was everything I had. She promised to go off to her sister's in Dublin with the money. No one will know she didn't take the child with her. She said you looked to make a right fine mother."

"Me?" Lucy said faintly. "Roddy, I don't know the first thing about being mother to a two year old. The children I looked after had nursemaids and nannies. I am a teacher . . ."

"Then you can learn, we can both learn. You see I realized this afternoon that it was what you needed. A child of your own. Not your sister's child who has obsessed you, but your own."

"He is not my own." Her tone was gentle.

"I know that. I don't mean him, necessarily. He just showed me what you needed. Babies, Lucy, lots of babies. And then you will have a family again."

"And what of him? What shall we do with him?"

He smiled; she saw his teeth flash white in the faint light. "Everything will sort itself out, you'll see. I think he needs a bath though and something to eat. He's going to be fairly cranky when he does wake up."

Lucy thought for a minute. "You stay here with him. I know my way around a kitchen. If he starts to cry, just give him your finger to suck on." Roddy made a face and Lucy grinned. "See I do know that much about babies."

She flung a shawl over her nightgown and went from the room, trying to assimilate the fact that the lost child of her dream was now sleeping on her bed. She stoked up the fire in the kitchen hearth, put two kettles on to boil, and went to the larder to find the sack of oatmeal.

Ten minutes later she was outside her bedroom, a scuttle of hot water in one hand and a bowl of oatmeal laced with honey in the other. Roddy opened the door when he heard her moving along the passage.

"You are a brick, Miss Parnell." He took the heavy scuttle from her and held the door for her to enter. He'd lit a candle, but had it shaded behind the bed hangings. The baby was stirring slightly, his grubby hands moving above his head.

Together they removed his sack dress and washed him all over with the warm water. His skin was a pale bluish white and wrinkled at his joints. Lucy had never seen a baby so thin. He never quite woke up while they fussed over him, but smiled several times. Lucy threw his dress and the tattered blanket into the fireplace. When she turned back, Roddy was attempting to swaddle him in his neckcloth. He blushed at her expression of amusement. "Well, the poor fellow needs some kind of nappie. It ain't dignified otherwise."

"We'll worry about his dignity tomorrow. Right now his behavior is what concerns me. He is too quiet."

"I thought that was a blessing. We don't want the whole household down around our ears."

She leaned over and sniffed the baby's pursed mouth. Her frown was thunderous when she stood up. "She's dosed him with gin, the old harridan. I've heard of mothers doing that when babies are teething to help them sleep. No wonder he's not waking up."

Roddy was aghast. "You mean she got him drunk? I wish now I had shot her."

"No you don't. But we can't feed him until he's full awake." She stood thinking a minute. "Tell you what, leave him here for now. When he's awake I'll feed him. I expect he won't mind cold oatmeal. In the morning we will decide what to do."

Roddy swept his cloak off the back of a chair and went to the door.

"Tell me I did the right thing, Lucy. I need to hear you say it."

Lucy got up from the bed and went to him. Her hands stroked along his shoulders to his chest, where they came to rest over his heart. "You might not have done the right thing, Roddy, but you did the humane thing. They are not always one and the same."

He raised one of her hands and traced a kiss along the palm. "I have to tell you something."

Her eyes widened. "I'm not sure I am up to any more surprises tonight."

"It's not a surprise," he whispered against her skin. "It's more of a declar—"

The piercing wail shattered the quiet and rose right up to the plaster ceiling. It grew in volume until the chamber was full of vibrating, tangible sound. Roddy and Lucy both gaped at the bed in dismay. The baby was turning red and squirming, his mouth open wide.

Lucy flew across the room and picked up the bowl of oatmeal. She tried putting the spoon to his mouth, but he pushed her hand away fitfully. She tried again with no success.

"Bet he has the devil of a hangover," said Roddy from the door. "Gin always does that to me."

"You're not being much help," she grumbled. "Think of something."

"Give him your finger to suck on," he drawled.

"You're going to be wearing this oatmeal in a minute," she said hotly.

"You already are." He motioned to the front of her nightgown, where some of the sticky gray porridge had come to rest.

Meanwhile the baby continued to cry, without air it appeared, since he didn't ever stop to breathe, but just keened out a continuous, undulating wail. Lucy tried picking him up, bouncing him on her knee, jiggling him on the mattress. Nothing worked. She tried feeding him the oatmeal again and found herself wearing even more of it.

"Sounds like he's got a pain in his belly."

"Roddy, if you can't be any more help than this—"

The door behind him swung open, nearly swatting him in the tail. Consuelo stood there, arrayed in layers of iridescent gauze, and wearing a frilled lace cap. She didn't say a word as she crossed the room and lifted the baby onto her shoulder, patting him all the while firmly on the back. There was a loud, resounding belch, and the baby immediately stopped crying.

"Told you he had a pain in his belly," Roddy said from over his fisted hand.

Consuelo's gaze swung from him to Lucy. She rattled off something in Spanish.

"English, Connie, if you please. We are none of us here conversant in Castilian."

"I said, whose child is this? And what is he doing in Miss Parnell's bedroom?" She looked down at the badly wrapped neckcloth and scowled. "And why is he wearing a cravat?"

Before either of them could answer, she carried the baby across the room and out into the hall, crooning to him all the while in Spanish.

Lucy was dumbfounded. Roddy looked smug. "See, I told you something would work out."

"You planned this? I don't believe it."

He shook his head. "I didn't plan anything. But it makes sense. There's Consuelo pining for a child, and there's a child pining to be looked after."

Lucy was doubtful. "Have you forgotten that Consuelo is a

Spanish noblewoman and that the baby is an illegitimate farm child?"

He took her hand and squeezed it. "I'll let you explain that to her, Luce. It should be interesting. And by the by, that was a very Yardleyesque observation. You could just be happy for her, you know. Not everything has to be neat and tidy to be good."

She moved away from him, rubbing her hands over her face. "I'm sorry. I had no right to say that. Consuelo will go her own way. I think that everyone in this place has caught that ailment."

"You'd better sleep now . . . I fancy tomorrow is going to be even more eventful than today."

He crossed the room to where she stood and kissed her soundly. "Good night, sweetheart." He went again to the door.

"Are you going?" she asked when he did not pass out into the hall.

"I was just wondering . . . do you think you're compromised now that the countess has seen me in your room, and with a baby, no less?"

"Go to sleep, Roddy," she said with weary forbearance. "I don't think she even noticed you were here."

Chapter Twelve

The next morning there was a soft knock at her door.

"The countess has asked to see you in the gallery, Miss Parnell." It was Mrs. Granger's voice. "She is taking the baby for his first outing."

Lucy quickly finished dressing and made her way to the portrait gallery. The countess was there, hovering behind the baby like a nervous mother hen, while he took halting steps along the carpeted runner. His thin arms angled out from the sides of the white linen gown he now wore. Owen and the Joker watched from the window bench, while Nonnie crouched at the far end of the carpet and coaxed the little fellow forward.

"Ah, Miss Parnell," the countess called out. "See how well he walks."

"Not much for talking though," Roddy said, coming up behind Lucy. He ran his hand along her spine. "Just checking to make sure all your buttons are done up," he whispered over her shoulder.

"I have a maid do my buttons now," she said between her teeth.

"Pity," he drawled as he drew her to where Nonnie was kneeling on the floor.

The earl looked up and grinned at them. "This is capital, Ram. He is a charming little fellow."

"Till he opens his mouth," Roddy said. "Then we'll all run for cover."

Consuelo shook her finger at him. "You are very wicked to say such a thing. He is a sweet *niño*."

"Isn't she even curious where you got him?" Lucy said to him under her breath.

"Apparently not. He's like manna from heaven, I suppose. Who questions that?"

The baby finished his progress across the floor and propelled himself into Nonnie's arms. The earl gave a startled chuckle, then rose and carried the baby closer to the wall of portraits.

"These are my ancestors," he said into the cap of fair curls. "My Uncle Theodore, my Great-Aunt Gertrude . . . my father with his parents . . ." Nonnie's voice faded. He staggered slightly and set the baby down carefully. The child clamored at his knee to be picked up again.

"By George," Nonnie was whispering in a hoarse, shaking voice. "Oh, by George."

Everyone in the room quickly moved to his side.

"What is it, Nonnie?" Roddy asked, all his glibness fled at his friend's stricken tone.

"Look," said Nonnie, pointing to the baby in the group portrait. When no one seemed to comprehend, Nonnie scooped the McFallon baby from the ground and held him up beside the portrait. *"Look!"*

Five pairs of eyes widened at the same time.

Nonnie's father, the sixth Earl of Steyne, in his long white gown, could have been the twin of the baby Nonnie held in his arms. The same blond curls, the same blue eyes, and the same promisingly large nose.

"Santa Maria," Consuelo muttered and crossed herself.

"I'll be damned," Roddy whispered.

"This is a miracle," Nonnie pronounced, his voice near to breaking. "Somehow, some way, this little fellow found his way back here. Where he obviously belongs."

"Does he have a name?" Owen asked. "We can't keep calling him 'this little fellow.' "

Everyone turned to Lucy. She bit her lip. "We never thought to ask." She didn't tell them that the old woman had referred to him only as "that squalling little toad."

"I think Connie should name him," Roddy said.

"Yes, I will name him. Ah, but these English names . . . so dry."

"You can name him in any language you like," Lucy said. "As long as we can pronounce it."

The countess took the baby from Nonnie and raised him up above her head. He gurgled as he'd done when Lucy lifted him the afternoon before. Lucy felt a momentary pang of envy—he had been her baby for the space of five minutes then, and again for an hour last night. But she gladly relinquished him now. He would never know want or neglect again. He would be loved and cherished, not only by the effusive Spanish woman, but apparently also by Nonnie.

"Salvador Lucien Rodrigo Swithins," she said. She grinned

across at Lucy and Roddy. "See, now he will never forget you. You are part of his name for all time."

"Swithins?" the Joker said with a tiny frown. "That's a bit precipitate. We can't know for sure that he's a Swithins."

Nonnie swept away his objection with an imperious wave. " 'Course he's a Swithins. Or a Gurney at the very least. He's got the nose."

Everyone went downstairs for breakfast, except Roddy, who lingered in the doorway and prevented Lucy from leaving.

"Talk to me, Luce. Are you cross with Consuelo for usurping you?"

"Not a bit, in truth. It occurs to me that if there was any purpose in my coming to Man, perhaps it's now been served. Those dreams were not meant to lead me to my niece, I think, but to lead me to the baby for Consuelo. How else can I explain that two separate encounters we had while looking for Susanne's child guided us to this child?"

"You still want things neat and tidy don't you?"

"Always," she said with a grin. "And that's not necessarily a fault." She reached up to tweak his disordered neckcloth. "We really need to see about getting you a proper valet."

He sighed. "It won't be long. I fear MacHeath is anxious to leave my service. He's hearing the siren song of the sea again."

He drew her onto the long window seat. "So you've given up your quest to find Susanne's child? I find that difficult to credit."

She leaned back against the window ledge. "I am tired, Roddy." She gave him a twinkling look. "I am not that young, you know."

"Oh, bosh!" he said. "You're getting younger by the minute."

"Well, I'm done trying to make up for the mistakes I made with my sister. I think it's time I laid her ghost to rest. If her child is here, I will have to trust that she is happy and well cared for. These islanders are good people for the most part—look at Reverend MacTell and Charlie Pace. More than a few people were worried about little Salvador. Even if they didn't succeed in turning that old woman into a better caretaker, at least they cared enough to try."

"But trying isn't doing. Still, I know what you mean. Good intentions are a beginning."

"Is that why you took him, Roddy?"

"I'm still not sure why I did. After we came back to Ballabragh it kept gnawing at me. I . . . I just wanted to make things right."

She took his hand. "You have, Roddy. I never believed that money could buy happiness, but you've just proved me wrong. But where on earth did you find two thousand pounds in the middle of the night?"

He fidgeted with his neckcloth. "There is something I should probably tell you . . ."

"Miss Parnell?" Mrs. Granger stood at the door of the gallery. "There is someone in the hall who wants to see you." Lucy's face fell. "It's not your brother this time," the housekeeper reassured her.

Lucy followed her down to the main hall. Charlie Pace was standing there goggling at the epic paintings and elaborate tapestries that adorned the walls.

"Miss Parnell," he cried, meeting her at the foot of the stairs, "I wanted 'specially to talk to you."

"Hello, Charlie," she said. "You're about early this morning. Who's tending the sheep?"

He pulled her down by one arm and whispered in her ear, "The truth is, they mostly tend themselves. But don't tell anyone."

Lucy looked across at Mrs. Granger. This morning the woman seemed to be almost in charity with her. "We would like breakfast in the library, if you please."

Mrs. Granger actually curtsied before she went off.

"She's a bit of a dragon," Lucy said under her breath as she led Charlie into the library. Owen had not yet taken up his daily residence there, and they had the room to themselves.

"She's my father's aunt," Charlie said, and added with a chuckle, "but she scares me too, sometimes."

"It's a pity we can't pick our relatives," Lucy said as she settled into one of the chairs and indicated that Charlie should sit opposite her. "Now what is it you want to talk to me about?"

"My mother sent me," he said. "To thank you for . . . um, intervening, with the McFallon baby. That was her word. I think it means rescuing. Anyway, we both want to thank you. He won't die now, will he?"

"I don't think so. He'll be well cared for in this house."

"Is the countess going to keep him, do you think?"

She smiled. "Ten strong men couldn't pry him away from her." Charlie looked reassured.

"But tell me, how did you know about all this? The McFallon woman swore not to tell a soul."

Charlie screwed up his mouth in distaste. "She was drunk this morning, wandering up and down the valley telling everyone she met that she'd gotten some nob from the big house and his lady to take the baby off her hands."

Lucy was still fighting off her blush at being called the nob's lady, when the breakfast cart came in. Charlie's eyes grew to saucer size.

"May I have one?" he asked, eyeing the honey buns with an open appetite.

"You may have as many as you like."

They spent another half hour talking; Lucy was surprised and delighted when Charlie expressed interest in the volumes in the library. It turned out Charlie had only a few books at home. "My mother sometimes brings me books from Castleton, but they are very dear."

Lucy thought a moment. "You must ask the countess if you can come here and read, Charlie. You know she invites her servants' children in for tea; I'm sure she would let you use her library."

The boy looked dubious.

"I will ask her for you." She gave a little cough. "I believe she owes me something of a favor."

Charlie's eyes lit up. "Thank you. And now I should go. My mother will need her dogcart back." He took Lucy's hand in his. "You are a very nice person, Miss Parnell. I told Mama she would like you very much if she met you."

Lucy walked him to the door and watched him drive off in a jaunty red cart pulled by a cream-colored cob.

She spent the remainder of the morning in the garden with Consuelo and Salvador. The countess was beaming, her joy barely contained, as she walked the child along the pebble paths. Lucy was reminded of the Ten of Pentacles, the Tarot card that showed a man and a woman walking with a child. She wondered if that happy scene would be replicated in her own life.

Though she and Roddy had not yet reached an accord, she had a feeling it was only a matter of time. He'd find some way to be alone with her—it was one of his greatest skills—and make his proposal. And she would not hesitate for even the space of a second in accepting him.

They would have a fine life together, she mused. He would no doubt want to settle near his family in Cornwall. When she had traveled there to visit the great house of Carillon, she had loved the drama of the spare, rugged terrain, so unlike any other county in England. Though it was not so different from parts of this island, rocky and windswept, with the sounds of the sea always close by.

She would take in students for extra funds, perhaps teach drawing or French to the children of the local gentry. Surely Roddy would not begrudge her that contribution. It was a good life she imagined, she and Roddy making their own way in the world, not dependent on his wealthy friends or her nipfarthing stepbrother for a single sou. He might go into the church or interest himself in local politics—he'd make a fine cleric or member of Parliament with his kind heart and ability to sway others.

She was busy organizing their lives in her head as she left the garden and returned to her room. Once there, she sat at the writing desk and composed a note to her stepbrother. If she was going to begin the healing process, this was a very good place to start.

"Dear Yardley," she wrote, "I have been to Parapet and seen what it was you wished me to see. I am still most distressed by what I discovered there. (*Ha*, she thought, *that was properly ambiguous.*) I now realize my quest must be at an end. My invitation to stay at Ballabragh has been extended to Saturday, after which time I will return to Manchester. It would be a kindness in you to return my purse and my ticket which were taken from my trunk. I know the countess would gladly furnish me the funds for my passage, but I am sure you don't wish me to be further beholden to the earl's family. I would also appreciate the return of my journal, which was likewise missing from my personal effects."

She signed it with a satisfied flourish. Let Yardley think she believed the words on the tombstone, let him think she was going back to her post in Manchester—it didn't matter any longer. She would do her utmost to have no further contact with him. The Abbots were a part of her life she intended to put behind her. Her heart sang as she went downstairs to the dining room. She was hoping to find Roddy there, but Owen was the only one at the table. He gave her a wide dreamy grin.

"So you weren't imagining that child after all," he said as he reached for a cutlet.

"No," she said. "Only it wasn't the child I was expecting it to be. But fate works that way sometimes."

He set his chin on his hand. "I also found the lady I was looking for," he said with a sigh. "And she was exactly who I expected her to be."

Her eyes lit up with delight. "Mr. Griffith, that is wonderful news."

"It was last night, during the storm. She walked right past me . . . I was drowsing on the window seat and fell over my own feet when I jumped up to follow her. She came back and spoke with me. She's an angel, Miss Parnell. I don't care if she's just a seamstress. She's the most beautiful woman in the world."

"So she's not a ghost after all."

"She's a widow who lives in Dorne Valley. Her name is Mrs. Pace . . . I was so awestruck I never asked her her given name." He grinned in such a besotted manner that Lucy laughed.

"I suspect you will discover that soon enough. As a matter of fact, I had breakfast with her son, Charlie."

Owen was shaking his head. "Daughter," he said. "Not son. She told me she has a daughter."

"Mr. Griffith, you must be mistaken. Ask Roddy. He met Charlie two days ago out on the moors."

Owen shook his head again. "Miss Parnell, I remember every word she said, they are 'graved in my memory. She told me she had to hurry home to her daughter."

Lucy thought a moment. "Perhaps she has more than one child, a boy and a younger girl. Charlie is so independent I doubt she had to hurry home to look after *him*."

Owen mulled this over.

"Does that upset the applecart, if she has two children?" Lucy asked.

"She could have a dozen and I would not mind. When she touched my brow, it was like the whisper of dawn . . . ah, and her scent was sublime, a glorious mix of gardenias and roses."

Lord help him, Lucy muttered to herself in amusement. Thank goodness Roddy did not moon about spouting such nonsense over her. Or if he did, it was not while she was in earshot.

The others came in then, and Roddy seated himself beside her. Nonnie announced that the afternoon would be spent in the attics trying on costumes for the fete. "In case anything needs to be altered," he said, "we can have the seamstress come in tomorrow to see to it."

They trooped up the three staircases, laughing and joking among themselves. Lucy was induced to try on the brocade gown that Nonnie had described to her that first night. She went behind a raggedy dressing screen, tied on the bone and wood panniers, and then shrugged into the bodice of the pink and green dress, drawing it on over her own gown. She was struggling into the voluminous skirt when Roddy peeked around the frame of the screen. "Need any help?"

She plucked up the feather-trimmed fan that had been packed

away with the gown and swatted him with it. "She'll do," he declared merrily over the screen to his friends, ducking away from a second stroke of the fan.

"Nonnie," she called out. "Would you kindly restrain Mr. Kempthorne?"

"Come out of there, Ram," the earl ordered. "Isn't fair that you get the first glimpse of the gown."

"Ain't the gown I'm interested in glimpsing," he murmured so softly that only Lucy could hear.

"Roddy," she muttered in warning, as he slid an arm around her and tugged her close.

"What?" he said, just before he set his mouth on her throat. Lucy moaned.

"What was that, Miss Parnell?" the Joker drawled from the outer room.

Lucy swung away from Roddy, neatly clipping him in the hip with her wide panniers. He beat a hasty retreat, laughing and promising dire retribution.

Lucy realized the brocade gown displayed little charm, layered as it was over her day dress. She began the whole procedure over again, laboriously undoing the buttons on her dress and slipping it over her head. She drew on the two sections of the gown and did up the tabs and hooks, thinking that although the wide panniers were awkward, the closures on the gown were a lot more manageable than those of her normal clothing.

The neckline was scandalously low—she feared if she took a deep breath her bosom would escape the lacy bodice altogether. This did not seem to be an issue of any concern to her audience however. When she stepped from behind the screen all four men stopped their lighthearted chatter and stood in an attitude of silent awe. Even the Joker was, for once, speechless.

"I say," Nonnie managed at last, his eyes roving over her with open approval.

"No," said Roddy abruptly. "I don't think so."

Lucy's smug satisfaction evaporated. "Mmm," she said. "I had a feeling I couldn't carry it off."

Roddy realized his mistake at once. It wasn't Lucy's lush attributes, now deliciously on display, that had spurred his outburst, it was his friends' open attitude of lust.

"No, Lucy," he said quickly. "You look perfectly wonderful—"

"Queenly," Nonnie said.

"Elegant," Owen added.

"Heavenly," the Joker breathed.

She turned to Roddy. "Then what is the problem?"

He bowed to his friends. "Gentlemen, if you will excuse us."

He drew Lucy back behind the screen, and then raised her hand to his mouth. "Lucy, my fair, clever, delectable girl. The gown is beautiful, you are beautiful . . . and if you don't take it off this instant, I shall have to shoot my friends. Every last one of them."

"But . . ."

"And every man in Peel who ogles you, and all the grooms and the footmen and any man who dares to look at you. It'll be a bloodbath, Luce. You don't want that on your conscience, now do you?"

She didn't know whether to be affronted or flattered. She looked down at her chest and frowned. "It is a rather extreme décolletage . . ."

"To say the least."

"Maybe a lace tucker," she suggested.

"Maybe a body-concealing cloak," he countered.

Her eyes danced; amusement now all she felt. How delightful that the breathtakingly handsome Roddy Kempthorne was eaten up with jealousy.

"Nonnie will be so disappointed. And it's his birthday, Roddy." She tugged a piece of pink satin from the screen and set it around her shoulders. "See it is not so immodest now. I'll have the seamstress make me a shawl out of it."

He considered this alteration judiciously. Most of her creamy chest was now obscured.

"Maybe. But you'll have to promise not to take it off." She was nodding when he added, "Until I ask you to."

"Oh, so you get to ogle me, but no one else?"

"Sweetheart," he said as he moved toward her and twitched away the pink satin, "this is not ogling . . ." He set his mouth to the rise of her breast. "This is worship."

If his friends had an inkling of what was transpiring behind the screen, they did not voice their suspicions. Each of them wandered off to a distant corner of the attic, and when Roddy and a slightly shaky Miss Parnell emerged some minutes later, no one commented on her rosy mouth, or the fact that she was again wearing her day dress with every button neatly in place.

They reconvened near the row of trunks that lay below an oriole window. Lucy was decreed final arbiter of the costumes. Draped in an old ermine cape, she perched in state on a barrel while Roddy's friends paraded before her. Most of the costumes, she saw, were not antiques, but rather relics from previous masquerade parties, done up to match specific time periods. The medieval surcoat the Joker had worn that first day was such a garment, its bright blue hue unfaded by the passage of time.

Nonnie tried on his Uncle Theodore's dashing hussar uniform, which he unearthed from a trunk of his late uncle's effects. While he struggled to close the frogged pelisse, Owen delved more deeply into the trunk, seeking the feathered shako that completed the uniform. He drew out a leather-bound diary and set it aside. Roddy, who was growing a bit restless, having determined his costume already, picked it up and began to thumb through it while his friends made their choices, guided by Lucy's discerning eye.

The Joker, who fancied he had splendid calves, chose a Highlander's outfit, complete with kilt, tartan, and feathered bonnet.

"Looks like the viscount gets to wear a skirt even if Miss Parnell doesn't," Owen chirped. He had chosen a highwayman's costume, clearly a leftover from a masquerade ball—the black velvet jacket bore the label of a Bond Street tailor. He was feeling very dashing and brave, now that he'd finally met his ghostly maiden, and the sweeping cloak and high boots suited his mood.

Lucy approved his choice. The bookish young man with the thin face now cut a romantic, nearly piratical figure. Nothing like black, she thought, to give a man presence. Yardley had known that for years.

Nonnie was still fussing with his frogs, his uncle's jacket being cut for a less robust man. Lucy soothed him with one hand on his arm. "We'll have the seamstress move them a bit."

"She's going to be busy tomorrow;" Nonnie said. "We'd best send someone to her cottage to alert her." He nodded toward Owen, whose back was turned, and then winked broadly at Lucy.

"Ah," she said. "That is a capital idea." She leaned toward the earl and whispered, "Have you known all along who his ghostly maiden was?"

He nodded guiltily. "Didn't take long to figure out. I've never met her, but the Widow Pace has been sewing for Connie ever since my stepmama arrived here. And she sometimes comes late at night. Connie's offered to send the mending to her, but the widow has a proud streak, likes to go her own way. At any rate, I thought it wouldn't do Snow a bit of harm to pine awhile. It got him out of the library, for one thing."

She grinned. "Out of the library, and headlong in love."

"There's a bit of that going around, I'd say." Nonnie gave her arm a squeeze. He was about to make some comment when Roddy gave a muffled cry from the window, where he stood clutching Theodore's diary.

"What is it, Ram? Some hair-raising adventure with Old Hookey on the Peninsula."

When Roddy met Nonnie's eyes, his face was grave. "I need a word alone, old fellow."

Owen and the Joker had never heard that tone in Roddy's voice before. They stood in baffled silence. Lucy, however, had heard it—he'd spoken that way at the foot of her sister's grave.

She took Owen and the Joker in hand and led them from the attic, casting Roddy a look of understanding before she went down the narrow stairs.

"Read this," Roddy said to the earl, marking a paragraph with his forefinger. "It was written while your father was here visiting Theodore . . . several weeks before your uncle succumbed to his wound."

Nonnie scanned the words, his face screwing into a knot. "Can't make out his blasted handwriting. Here, you read it to me."

Roddy took back the small volume. "I am sorely troubled," he read in a soft voice. "My brother attends me by day, dutifully playing endless games of piquet and amusing me with tales of London. But his nights are spent away from the house. I chose at first to believe it was his grief that kept him away, perhaps setting him to roam the moors. The loss of his third child this spring sits heavy on him, and the melancholy that besets his wife—she with her Iberian nature that takes things so much to heart—has made him fretful. And now my own imminent death, which, though we joke about it, cannot be long in the future, must be a trial to him."

Nonnie interrupted his friend. "What's this to do with anything? I remember when my father came here that summer. We had a feeling Theodore would not survive the wound to his chest. He was near recovery several times, but the damned thing kept reopening."

"Let me continue," Roddy said. "There is another entry, a week later."

"I feel the hands of mortality clutching at me while I sleep. That I will wake to greet each new morning becomes my only prayer. I have received news of my brother's nightly wandering, most unhappy news, and yet I fear to accost him. It came to me from my valet, who has family in the Dorne Valley. There is a young woman living there, a beauty, by my valet's account, who met my brother while he was out shooting. They have been trysting now for weeks . . . meeting in the woods near the girl's farmstead. Oh, wicked man, that could so ill use his grieving wife and worthy son. But, no, I dare not judge him, not when I am so near my own time of judgment."

Nonnie sat down hard on a trunk. "It was the McFallon girl, wasn't it?"

"So it would appear."

"That would make little Salvador—" Nonnie choked and could not continue.

"Your father's by-blow," Roddy finished for him gently. "Lord, I'm sorry, Nonnie. Don't take it so hard."

"Hard?" Nonnie cried, rising to his feet. "Sweet Jesus, Ram, I am overcome with happiness."

Roddy started back. "You are?"

"Oh, yes," he said with a wide smile. "It means the child is my brother, truly my brother. Baseborn or not, it don't alter the fact. I knew he had the look of a Swithens."

"And what of Connie? How will she take this news? Discovering that the husband she loved was off sporting with a farm girl while she lay grieving at Steyne."

Nonnie thought about this for all of three seconds. He took Roddy by one shoulder and said, in a man-to-man voice, "Don't like to speak of this, old fellow, but the pater had *chères amies* all over the place. London, Steyne, even one in Brighton. Consuelo knew—she has a rather Continental attitude about such things, I gather. She never doubted that my father loved her, which is what counts, I suppose. He just felt a need to . . . sport now and then. Never got any offspring that I heard of, though, at least before now."

Roddy looked dubious.

"She'll want to know that the boy is my father's get," the earl assured him. "Trust me on this, Ram. Her joy will outweigh any jealousy she may feel."

Roddy hoped his friend was right, though it probably didn't matter. If Nonnie waited a few days to tell her this news, she'd have become so enamored of the child that finding out he was the son of the archfiend Bonaparte himself wouldn't deter her from keeping him.

Still, Roddy had a hard time understanding that sort of laxity in a marital arrangement. His father had been devoted to his mother from the time they met, so the openly loose morality of some married members of the *ton* disturbed him. When he was wed there would be no question of *chères amies* or alluring farm girls. Not if the woman he married possessed the greatest allure of all, which was to say that he loved her with his whole heart. And if the woman he married was a challenge, a moody, dour, crusty female who required his kisses and his gift of joy on a daily basis, all the better. A woman like that would surely keep a man too busy to stray.

Perhaps it was time to seek out Miss Parnell and get down to some serious business. There were quite a few things he needed to tell her.

Chapter Thirteen

L ucy sent Owen off to the Widow Pace's farm to request that she come to the house the following day. Owen went riding away with a lopsided grin on his thin face.

"There goes a happy fool," the Joker pronounced as he came up beside her in the stableyard.

She turned to him with a knowing expression. "Do I detect a smidgen of jealousy, my lord?"

He looked away from her probing gaze.

"You are not such a cynic as you like the world to think," she remarked.

"No," he said with a dry laugh. "You've seen through my many facades, Miss Parnell. I am neither a practiced seducer nor a jaded cynic."

She squared his shoulders with her hands and looked him in the eye. "What then, Viscount Broome?"

He shrugged. "Just another layabout in the *ton*, I expect. With too much money and not enough energy to accomplish anything."

"What would you like to accomplish?"

His face clenched in bewilderment. "Never thought about it. Never had to."

"You might begin now, thinking about it, I mean. If Owen has his way with the widow, he won't long be a part of your circle. "

"No, he'll whisk her off to Wales, never to be seen again."

"And I fancy Nonnie will stay on here, or convince Consuelo to return to Steyne. He'll be too busy raising up young Salvador to bother with London for a while."

"I see what you're getting at. Everything is changing, isn't it? When we came over here on the ferry, I felt sure we would go on, the four of us, forever. Friends, comrades . . ."

"The world alters, Gregory," she said softly. "And we must bend with it or be lost. I am only myself coming to grips with that."

"You've a pleasant future ahead of you, at any rate," he said, and then blushed. "Or hasn't my ramshackle friend declared himself yet?"

Lucy's cheeks drew in. "I believe young Lochinvar is still wandering about in the moat."

The Joker hooted with laughter. "He'll find a way to climb out, mark my words."

"I may have to help him . . . though it won't be the first time."

The viscount moved past her toward the sprawling stable building. "One more thing, my lord," she called out to him. He turned with an amiable, curious expression. "I keep meaning to ask Roddy. About the names you have for each other. I know that schoolboys often give each other silly names, but—"

"It was my Uncle Arkady who named me," he said as he toyed with his riding gloves. "In his library he has an antique pack of playing cards from the time of Henry VIII. He swears that as an infant I looked just like the joker in the pack."

"And you kept the name past childhood?"

He sucked in one cheek. "If you'd ever met my uncle you'd know that he has a way of not letting things go. A bit of a needler, he is. Once he started calling me the Joker, soon everyone else had taken it up. Well, except for Mama, but then she's one of the few people who pays my uncle no mind."

"And what about Snowball?"

"That *was* from our schooldays. He was a sickly stick of a boy back then, and bookish as an owl. He got an enormous amount of ribbing from the other students at Eton. One bully in particular made it his life's work to torment our Owen. Roddy got it into his head that Owen should challenge him to a fight, to put an end to things. The boys all thought it was a prime joke; they knew Owen had a snowball's chance in hell of beating the other fellow."

"Ah, it makes sense now. And what happened? Did Owen challenge him?"

The Joker nodded. "Challenged him, met him behind the cricket pitch, and had the tar beaten out of him with half the school watching."

"So he lost then, did he?" she said sadly.

"No," the Joker said. "Not exactly. Because, you see, he was still standing when it was over. He was bloody and tattered, but he was still on his feet. Boys are very impressed by that sort of grit. Well, the bully was, at any rate."

"And how do you know that, Viscount Broome?"

The Joker gave her the fleeting glimpse of a warm, surprisingly sweet smile before he turned away. "Why, because I was the bully, Miss Parnell."

Lucy went back into the house to look for Roddy—she wanted to know what he had found in Theodore's diary—and was met outside the library by a footman bearing a note on a silver tray. She recognized Yardley's elegant backhand script at once. She stepped into the room, tore open the letter, and read it through quickly. And then read it again, to make sure she wasn't experiencing a very bad dream.

"Dear Sister," he had written. "I regret that you should have had to look upon that double grave. As you know, I did everything in my power to keep you from that sorrowful place.

"I also regret that I know nothing of your purse, your ticket, or your journal. Though I felt the need to remove your trunk from the inn, I certainly did not overstep propriety by examining its contents. However, one of the maids here did begin to unpack it before she was advised that it was not necessary—when questioned, she reported that both purse and ticket were among your things, though there was no journal. It is my advice that you question the party who was responsible for removing the trunk from my care. I fear that is where you will find the culprit.

"I will be relieved when I hear that you have returned to Manchester; my letter to the Burbridges was never posted, so you will be free to resume your responsibilities there until you wed Sir Humphrey. I would wish a more hasty departure for you, but in light of the shock you experienced in Parapet, I understand your need for additional recuperative time. This I will allow out of my own kind heart.

"Permit me to furnish you with one additional caution: Mr. Kempthorne's attendance on you has not gone unnoticed by me—and it is clear you have formed an attachment to him. Be warned, sister. Your penniless young man is not what he seems. I have made inquiries with the Wibberlys and discovered that he is the son of Gerald Kempthorne, one of the wealthiest men in Cornwall and the owner of Carillon. Young Mr. Kempthorne's portion is nothing less than ten thousand a year according to Mrs. Wibberly. She has two marriageable daughters, and so has made acquiring this information her maternal business.

"I fear that if you harbor any expectations of matrimony in that direction, you will be severely disappointed. Men of Roderick Kempthorne's position and wealth do not ally themselves with

portionless spinsters. I need not warn you that what they do offer
are other, far less savory arrangements."

He'd had the temerity to sign it, "Your loving brother."

Lucy fell back into a nearby chair. Her brain felt as though a
hive of angry wasps was buzzing through it. How could she have
been taken in by Roddy? And, oh, dear God, how could she have
let herself play such a willing foil, allowing him liberties practically under the noses of his friends? It was shaming, it was humil-
iating, it was deplorably loose.

She twisted Yardley's note in her hands, wishing it was
Roddy's fine neck. She forgot all his helpfulness, all his comfort.
She pushed away all thoughts of his blazing kisses and forced herself to think only of his many deceptions. It was he who had taken
her money and her purse, she knew it as a certainty She also had a
creeping suspicion that he'd found her journal. And doubtless read
it, read her glowing, schoolgirlish praise for his beauty and his
easy manners.

Worst of all, he had never once mentioned that his family was
wealthy or that he had grown up in one of England's great houses.
No, he had let her make a fool of herself, lecturing him on his im-
prudent wagers and rattling on about how fortunate he was to visit
his friends' elegant homes. He'd been raised at Carillon, for
heaven's sake—the house the Prince Regent had declared finer
than any other place in the kingdom.

Such a variety of intense emotions flooded through Lucy that
she sat unmoving for nearly a minute, waiting for one of them to
take the fore. Anger, embarrassment, shock, betrayal, all rioted together inside her head. Her heart did not do battle with her head to
be heard—in that space she felt only a numb, incoherent ache.

Finally anger moved to take center stage. She had been duped
and manipulated, and so anger was the most tangible of her emotions. She wanted to hike up her skirts and run from this house.
She knew she could go to the Wibberlys' and throw herself on
Yardley's smug mercy. That course was less intolerable than having to confront Roddy Kempthorne on his deception.

She was heading for the door when Roddy appeared on the
upper landing.

"Ho, Luce," he said. "I've been looking for you. Wait till I tell
you what—"

She looked up at him, every ounce of her misery written plain
on her face. He instantly hurried down the stairs and caught her before she could get the ponderous door open.

"Don't!" she cried, reeling away from him. "Don't touch me."

He drew back, his hands splayed before him. "Steady on, Lucy."

"I'm leaving," she cried, tugging at the huge wrought-iron door latch. It wouldn't budge. Roddy reached past her and engaged the thumb lever. The door creaked open.

"Thank you," she said stiffly. She marched out onto the covered porch and down the three shallow steps to the graveled drive. Roddy followed behind her.

He didn't say a word as she stood gazing down the long, winding driveway. He could hear the sharp susurration of each indrawn breath, a sure sign that a female was not far away from tears.

He touched her arm. "What's happened to you, sweetheart? Who did this to you?"

She spun on him with blazing eyes. "You did, Roderick Kempthorne of Carillon."

He winced. "Oh. I see you've discovered my little secret." His voice lowered. "It was never my intention to keep it from you, Lucy. You just got this corkbrained notion that I had no money. It tickled me, actually. I've become so used to chits chasing me for my fortune."

Her scowl was deep black. "*This* chit is not chasing you, you insufferable peacock!"

"That's not what I meant," he said quickly. "Only I never had a chance to tell you how it stood."

"You had time to badger me with kisses though, didn't you? Plenty of time to play at wooing me—"

"Damn it, Lucy," he growled. "Is that what you think, that I was playing?"

"It's all you know how to do. Play a May game, have a lark. I must have been so amusing to you—the pitiful spinster, so grateful for your attention, so hungry for your kisses. How you must have laughed with your friends over me."

"God, no. Lucy, no." He reached out to her, his fingers trembling from his distress.

But she was already walking away from him, striding down the drive with grim determination. He sprang forward and caught up with her. "You can't walk out of here; you'll still be on the moors when night falls. Let me call for a carriage if you are so set on leaving."

She shook her head. "I will hail a farm cart or a tradesman's van. Do not trouble yourself over me."

"But where will you go?"

"I am going to the Wibberlys'."

"You're mad!" he uttered.

She spun on him. "Yes, I think I must be mad. To have trusted you, to have put my faith in your honesty and integrity."

"Please, Lucy. Hear me out. I did not deceive you. I just neglected to tell you something. Not the same kettle of fish at all."

She clenched her hands to still their shaking. "And when, when were you going to reveal to me that you are the son of the wealthiest man in Cornwall?"

"I began to tell you this morning in the gallery, but Mrs. Granger interrupted us. I never thought you would take it like this; it ain't exactly bad news, you know."

"It is to me. It is the end of everything for me." Lucy realized she had just disclosed a deal more than she intended. Still, she might as well hang for a sheep as a lamb. "Your wealth places us at the opposite ends of society," she added in a mournful voice.

His face darkened. "I rather think that is for me to determine."

"No," she said, "it is for the world to determine. I will be thought a climber of the worst sort were I to encourage you. I have spent the last seven years of my life refusing to be beholden to anyone. I am not about to start now."

"Beholden?" he cried. "Is that all it boils down to? Who is beholden to whom? That's a dreadfully narrow view, Lucy."

"It is the truth, nevertheless. I want none of you, Roddy. Now go away."

"You dismiss me over something as trivial as money?"

"I dismiss you over something as serious as deception."

He circled around her, noting the tension in her posture and the stark whiteness of her complexion. He still couldn't believe she was throwing him over because he was rich.

"It's not just the money, is it, Lucy? You wouldn't be that cruel, to reject me over some idiotic quirk of birth, just because I happened to be born into a wealthy family."

"No," she said, trying to restore her equanimity. "That was only the first of your crimes."

"Gad, you *are* a starchy governess when you get to lecturing a fellow." He ran a hand through his hair. "So tell me now. What other sins have I committed against the sainted Lucy Parnell?"

"I don't have to listen to your insolence, sir." She pivoted on her heel and again started walking.

"Tell me!" he cried. "At least tell a man what he's charged with before you put his head in the noose."

She came stalking back to him. "You put your own head in this noose, Mr. Kempthorne." She paused to take a breath. "When my trunk was stolen from the Wibberlys' home, my money and ticket were still inside. I have Yardley's assurance on that." Roddy scoffed, and her eyes flashed. "Yardley rarely resorts to outright lying; misdirection is more his style. So I must conclude that someone in this house took my things. And there was only one person who had the opportunity."

Her piercing gaze left him in no doubt to whom she was referring. He hung his head and said in a dull, empty voice, "I was going to return them. I only took them to keep you from going back to Peel." He raised his eyes to her pale face. "Because I couldn't bear it if you left."

"Because you wanted to win your wretched bet, you mean."

"Hang the bloody bet!" He snarled. "I lose that much at faro in a night."

She put up her chin and said in a searing voice, "Then I also gather two thousand pounds means little to you. I was so in awe that you'd beggared yourself to buy Salvador. But I suppose you've spent that much on a racehorse. Or to keep a ladybird in ball gowns. There was no nobility in what you did, Roddy, I see that now. To you that baby was just another fanciful purchase."

He walked several paces away from her, trying to calm himself. How could she be so cruel, when everything he had done had been with her good in mind? He wanted to strike out at her, to hurt her in the same way she'd just hurt him. Then he remembered his mama's words, that he must resist answering anger with anger. He added his own corollary—especially with someone you loved. And if Lucy was lashing out at him, he reckoned she must be in enormous pain. He had to make things right with her, even if it meant forfeiting a bit of his pride.

He walked back to her, his arms down at his side, his manner subdued. "We are both overwrought, Lucy. This week has been a whirligig for us all. Come back to the house and we will talk later tonight." He watched her expectantly, hoping for some sign of relenting.

Her eyes softened for an instant, and his heart leapt. Then she scowled and all was dust.

"There is no point to that. I will not ever change my mind." She crossed her arms over her chest.

He stood there in silence, his mind reeling from the bleak realization that she was indeed going away.

"Then wait here and I will fetch your things," he said at last. "I will ask John Coachman to drive you back to Peel." He leaned toward her. "You don't really want to go to the Wibberlys' now, do you?"

"No," she said.

He strode off down the drive and disappeared through the front door.

Lucy went to lean against one of the wooden posts that lined the drive; she was weaving on her feet and feared she might collapse before Roddy returned. It had been the most draining encounter of her life, bar none. Her future lay before her in ashes and she prayed she could hold back her tears until she was safe in her room in Peel.

Tomorrow she would take the mail coach into Douglas to await the ferry to Liverpool. Once she was away from this side of the island, she knew she would be more at ease. Even in Peel she would feel too close to Roddy, too close to the potent tug of Ballabragh. She'd thought she'd found peace at last inside the great stone house. But it had been a false hope. Peace did not emanate from a house or from another person. It only grew from within. Lucy was not sure she would ever be at peace again.

Roddy came down the steps and walked toward her carrying her trunk under his arm. "I've called for the carriage," he said. He set the trunk down at her feet and opened it. "Here," he said grimly. "Have a look. Make sure it's all here."

She knew he was baiting her, but she did look. Her purse and the packet with her return ticket lay there atop her folded gowns. The journal lay there as well. Her eyes narrowed.

"So you managed to get your hands on my journal, I see. Yardley told me it wasn't in with my other things."

"You'd left it at the Greene Man," he said without looking at her.

Lucy recalled hiding it under her breakfast napkin when Yardley had come through the door. "And when exactly were you going to tell me this?"

He shrugged, to all appearances immune to her sarcasm. "I'd have gotten around to it."

"I suppose it's too much to hope that you didn't read it."

"Just the few bits that had to do with me."

"Oh, and *that* is supposed to console me."

"Damn it, Lucy. You wrote some very nice things about me."

"Which are no longer true," she snapped. "I have no tolerance for sneaks, Roddy. I admit it was amusing when you stole my trunk back from Yardley, and it was necessary for you to break into Plimpton's files. Still, I trusted you not to turn that larcenous streak against me." She smiled a tight, pained smile. "It seems I was foolhardy to think that."

"Let's not start that again. Please. You think I deceived you, when all I did was sort of waylay you. If you had gone back to Peel you'd never have found Susanne's grave, you'd never have discovered the McFallon baby—who is Nonnie's natural brother, by the way. I got you to stay on to good purpose and still you rail at me."

"It's not your intentions I am faulting, Roddy. It's your methods."

"Needs must, when the devil drives," he muttered. "I saw the way to keep you here at Ballabragh and I took it."

"It was badly done," she responded. "You might have asked me to stay . . . has that ever occurred to you? A simple request."

His mouth twisted in anger. "I forgot. That you want everything neat and tidy. But I am not made like that. I do things haphazardly, you see. On the spur of the moment."

Her eyes held his. "Which is precisely what I have come to realize—that we are too different." The jingling of harness chains distracted her from the defeat in his indigo eyes. "Here comes the carriage," she muttered as she crouched down and closed up her trunk.

He drew her to her feet. "Stay, Lucy. I'm asking you now. Please stay."

This time she knew better than to gaze into his eyes. "No," she said, backing away from his touch.

"I didn't mean to deceive you," he said earnestly. "I wouldn't hurt you for the world. You must know—"

"*All* men are deceivers," she interrupted him fiercely. "My sister's lover deceived her into running off, my stepbrother deceived me over the child's death . . . even Sir Humphrey deceived me by spying on me and reporting to Yardley. And now you haven proven yourself to be as bad as the others. I am surrounded by rogues, it appears. Only my young professor was true to me, true and trustworthy . . . and I spurned him." Her voice began to break.

"He deceived you more than anyone else," Roddy growled softly. "No!"

"Oh, yes he did. He said he loved you . . . but that was a lie."

"It was not a lie."

He stalked toward her. "It was a lie, Lucy. If he loved you, he'd have never gone away without you, never left you behind at Yardley's mercy. When you love someone you fight for them, you fight to be with them . . . because . . . because life without them is unthinkable . . . it is intolerable."

"You are a wretch!" she cried. "To rend from me the last sweet memories I had left."

"Then we are even," he bit out. "Since you have destroyed mine as well."

He didn't wait to see her off—where was the purpose of that? He went to the stable, saddled a horse, and rode out at a breakneck pace over the moors in the opposite direction from where Nonnie's carriage was carrying her inexorably toward Peel.

Owen topped the gentle rise that overlooked the Widow Pace's small stone house. A fire rose up from the river stone chimney, a promising portent that his divinity was at home. There was a paddock with a shed at the rear of the house where a cream-colored cob was browsing in the sun. The horse's pale coat was the same blond shade as Mrs. Pace's hair. Owen sighed. He really had to control this urge to compare everything he saw with his beloved. The sun was her smile, the moon was the light in her eyes. The very air he breathed was nectar because she too breathed it.

It was bad enough he possessed the Welsh penchant for melancholy reflection, but he'd never suspected till now that he also had the national tendency for flowery, romantic piffle. If he wanted to impress her, he thought as he urged his horse down the hill, he would do better to behave like an accomplished gentleman rather than a giddy, lovesick schoolboy.

He knocked once, and then called out, "It's Owen Griffith. I've come from Ballabragh."

The door opened and when he saw her, he instantly forgot his resolve to stay calm. She was more beautiful in daylight than she had been in candlelight, a confection of creamy skin, celadon eyes, celestial blond hair. His heart began to beat halfway up his constricted throat.

Her eyes lit up when she recognized him, but then she schooled her face into a cautious frown. "You should not have come here," she said stiffly.

"I have a message for you from the earl," he said quickly, before she could shut the door. "You are needed at the house tomorrow. There are some costumes that need altering for the fete."

"Very well," she said, then added wryly, "though he might have sent a servant to deliver it."

"I have a message of my own, as well," he said in a low, halting voice. "I am here to ask if you will . . . if you will . . ."

"What?" she said, cocking her head. "If I will what?"

He took a step toward her and tripped over the raised stone threshold. She stumbled back in alarm as he sprawled forward onto his hands and knees.

Owen sat up slowly and set his hands over his face as he gave a rueful moan of laughter. "You must think me the worst clodpole on the planet."

She knelt down beside him and touched his brow as she had done the night before. "The first time I saw my husband," she said, "he was riding along the narrow lane where I was walking. He kept looking down at me as he passed by . . . a low branch caught him right here." She touched Owen's midriff. "He landed on his bottom in a mud puddle. I laughed for nearly a minute. At the handsome gentleman in his fine uniform sitting there in the mud."

"And still you married him?"

"Because he laughed at himself, you see, as you did. It is a rare man who can laugh at himself. My Carlton was a very rare man." As she helped Owen to his feet, he saw that her eyes had misted over slightly. They now looked like the sea before a winter storm. She led him to a small pine table. "I think we could both use a cup of tea," she said as she moved toward the hearth.

Beyond this room he saw another chamber, where the sunlight poured in through a row of windows. It was an extravagance, all those windows, but then he noticed the loom, partially hidden by the door frame, and realized that she needed the light to work.

"Have I interrupted you?" he asked, motioning toward the loom.

"Not at all. I was merely sorting my yarns. Tedious work," she said with a quick grin. "I am happy for the excuse to play truant."

"You are here alone?" he said. There were signs of children in the room—a primer lying on the settle, a stick dancer canted in one corner and several childish drawings of sheep propped on the mantel shelf—but no sound of children in the small house.

"Charlie and Samson are off at the end of the valley. Charlie is looking after Mrs. McFallon's sheep now that she's gone off to Dublin. And Samson just tags along—the two are inseparable."

If Owen thought Samson was a peculiar name for a female child, he did not express his misgivings. In his eyes, everything the widow did was beyond criticism.

Her initial cautiousness soon relaxed while they talked over tea, which in turn calmed his nerves. He spoke enthusiastically about his family in Wales and his interest in ancient Rome, and then asked Mrs. Pace about her own life. She made no mention of her childhood or family, but instead told him about her time in Spain, of how the deprivations of army life had been greatly tempered by her admiration for the Spanish people.

"The women fought beside their men against the French invaders," she said intently. "I found that inspiring. I became friendly with one of the woman guerrillas—that was what the Spanish soldiers were called—and she gave me a pair of leather breeches to wear. Much more practical than skirts for long stretches on horseback or for tramping across rough country."

"What did your husband think of that?" Owen asked. He was trying not to picture Mrs. Pace in leather breeches. It was too provocative. He could barely stand to look at her in her dimity gown with its demure lace tucker.

Her eyes lit up. "He said I made a proper little soldier. Carlton was the most tolerant person I have ever known. I valued that in him above everything else. He never judged, never issued orders, well, at least not to me." She grinned. "He was an officer, after all. But his men adored him, too."

Owen reached out to touch her hand. "How very sad that you lost him."

Her mouth tightened. "It was a blessing just knowing him. And another blessing of a sort that when he was killed I was already carrying our first child. It gave me something positive to focus on. A woman's will to survive and thrive becomes overwhelming when she has that spark of life inside her."

Owen felt his own eyes mist over. Her words had touched him in some deep, basic place. He'd thought Miss Parnell a brave soul for standing up to her stepbrother and coming here on her own to find the lost child, and now Mrs. Pace's tale had moved him nearly to tears. It seemed to be his week for meeting courageous women.

They continued talking for over an hour, and then Mrs. Pace glanced up at the mantel clock and gave a small chirp of surprise.

Owen rose at once. "I am sorry to have kept you from your work, Mrs. Pace. I have enjoyed talking to you very much."

She held out her hand to him, like any lady of the manor, and he took it and raised it to his mouth.

"Dear, Mrs. Pace," he murmured. His eyes met hers. He read a shimmering joy there and his heart sang at the sight. "Would you . . . do me the honor of coming with me to the fete on Saturday."

She drew her hand away as she shook her head. "That is very kind, sir. But I do not go into Peel. I rarely leave the valley. Except for Mr. MacTell, the vicar, you are my first visitor in months."

He pondered this for a moment. "Is there someone in Peel you wish to avoid?"

"Yes," she said in a low voice. "In truth there is."

Owen was not so easily dismissed. He had come this far and would not be thwarted. "We will all be in costume," he pointed out. "You could wear a domino and no one would be the wiser."

He saw a fleeting expression of eagerness cross her face and, bolstered by this, he continued, "We needn't stay very long. I only want . . . want to . . . ."

She was laughing now. "Yes, Mr. Griffith?"

"I want to dance with you," he whispered gruffly. "More than I can say."

"And no one will know it is me?"

"Except me." He gazed at her intently, his eyes brimming with naked hope. "And that's all that matters, isn't it?"

She leaned forward and set her hand on his cheek. "Very well, sir. I will dance with you in Peel."

Owen left the widow's house in a daze of happiness. She was not only beautiful, she was warm-hearted, spirited and—what a delight—intelligent. She had actually known about the Roman settlements in York and had expressed unfeigned interest in his research. He had loved her for her beauty since the first night he'd seen her, but that superficial attraction now paled beside the awe and wonder that her conversation and her manner had evoked in him. She was a woman of strength and will, who had survived a terrible loss and still managed to carve a life for herself on this rocky island.

Romantic love alone was a potent thing, he knew, but when that love was combined with admiration and respect, it was nearly impossible to revoke.

It was not until he was trotting down the drive to Ballabragh that Owen realized he had again forgotten to ask the widow her given name, in spite of the time they'd spent talking. One part of their conversation did return to vex him. Mrs. Pace had told him her husband died while she was carrying their first child. He wondered then who the devil had fathered the daughter with the unlikely name of Samson.

* * *

Lucy managed to hold off her tears by sheer force of will until she had reestablished herself in the Greene Man. She muffled her sobs in a feather pillow and prayed that her landlords did not have acute hearing. The tailless cat sat aloof at the end of her bed and watched her with half-closed eyes, as though he possessed all the answers to all the questions in the universe, but had second thoughts about sharing them with a mere human.

Once she had cried out all her pain and humiliation, she lay back on the bed, fighting off the effects of a throbbing headache. *This is Yardley's doing*, a small voice prompted in between the aching throbs. She tried to rebut the voice, but it was persistent. It sounded remarkably like Roddy Kempthorne.

No, for once she knew Yardley had the right of things. Roddy had played her for a fool. Even if he was acting on his desire to keep her at Ballabragh, that did not excuse the underhanded way he had coerced her. She'd experienced enough coercion and manipulation in Yardley's home to last her six lifetimes. Surely Roddy should have known that was no way to endear himself to her. Rather, it was the one thing guaranteed to make her flee away in anger.

She got up from the bed and dashed some water over her face from the basin on the washstand. She'd have to get the schedule for the mail coach and order up some supper. And then she'd write a brief note to the countess, thanking her for her hospitality. There was no reason Consuelo should suffer rude treatment—she had done nothing to deserve Lucy's ire.

By tomorrow night she'd be in Douglas and well away from any temptation to forgive Roddy and return to Ballabragh. Forgiveness was not an option when a man had proved himself false.

She wondered then how Susanne had managed to stay with her lover after he refused to marry her. Ah, but Susanne had always been less bound by the rules of society than Lucy. She had flouted the protocol of mourning when their stepfather died and worn colors after only three months had passed. Lucy always suspected she'd done it to irritate Yardley. Still, it was difficult to credit that a gently bred young woman could live in sin with a man, travel with him openly to Spain, and continue as his camp follower once he rejoined his regiment. That was not the Susanne she had known, but some aberration.

Chapter Fourteen

Roddy was wearing a hole in Consuelo's carpet, pacing back and forth in open agitation, all the while venting his frustration with a flow of clipped, angry words. She lounged on her divan and listened to these verbal pyrotechnics with great patience, stirring herself now and then to reach for a sweetmeat.

Once Roddy had run out of steam, he threw himself into a slipper chair and lay back, glaring at Consuelo from beneath his furrowed brow.

"Well?" he said. "No Iberian insights today, Connie?"

She moved one shoulder up a fraction. "You are not in a mood to listen to anything I might say. It is always so with men—you snarl and protest and are generally very exhausting, but your ears remain closed to anything but your own words."

"I'm listening," he protested. "Why the devil do you think I came up here?"

"You needed an audience," she said simply. "And because you know you cannot express these things to your friends without making yourself a target for their mirth."

"And you're not laughing at me behind your dark eyes?"

"I am not amused, Rodrigo. You hurt someone I had begun to care about."

"She hurt me," he cried. "She called me all manner of wretched things."

"And you didn't deceive her? You didn't take her money or read her journal? You didn't allow her to go on assuming you were penniless?"

His brow lowered another inch. "I had very good reasons for what I did, which I explained to her. But she wouldn't listen—I see now what you mean about a person closing their ears. Only in this case it was a female."

"Both sexes turn stone deaf when they are angry. I did not mean to imply otherwise. But females generally get over their snits more quickly."

Roddy's eyes brightened. "You're saying I should ride off to Peel now?"

"Not *that* quickly," the countess said with a chuckle. "I'd say give her a day or so to sort things out."

"But she'll be gone," he protested. "Back to England. Or to Douglas at the very least. And I want her here, Connie. Not jaunting over the countryside."

She leaned toward him, arranging her skirts over her outstretched legs. "And why is that, Rodrigo?"

Roddy looked away, toward the windows, where the draperies had finally been drawn back. Sunlight pooled on the dark carpet, and sparkled off the red glass candleholders. "Because," he said softly, "she needs looking after."

Connie gave a short bark of laughter. "She is the last woman I'd think needs looking after. She has battled a formidable rogue for most of her adult life and come away stronger for it. You're going to have to be more than her protector, Roddy. You need to give her something more substantial."

His face was clouded with confusion. Consuelo let her eyes wander to the elegant day bed that had been placed by the rear wall, where young Salvador lay sleeping. Indeed, the fractious child had slept serenely through Roddy's entire diatribe.

Roddy saw where she was looking and he nodded.

"I want to be her family," he whispered. "And to draw her into my own family."

"A nice sentiment, but she values blood ties, this one."

"Babies," Roddy said with determination. "I want to give her babies."

Consuelo grinned. "Another very nice sentiment. And one I favor myself."

Roddy moved from his chair and came closer. "What is it, Connie? What part have I left out? I will be her husband, the father of her children. What more can I give her?"

Consuelo gave a melodramatic sigh and muttered something in Spanish. The baby stirred then, and Roddy went to the narrow bed and scooped him up. He snuggled the child under his chin and whispered, "What the devil is she talking about?"

Salvador reached up and twined his fingers in Roddy's thick hair, cooing in delight. Roddy smiled and turned to the countess. "He's happy now, isn't he?"

"He knows he is loved," she said. "That's all it takes for happiness to begin."

Roddy scowled at her over the baby's head. "Is that what this is about? Of course I love her. Haven't I been saying that, all along?"

"Saying it to whom, Rodrigo?"

"Well, I thought it was obvious. And no, don't shake your head and make a face, Connie. Perhaps I have not come right out and said the words, but, good Lord, it's what I've felt nearly from the start."

"Then I suggest you start saying it. Most especially to Miss Parnell. And in order for you to do that, I think it is best that we keep her in Peel." She motioned with one hand. "There, go to my desk and write down what I tell you."

Roddy carried the baby over to the divan and set him down. Salvador crawled immediately into Consuelo's arms and began to play with her bracelets. "Mama," he gurgled as he gazed up at her.

As Consuelo dictated her note to Roddy, she stroked one hand over the baby's fair curls, which were so reminiscent of her late husband's. She knew in her heart that the boy was his—knew that the earl had been here on the island at the time the child had been conceived. That some might think he had betrayed her did not trouble her one bit. Her lord had been a man of lusty appetites and so she could not fault him for the very quality that had made her love him.

Still, there were some betrayals she could not take lightly. Betrayal of a confidence, for one.

After she finished her dictation, she was silent for a time, playing idly with the child in her lap. Roddy stood beside the desk and watched her, saw the emotions warring in her lovely face.

At last she spoke. "I think that when you are trying to heal a breach with someone, it is best if you arrive bearing a gift. And I have something for Miss Parnell that she will like very much."

"And what is that?"

Consuelo looked up and smiled a bit sadly. "The truth, Roddy." He leaned forward intently. "The truth about her sister and the child."

Lucy returned to the Greene Man late Friday morning, muttering every wicked oath she had ever learned. The man at the coaching office had not been rude, but he had been firm: there were no seats left on any of the coaches going to Douglas. Not until Sunday. Lucy had stood there with her mouth open in disbelief. Surely on the day before the earl's fete people would not be leaving Peel, not in such numbers that the coaches were completely booked.

As she walked along the waterfront, she'd had the notion of hiring a boat to carry her to the other side of the island. But the boatmen had shaken their heads.

"Sea's too rough," they all chorused, as if prompted by an unseen choirmaster. Lucy had gazed beyond one burly fisherman's shoulder and pointed to the serene blue-green water on either side of Peel Castle.

"Rough?" she had echoed. "I could take a rowboat out there, it's so calm."

The man had begun muttering about know-it-all off-islanders. "'Tisn't calm down around the point. We had a storm th'other night, or have you forgotten? There be currents and eddies . . ."

Lucy had gone off then, determined not to be defeated. She had inquired at the town livery if she might hire a horse to ride across the island. The liveryman had been most apologetic. All his hacks were spoken for, he declared. Every last one.

Lucy went from his office, but loitered awhile near his open door, trying to think of another means of travel. Pity there were no hot air balloons on the island. A young laborer went past, giving her a curious glance, and then leaned in through the open door.

"Got a nag for me, Jasper? I need to see about the wood for the mayor's podium. Blasted lumber mill still hasn't delivered it yet."

The instant the man rode off, Lucy accosted the liveryman. "You told me you had no horses to let," she cried. "That fellow just waltzed in here and got one."

The man smiled tolerantly. "Well, a'course he got one. I had one horse set aside for emergencies."

"This is an emergency. I need to get to Douglas."

"No, no. *That* was an emergency—the mayor's podium needs to be built in the square. To honor the Earl of Steyne, you see."

So Lucy was cursing under her breath in frustration as she walked back to the inn. She knew it was not possible, but it felt distinctly like the entire town was conspiring against her. She had a thought to ask Mr. Greene for the use of his dogcart, but suspected the fat pony that stood eating its head off in the inn's stable would not get her much past Ballabragh—the last place she could afford to be stranded.

There was nothing for it, she would have to spend tomorrow barricaded in her room, or at least once the fete began. She was taking no chances of running into Roddy or any of his cronies dur-

ing the festivities. And for further insurance, she would tell the
Greenes that she wanted no visitors. That should do the trick. She
would find a book or two in the town's circulating library and
spend the day reading.

Mrs. Greene seemed distracted that evening while she served
Lucy her supper in the dining parlor. When Lucy asked her what
was wrong, the woman raised her eyes to heaven and said, "It's
just like the girl to be taken with the grippe the day before the
fete."

"You mean Abby, your kitchen maid?"

"The very same. Sneezing and snuffling all morning, she was,
and by this afternoon, red as a beet from the fever."

"Poor girl," Lucy murmured.

"Poor nothing. She's left me with six dozen scones to prepare
for tomorrow." Lucy recalled that the Greene Man was to keep a
tea service going during the course of the fete. "And my sister
won't be here till morning."

"I can help," Lucy said, setting down her napkin. She had not
been looking forward to an evening alone in her room. Too many
hobgoblins in the shadows for one thing, the sort with dark hair,
blue-violet eyes, and winning smiles.

"Truly, miss, you wouldn't mind? It's a lot to ask . . ."

"Nonsense," said Lucy, rising from her chair. "I used to help
out in the kitchen sometimes when I lived in Ceylon. My papa expected me to pitch in, you see."

"Well, we won't be making anything heathenish here, just my
raisin scones."

Lucy followed her into the tidy, whitewashed kitchen. All the
ingredients had been laid out, dozens of eggs, a block of white
lard, a pitcher of cream, and a vast crock of flour. Mrs. Greene
swept a gingham pinafore over Lucy's head to protect her gown.
Not that it mattered—it was one of her own dresses she now wore,
gray and drab. She had packed up the gown she'd arrived in and
sent it back to Ballabragh with her note to the countess. She no
longer had a need for pretty things.

Mrs. Greene watched her with some misgiving at first, but
when Lucy demonstrated that she knew how to use a sifter and
measuring cup, the landlady relaxed. Lucy tried not to think while
she worked, tried to put away all thoughts of Roddy. He could no
longer mean anything to her. Even her young professor had eventually faded from her thoughts, though much of that was due to her
distress over Susanne's abrupt departure. But she knew Roddy's

image would dissolve with the passing of time, however deeply it was currently etched in her mind. And he would surely forget her. A man who looked like Roderick Kempthorne would have no lack of ladies to distract him. Ladies with money and position. Prettier ladies, younger ladies—

"Please, miss," Mrs. Greene cautioned her from across the table, "you mustn't stir the batter so hard. You'll take all the plump out of it."

Lucy realized she had been whipping the wooden spoon through the mixture with a vengeance. "Sorry," she said and began to stir the batter with sedate strokes.

Roddy stood in the garden behind the inn and watched Lucy through the kitchen window.

He had been in Peel since the night before, when he'd come to deliver Consuelo's note to the mayor. He'd slept at the Turning Stone, an inn at the other end of town, and spent the early part of the morning making sure, just in case Connie's request to the town's fathers didn't work, that Lucy did not find a way out of Peel. This was accomplished by the judicious use of bribes to the locals—he had not made the mistake of leaving Ballabragh with an empty purse this time. Lucy would loathe him even more, he reckoned, if she learned of this, but he couldn't afford to be less than ruthless in keeping her here.

He smiled as he watched her wrestle with the large mixing bowl she held under one arm. There were smudges of flour on her cheeks, and a long tendril of brown hair was dancing against her chin. She blew at it impatiently, and then swiped at it with her forearm, distributing even more flour over her face. The tendril would not be tamed. She narrowed her eyes and wrinkled her nose in annoyance, and then returned to her stirring.

"Luce," he crooned under his breath, still completely charmed by her in spite of her display of temper. He'd wager she hadn't smiled once since she'd left Ballabragh. Which served her right. It was his job to see to that, if she only knew it.

He wanted to approach her but knew it was too soon; Connie's advice had been to wait until tomorrow, when the festive mood engendered by Nonnie's birthday party would likely soften her resistance. Still, it was dashed hard watching her from the other side of a window. And it was even harder not to rush inside and tell her what he had learned about her sister.

Connie's startling revelation was what had kept him in Peel. He wasn't sure he wanted to face the countess so soon again; he was still simmering over what she had done to Miss Parnell. The countess had expected his anger and his shock. She told him she expected everyone to be angry with her for a time.

"What I did was out of friendship for another," she had explained. "Now I have broken my silence and there will be blame from all sides. But I am weary of keeping secrets, *cara*."

Once Roddy had heard her tale, he agreed that she had reasons for going cautiously. But it did not lessen his vexation with her. If she were going to break a promise, he didn't see why she had to wait five long days to do it. Surely Lucy had deserved the truth sooner than that, and he made no bones about saying that very thing to the countess.

She had been unrepentant. "Sometimes, Rodrigo," she had pronounced, "it is what we learn on the journey that matters more than the goal."

"So for that you made Lucy suffer, you put her through a sort of hell? It's not like you at all, Connie."

"I needed to know the heart of this person, this stranger, before I could trust her with the truth."

"And now?"

The countess's gaze had drifted to the day bed, where Salvador again slept, clutching a large stuffed lamb. She smiled serenely. "Oh, yes. I know her heart now. It was to her heart that the Madre de Dios sent the dream of the lost child. It was Lucy's heart that urged her to find him and bring him to me."

Roddy forbore to point out that he was the one who had brought the boy to Ballabragh.

"I think," Consuelo continued, "that your lady has a better heart than me. But it is still a sad heart, yes? *El corazón dolorossa . . . tu comprende?*" He nodded briefly. "And so you must give her time to deal with her feelings for you before you tell her about Susanne. There is great joy in store for her if she listens to her good heart . . . the Tarot has shown me this."

Roddy was still puzzling over the things Consuelo had revealed to him. And puzzling over Consuelo in general. He'd thought Lucy a complicated woman, but she rarely confounded him the way the countess did. Consuelo clearly believed in God, but also gave credence to the predictions of her Tarot cards. Her indolence was monumental, yet when she stirred herself, her energy was boundless. She was the most compassionate woman Roddy had ever known, and yet she had cold-bloodedly kept from Lucy the thing she most wanted to know.

He finally attributed this paradox to her Iberian blood. The same nation that had produced his mother's favorite literary hero, that truly ramshackle knight, Don Quixote, had also given rise to the infamous purges of the Inquisition. Thank goodness the British were not so dashed bloodthirsty, he thought, and then chuckled at his own naïveté.

When Lucy left the kitchen after the last tray of scones had been placed in the wall oven, Roddy moved away from the window. He stepped carefully past the Manx cat who was standing guard over the flower bed. "Tell her I wish her a good night," he muttered to the beast. "Which is more than I shall have."

Lucy slept fitfully in her narrow bed. Though the dream of the crying child had vanished once Roddy had taken Salvador from Dorne Farm, she was now beset by a new dream. She was lost on the moor at night, running panicked through a billowing fog. She could hear Roddy calling her, but wherever she turned there was only the shifting whiteness around her. Charlie Pace appeared out of the mist, wearing her cream-colored pelisse over his woven vest. He motioned her to follow him and she staggered along in his wake, still following the sound of Roddy's hoarse calls. Suddenly Charlie disappeared and she felt herself falling, her arms flailing in the air. As she fell, she looked up and saw Charlie and Roddy peering over the edge of the cliff. There was a woman beside them, her pale hair whipping around her head.

"Susanne!" she cried out in her dream. *"Susanne . . ."*

Lucy awoke with a start. She was shivering in spite of the comforter that was cocooned around her.

"Blast," she muttered as she sat up and drew her knees to her chest. It was bad enough she'd been haunted by a strange child, but now she was being haunted by Susanne. Even after her sister's death she had not dreamed of her. Though she wondered now whether that was a healthy thing. It seemed she had shut away all her memories of her sister with her passing. She had grieved for months, but had never once relived a happy time or mused over a shared joke.

"I miss you, Susanne," she said into the darkness. "I miss talking to you and laughing with you. Remember the time we took Yardley's gold watch and hung it around the neck of Mrs. Crane's prize sow at the fair? He was furious that we could behave so childishly. But it was worth it, wasn't it? It's a pity you couldn't have seen his face when Roddy knocked down his bullyboy. His eyes fairly popped out of his head." She grinned again at the image.

"You'd like Roddy, Susanne. He reminds me of you at times. He is not very bookish, would rather be doing things than reading, just like you. And he has the kindest heart . . . he rescued the baby from my dream, did you know that? Well, I suppose you do know, if you are anywhere where you can watch us here on this little planet."

She looked up at the night sky through the mullioned window. "I just want to say one thing more. Forgive me for not finding your daughter. Perhaps I will marry Sir Humphrey after all, and then we can return here and begin the search again. He is very amiable, you know."

Bah to amiable, a woman's voice muttered in her head. She couldn't tell if it was Consuelo's voice or her sister's.

"That's fine for you to say," she protested peevishly. "You've both had men in your life who cared for you. I've only had my professor, and from what Roddy says, he didn't care nearly enough."

Roddy cares for you very much, the voice insisted. It was starting to sound more like the countess now. Lucy wondered when she had acquired this new, unsettling ability to carry on conversations with people who were miles away.

"It doesn't matter," she said aloud. "He and I would never suit. He is too rich, too young, and far too attractive. I would spend my whole life wondering when he would leave me."

He ain't your father, Lucy. Oh, Lord, now the voice sounded like Algernon. *He ain't your sister or your young professor. When Roddy says he's going to stick, there's very little that can unstick him.*

Lucy dragged the comforter from her bed and settled into the room's lone chair. It was hours yet till dawn, but she knew she was too upset to sleep. The disembodied voice had just awakened her to the fact that Roddy meant as much to her as those three people combined. He protected her and comforted her as her father had always done. He was as dear a friend as Susanne had been. And she longed for a future with him the way she'd prayed for a life with the professor.

No wonder I love him, she thought with a wide yawn. He was everyone she had cared for and lost, in one charming, slightly tat-

tered package. Then the enormity of what she'd just admitted to
herself hit her.

She loved Roddy Kempthorne.

At some point in the last few days the affection she felt for him
had deepened to a much stronger emotion. No wonder she had
erupted in anger when she read Yardley's letter. It was one thing to
be betrayed by a friend, a person you were merely fond of. It was
quite another to find you had been deceived by the man you loved.

"What a coil," she murmured into the folds of the comforter;
"There I was, planning our life together, Miss Neat and Tidy, without once examining what I felt inside."

Feelings were not something to be sorted and arranged, she
now knew; that was a Yardley way of thinking. Feelings were
meant to be experienced, even reveled in.

Poor Roddy, how she had ripped up at him in the drive yesterday. And all because he'd contrived to keep her in the very place
she'd wanted to stay. With him. She'd see him tomorrow, seek him
out at the fete and tell him how she felt. She would shout it from
the top battlements of Peel Castle if necessary. It occurred to her
that Consuelo had been imprecise when she'd accused men of having stubborn hearts. In this instance it was Lucy's heart that had
been stubborn and hidebound. But Consuelo had been spot on
about one thing—Roddy's physical overtures to Lucy, his kisses
and caresses, had been the lure that led to love. He had somehow
gotten past her defenses and stolen her carefully guarded heart.
But then Roddy had always been a deft thief.

She was smiling in the dark when the voice of reality crept up
on her—not Yardley's grim reality, but that of her own prudent nature. It would never work out, she saw after some serious reflection. The problems were myriad. Roddy was many years her
junior. He was a wealthy town beau, used to sporting with his
friends, accustomed to amusements and diversions. Even if he had
intended matrimony, which her instincts told her was not a rash
hope, she suspected domestic life would chafe at him.

But those were minor considerations compared to her chief
concern. She had been contemplating a serene, happy existence
with a friend, but now saw that her love for Roddy changed everything. If he did not return her love, if all he felt for her was desire,
then she would wither eventually, like the parched tea plants await-
ing the monsoon rain. And it was inconceivable to her that he
might love her. Aside from her age, she was waspish and moody,
not accomplished in the social graces, and possessed neither great

beauty nor wealth. She knew he was fond of her and enjoyed kissing her, but those were hardly recommendations for a future together. There had been moments they'd shared where she might
have read love in his simmering gaze or felt it in the intensity of his
words. But those moments faded now, eroded away by her growing conviction that when you loved someone it was easy to imagine, to pretend almost, that they returned your love.

She could not tell Roddy how she felt after all. How could she
bare her soul to him and risk facing a humbling rejection?

Love you? She could hear his amused drawl. *Sweetheart, it ain't
good* ton *to be in love with one's wife. Just isn't done.*

She would do better to ally herself with a man like Sir
Humphrey. At least they possessed a balanced regard for each
other, a bit lackluster, it was true, but that meant there was less potential for pain. She had been in torment since she'd driven away
from Roddy and never wanted to experience such feelings again.
Only a fool would willingly seek out a top-heavy, one-sided marriage.

If Roddy sought her out before she left on Sunday, she would
do everything she could to discourage him. She'd had years of
practice with Sir Humphrey

Coward! It was that dratted, disembodied voice again. Only this
time it was definitely her own voice that spoke the words.

Give him a chance, it intoned. *Let him have his say. If you let
your fears guide you, you will never find true happiness. You
learned that lesson when you lost your professor. Furthermore, Susanne didn't run away because of your scotched romance—Roddy
was right about that. She ran away because she refused to be
cowed by Yardley. She went away with a virtual stranger because
she had never been afraid of anything one day in her life. And she
had a life, Lucy—she had a loving man, she bore a child, she experienced a world of new things. If that life was leagues beyond your
own drab existence, it is because she reached for it and took hold
of it.*

Lucy brushed back her tears. She had never reached for anything. Even taking her first governess position had been a reaction
to Susanne's death, not the result of any strong desire to teach.
That she was good at it was merely a coincidence.

Her thoughts tumbled inside her head, making it ache and
throb. She had no idea now what to do with Roddy. Hold him off
or encourage him. Seek him out or wait for him to find her.

Roddy will know what to do, the voice assured her.

"He'll want to kiss me," she said aloud peevishly.

The voice purred, *And you should let him. There's been far too little of that in your life. And, when he does kiss you, think about why. Think about why a man who looks like he does is forever kissing you. And if you think it's merely desire, then you should go back to Manchester and marry Sir Humpty Dumpty, because that's all you deserve.*

Once again the voice had changed in midstream. It had been Roddy who finished the thought.

"Roddy," she whispered mournfully. She hoped to God he knew what to do. She hadn't a clue.

Chapter Fifteen

Sometime near dawn, Lucy crawled back to her bed. She was coughing and wheezing, and her eyes felt like they had sandpaper beneath the lids.

"It's the grippe," Mrs. Greene pronounced when she came into the room with Lucy's breakfast. She'd taken one look at her lodger's swollen eyes and red nose and knew for certain what ailed her. "You must have caught it from Abby."

"I can't have the grippe," Lucy croaked hoarsely. "Today is the earl's fete." She felt all her plans for the day, however amorphous, evaporate.

"Fete or no fete," the landlady staid sternly, "you are not leaving your bed. Here, let me feel your forehead. Ah, hot as a griddle, just as I suspected."

Lucy moaned and pulled the covers up to her nose.

"Sit up if you can and eat your breakfast." The landlady set the tray on the bed, and then returned shortly carrying a hot water bottle, a packet of horehound drops, and a small stone crock.

"I've brought you some liniment for your chest," she said hovering over the bed.

"My chest?" Lucy echoed. "I don't want liniment on my chest."

The landlady merely sniffed and looked adamant.

Lucy lay there all morning in a funk smelling of camphor and horehound, though by noon her nose was so stuffed up she could smell nothing at all. Mrs. Greene or her sister, Mrs. Kettle, looked in on her every so often. Mrs. Kettle made dire predictions about how often the grippe turned to an inflammation of the lungs. Since this was what her mother had succumbed to, Lucy's spirits were at a particularly low ebb by mid afternoon.

The sound of revelry began to filter up to her room at about four o'clock. There were merry shouts from below her window and in the distance she could hear fiddle music. She climbed from her bed to use the chamber pot, and then tottered to the window. In the cobbled lane below her, people were already milling about. A few men and women strolled arm in arm, but most of the crowd was walking in loose-knit groups. Vendors had set up stalls along the waterfront. There was a couple selling crockery directly across from the inn, and beside them an old man was tending a lemonade stand. She wondered if Mrs. Pace and Charlie had a stall here selling woven goods.

Mrs. Greene came in and found Lucy leaning against the window. "Back in your bed now, miss."

"It looks like they are all having a wonderful time," she said wistfully. "And there is a man selling lemonade near the pier."

"I will fetch you a glass, if you like. But you must climb back into bed."

Lucy sighed and crossed the room. It was still an effort just to walk. Mrs. Greene went bustling out. Lucy had fallen into a light doze by the time she returned bearing a frosty glass in her hand.

"It's that vexing," she said, as she helped Lucy to sit up. "I met up with Mrs. Twomby by the lemonade stand, and she got to nattering about her son, the mayor. You'd think the man was the prime minister himself, to hear her talk."

Lucy smiled up at her weakly.

"The point is that while I was out you had a visitor. Now I know that nothing cheers up a sickroom like having a friend in to chat, even if it is a young gentleman. I am not such a stickler when a person's health is involved. But Mr. Greene recalled your orders from last night, that you were not receiving anyone today. So that's what he told him. Sent him right off."

It took Lucy several seconds to process the landlady's rambling speech. "Who was here?" she asked in a husky whisper.

"It was that charming Mr. Kempthorne—" Lucy's heart sank. "And he had a boy with him. A young sprat, as Mr. Greene called him. Both dressed like play actors, by my husband's account."

"If he returns," Lucy managed to rasp out, "would you ask him to come up. It's important."

"Lord love you, miss, it's always important when a handsome man comes to call."

She left then, and Lacy leaned back against the headboard and sipped her lemonade. It was no more sour than her present mood. Roddy had come to speak with her and had been turned away. By her orders. Who would blame him if he never came again? she thought dismally. Even Lochinvar himself would eventually lose his enthusiasm for a damsel who remained so far out of reach.

She tried to sleep but the fever made her restless and the sound of merrymaking in the street below was a constant distraction. A prankster had apparently released some livestock in the town—she heard the lowing and baaing as the strays ambled along the lane, and the catcalls and whistles of people shooing them away. The distant music had grown in pitch, it sounded like an entire band was playing now, the fiddles joined by fifes and drums.

Since sleep was not an option, she lit the single candle on her bedside table and picked up the book of sermons she had borrowed from Mrs. Greene. It was not an inspired choice—the ponderous prose was like literary molasses to her aching head.

He will come, she murmured to herself as she clasped the book to her chest. It was not like Roddy to be kept away by anyone as paltry as a landlord. After all, he was capable of confounding Oxford dons and weaselly lawyers. He bested hired thugs and vicious old women . . . he had a one-armed valet . . . he lived in the most wonderful house she had ever seen. . . .

Lucy realized she was in a delirium, her thoughts leapfrogging haphazardly from place to place. She snuggled down under the covers and wished Roddy were beside her. He would hold her and keep her warm. He would stroke her hair and sing her to sleep.

She did fall asleep then, and dreamed that he was serenading her, his voice lilting and sweet. When she awoke some time later, she realized that a man was, in truth, singing below her window. In Spanish.

She pushed back the comforter, which felt like it was weighted with lead, and staggered to the window. It was full dark and there were torches lit along the waterfront. The flames danced in the air, and then again upon the water, where they reflected off the inky surface. The singing had stopped and Lucy could now hear the voices of several men directly below her window. There was suddenly a muffled banging against the side of the inn.

"Steady, now," a tenor voice called out. "A bit more to the left." The thudding came closer. "No, now to the right."

Lucy pushed open the window and leaned out. There was an ornamental stone balcony below the window. The top end of a ladder was leaning there.

"I'm still asleep and dreaming," she muttered, fighting off her alarm. "That's what this is."

A few seconds later, Roddy's head appeared at the top of the ladder. He was wearing a new version of the wide-brimmed hat that had been sacrificed to the demon ram. This one had a red feather.

"Hello, Lucy," he said cautiously. His eyes glittered in the darkness.

"What in blazes are you doing?" she hissed. "Mr. Greene will have the bailiff after you."

Roddy was unperturbed. "The bailiff is passed out under the mayor's podium. Along with the mayor and a few sleepy cows." He chuckled. "It's a topping party, sweetheart."

She uttered a cry of protest when he grabbed on to the balcony and hoisted himself over the edge. As he cleared the ladder, it slid off to one side and then slowly tipped over. Lucy heard the men below shouting in alarm as they scrambled away.

Roddy looked over his shoulder and grinned. "Sorry," he called down to them.

Lucy backed into the room as he came through the window. He was dressed exactly as he had been when she'd first seen him, minus the mud. He was carrying a wrapped package under one arm. Lucy looked down at her own apparel and realized her thin lawn nightgown was hardly appropriate for receiving visitors. Not to mention her hair was a tangled mess, having escaped from its neat braid while she slept. She imagined her face was grotesque—with its swollen eyes, ruddy nose, and fever-reddened cheeks. This was not the reunion she had pictured in her mind. Not by a long shot.

"Go away," she said thickly. "I don't want to see you right now."

"Been crying?" he said genially. "You sound like a foghorn."

"I have the grippe," she pronounced crossly. "I can't imagine why you would think I'd been crying."

"Oh, can't you?" He came nearer and she retreated until she was up against the arm of the chair. He drew so close she was able to detect that he'd recently been intimate with a whiskey bottle. Very intimate.

"You're foxed," she said as she ducked around him and fled to the window.

He nodded slowly, as though his head might become dislodged from his shoulders if he moved it too quickly. "I am foxed . . . and have been since you turned me away earlier. Intend to stay this way indefinitely." He plucked at the lace at his cuff. "Only one thing will sober me up."

"A bucket of cold water over your thick head?" she asked archly. And then sneezed violently three times.

His gaze darted to her face. "You really are sick, aren't you?"

She nodded miserably. "And if you were any sort of gentleman, you would go away and leave me to my bed."

"That's the last thing I'd leave you to," he muttered under his breath as he tossed his package onto the comforter. "Your lonely bed."

Lucy turned away from him. "I haven't the energy to brangle with you, Roddy," she complained wearily. "Now I believe you can find your way out."

He came up behind her and laid one hand on her shoulder. "Still angry, then?"

She refused to answer. It wasn't anger she felt now, it was mortification. She must look like a banshee with her wild hair and long, wrinkled white gown. A puffy-faced, drippy-nosed banshee. Hardly the stuff of fairy tales.

He was doing something with the unbound strands of her hair, winding his fingers through them, tugging on them gently. Then his fingers moved to her nape; he began to massage the tense muscles there, his touch firm and soothing.

"I'm sorry, Lucy," he crooned over her shoulder. "Sorry I hurt you. You see, I know now how you felt. I suffered similar treatment from Connie the night you went away—it left me feeling betrayed and deceived. And dashed angry."

Her curiosity got the better of her and she turned to him. "Connie? Whatever did she do to you?"

"I'll get to that in a minute. I just wanted to tell you that I understood. It's the very devil when someone you trust misleads you. So I don't blame you for going off in a huff. I left Ballabragh in the same state. Been cooling my heels here in Peel till this morning."

"You have?" she said wonderingly. And then her suspicions rose up. "Does that have anything to do with why I couldn't get so much as a goat cart out of this place?"

He set his jaw. "What do you think, Lucy? That I would just let you leave here and disappear into the wilds of Manchester? That I would let you go without a fight?"

She was about to rail at him for his continued interference in her life, when the last part of his response filtered into her fevered brain. He'd said those same words to her two days ago. *If you love someone, you don't let them go without a fight.*

"Oh," she said in a low, awestruck voice.

He swept off his hat and knelt down before her on one knee. He reached for her hand while his eyes held hers, dazzlingly blue. "I

am not neat and tidy, Lucy," he said softly. "Never have been. And
I know that's what you think you want, someone who marches
along in a proper manner. Someone staid and predictable, like Sir
Humpty. But don't you see, you've had that safe tidy existence, sequestered in Yardley's home, or living the half life of a governess,
and it hasn't made you happy. You deserve a whole life, sweetheart."

His grip on her hand tightened as he drew it to his mouth and
kissed the palm.

Lucy felt the thrill jolt through her like summer lightning. She
laid her other hand upon his sleek hair. He raised his head and
looked at her. His eyes were brimming with hope.

"I can't promise never to hurt you, or never to deceive you. I
may be a fool, but even I know such promises are often broken.
But I do promise never to stop caring for you." He paused and
drew a long breath. "Take me, Lucy," he said hoarsely "Take your
ramshackle boy and let him love you."

His sweet words pierced the last layer of her armor. Lucy's
knees, which were already shaky from her illness, gave out completely and she tumbled down into his waiting arms. She was crying now, the tears obscuring everything but the clear light of
affection in his bright eyes.

He crossed his arms over her back, holding her tight while he
rocked her gently. "My dearest girl," he said into her hair.

"I'm the fool, Roddy," she said between little sobs. "Not you.
You are wise and kind and . . . and I . . ."

A sneeze interrupted her. He fished his handkerchief out of his
pocket and dabbed tenderly at her cheeks before he handed it to
her. She blew her nose as delicately as she could.

"That's why I need to keep you around," she drawled, tucking
the linen square into the sleeve of her nightgown. "To furnish me
with dry handkerchiefs."

For that, and for so much more, her eyes declared.

He read the message there in those green-gold eyes and he
smiled. "I expect you won't be needing them so often, sweetheart.
I mean to keep you happy."

"I am happy," she protested. "Don't you know that, you with
your three sisters? We always cry when we are happy."

"I seem to have forgotten," he said in a gruff whisper. He had
forgotten everything but how blessedly wonderful it felt to hold
her in his arms. She was slim and softly rounded and she smelled
of—

He crinkled up his nose. "What *is* that scent you are wearing."

Lucy winced and then chuckled. "It is camphor liniment . . . and horehound."

"Nectar," he breathed as he ran his mouth along the soft length of her jawline.

"You are besotted," she said.

"Hopelessly," he replied.

She took his face between her hands and traced her thumbs over the faint indents where his twin dimples lurked. They deepened into crevices as he smiled and she felt her heart surge.

"You are so beautiful, Roddy. No, don't"—her fingers at once smoothed away his imminent frown—"you are. There is just no other word for it. You are a perfect work of art, like Michelangelo's *David*."

His brows raised. "Another playwright, Lucy?"

She muffled her laughter against his shoulder. He was grinning over her lowered head. It was such pleasant work, making his lady smile. Of course he knew who that Michelangelo fellow was . . . painted the ceiling in a church somewhere. Rome, maybe. He'd have to ask Snowball.

He drew the spill of hair away from the side of her face and ran his lips over the pale shell of her ear, sucking slightly on the delicate lobe. He heard her low, indrawn gasp, and it sent the blood coursing through him like wildfire. There were secrets here waiting to be revealed, a bounty of secret places for a bold, tender explorer to discover. Might be a lifetime's work.

She trembled as he traced his open mouth down the side of her throat; he felt her arms slip around him beneath his brocaded coat, the warmth from her splayed fingers spreading through the thin lawn of his shirt. He set his teeth against the creamy skin of her shoulder where the gown had slipped off, and bit down slowly. Lucy gasped again and then moaned a long, shuddering sigh.

He had her on her feet then, swept her up, and set her back against the wall. His body leaned into hers, all his weight, all his hungry yearning canted against her softness. Her breasts and thighs cushioned him, as she arched away from the wall, her hands twined around his neck. He pushed her head up with his chin, his eyes blazing now with desire.

"Kiss me, Lucy," he growled softly.

Her eyes were smoky with passion, they'd turned a deep, shimmering shade of gold. He felt a fleeting stab of amusement—by God, the Joker had been right for once.

"Kiss me," he said again. He needed to know, needed to be sure. That she was not just responding to his lovemaking, but that the fire burned within her as fiercely as it did in his own soul.

"But I have the grippe," she said huskily. Her eyes pleaded with him to understand. "You will catch it."

He tightened his hold on her, thrusting his body against hers until only the tips of her toes were on the floor. "Then give it to me," he breathed, his mouth scant inches from her own. "Give me the blasted grippe, Lucy."

Lucy sighed. Served him right if he ended up in bed with a wretched head cold. But then, as their mouths met, as she felt the heat course through her and replace the fever that had made her bones ache with one that made her whole body throb, she forgot logic and reason. She tasted him, the sweet tang of brandy and the other taste that was completely Roddy. Her mouth angled below his, hungry now, open and pliant. She probed delicately with her tongue, drifting it along his lower lip, and then exploring the dark recess of his mouth. He cried out softly then, his hands rough where they tangled in her hair.

He swung her away from the wall and bent her back over his arm. Neither one was leading now, they were equally paced, matching passion for passion. His urgent gasps mingled with her throaty cries as they plundered each other's senses. Lucy reveled in the lean strength of him, the long fingers that caressed her with such delicate skill and such deft purpose. His mouth was in turn gently ardent, and then fiercely hungry. She responded with her own mindless hunger, dragging a halting moan from him as she ran one hand down his muscular chest and over his lean belly.

Grasping her head between his hands, he took her mouth with such blazing appetite that she feared she would swoon. When he broke their kiss, his eyes were wild and dark. It was a buccaneer smile he flashed at her—rakish, potent, and breathtaking. "You kiss like a wanton, Miss Parnell," he said in a shaking, amused voice. "Will you marry me?"

"Is that your only requirement?" she asked in feigned irritation.

"It's the chief one," he said, trying to keep his dimples at bay. "Well then?"

She pondered a moment. "It's not really fair," she said. "I have no point of comparison. Of kissing, I mean."

His hold on her tightened and he shook her menacingly. "The devil you haven't! If your young professor and your festering Sir

Humpty have neglected you in that area, it is their loss. Now, I asked you a question, and if you can't—"

The bedroom door opened and Mrs. Greene came in bearing a tray. Her eyes widened at the sight of them, standing entwined at the far side of the bed.

"I have a visitor," Lucy said lamely.

"I think she can see that," Roddy said against her ear. He took the opportunity to nibble at a patch of skin and she giggled. He addressed the landlady without releasing his hold on Lucy. "Mrs. Greene, you look like a lady of good sense. Wouldn't you say that Miss Parnell was soundly compromised?"

The woman nodded enthusiastically. "Appears that way to me."

"See," he said to Lucy. "You have to marry me now. Otherwise your reputation in Peel will be in tatters."

Lucy's mouth drew up. "I think that was accomplished when half the town watched you climb through my bedroom window . . . Very well, I know when I am beaten."

"Not beaten, sweetheart. I just wore you down. I warned you about that."

Lucy realized she would probably spend the rest of her life being worn down by his persistent charm. Somehow it sounded like a splendid prospect.

Roddy kissed her swiftly on the cheek and then handed her over to Mrs. Greene. He motioned to the package on the bed and said, "Get her dressed, if you please, ma'am. We've some business in the town."

"But Miss Parnell is ill," the landlady cried. Her eyes went to Lucy, who was flushed and shaking. Lucy set a hand to her cheek. It was still tender from Roddy's kisses, but it felt cool beneath her palm. And the only ache she now felt in her stomach was one of giddy joy.

"I believe I am feeling much better," she pronounced in wonder. Roddy had kissed the fever right out of her.

"Capital," said Roddy from the doorway. "Now make haste. There is someone I want you to meet."

Chapter Sixteen

Yardley was just sitting down to dinner with the Wibberlys when the note from the lawyer arrived. The footman carried it in to him with apologies. "It says 'Urgent,' sir," he whispered as he lowered the silver tray.

Yardley excused himself as he rose from the table. Mr. Wibberly looked across at his lady wife and raised his brows. She shrugged and then pinched her eldest daughter, who had commented under her breath that it must be a love note. Her youngest daughter, Serena, was not at table, having come down with a sick headache. She had taken to her room and asked to be left alone to sleep it off.

Yardley went out to the hall and slit the wafer that sealed the note.

"It is as you and I suspected," Mr. Plimpton had written in a hurried scrawl. "My men exhumed the grave and found the coffin weighted only with sacks of dirt."

Excitement surged through Yardley. Susanne was alive after all! He was somehow not surprised. He'd never been able to picture all her vitality and spirit doused by something as commonplace as death. His heart was racing in his chest as he read on.

"You must come to Peel this evening. Everyone in the district will be there for the earl's fete, and I suspect your stepsister and her child will be among the celebrants. I have made inquiries today and was unable to discover a woman fitting Susanne's description who has a daughter. There is, however, a fair-haired widow with a young son. A Mrs. Pace. Is it possible that, since your niece lied about her own demise she also saw to it that you were misinformed as to the sex of her child?"

Yardley licked his lips. He'd always bitterly regretted that he had no son. No diminutive version of himself that he could shape and mold. He and Sophia had been unable to have children, one of the reasons Susanne's scandalous pregnancy had infuriated him.

He had wanted no part of her bastard daughter, but if she had borne a son it became a whole other matter. He would take the child as his ward and raise it as his own. And bring Susanne back to his home. Sophia would jib at that, but he was master in his own house, after all. The specter of scandal faded—he could live without the promotion to dean—at the thought of having the delectable Susanne once again under his roof.

He called to the footman, who had been hovering at the end of the hall, and ordered the coach. Then he reentered the dining room to explain to his host that he had been called away to Peel.

Roddy had Lucy's arm firmly tucked in his own as they made their way through the town. It wasn't only the jostling, rowdy crowd that made this a necessity—she was still shaky on her feet from her illness, though she claimed she felt just fine.

It was after ten, but the festivities had not diminished. Jugglers and tumblers performed at the cross streets. Revelers spilled noisily out of the open doors of taverns and restaurants, The band playing in the town market square added to the general din of people laughing and calling to each other. There were vendors selling merchandise of every sort. Lucy kept stopping to gaze at the pretty bits of lace, the blown-glass window ornaments, and the jars of candies and sweetmeats in the various stalls. Roddy bought her a long stick of peppermint candy for her throat. She broke it in two and set half in her pocket to save for later.

They turned one corner and saw up ahead of them a flock of sheep, ambling along the thoroughfare like a group of ladies out for an evening of window-shopping. Samson broke from the middle of the herd and came trotting up to them.

Roddy rubbed his knuckles against the bony forehead. "Hello, old fellow. Been keeping out of the brambles?"

The ram snatched a bit of lace from his cuff and began to chew it.

"Come along, Androcles," Lucy muttered. "You've got me agog with curiosity now."

Roddy grinned. They made their way down a narrow alley that opened onto the square. If Lucy was disappointed that he didn't stop in this dark, secluded spot and steal a kiss, she didn't express it. She could feel the excitement simmering off him. Whatever it was he wanted to show her, it was something special. He had assured her of that. Yet she still had doubts.

The cobbled market square was not large. People were crowded into it, right up against the podium where the band played. There were couples dancing off to one side, their steps measured by the mass of people gathered around them.

Lucy craned her head up. She thought she could make out Nonnie jigging furiously with a plump, pretty girl who was dressed as a milkmaid. And surely that was Owen dancing with a woman in a black domino. It was not unlike the domino Lucy wore over her own gown, except that hers was crimson. It had been in the package Roddy had carried into her room—a sweeping crimson cloak and a matching satin mask. She'd never been masked before, it made her feel dangerously liberated. She'd shared this observation with Roddy, who had laughed and told her that was the whole point.

Ahead of them the crowd parted for an instant, and she saw the countess surrounded by a bevy of children. All of them were draped in green and yellow gauze and wearing wire wings.

"She fancied herself as Titania," Roddy whispered close against her ear. "You know, from that Shakespeare play. Tricked out all the servants' children as wood sprites." He chuckled. "Nonnie says she had him and the Joker up half the night gluing gossamer onto wire for the wings,"

"I'd have given a guinea to see that," Lucy said. "And where was Owen? Didn't he help them?"

Roddy's face tensed. "He was . . . consoling the Widow Pace."

Lucy felt her stomach knot. "Consoling? Lord, Roddy, don't tell me something happened to Charlie."

He quickly patted her hand. "No, no. Nothing like that. She just had a bit of a shock, you see. You'll understand in a minute or two, if I can just get Consuelo's attention."

He stood on tiptoe and raised one hand. "Ho, Connie! We're over here . . ."

The countess moved through the crowd like a great ship of state, her shimmering skirts belled out around her, her attendants capering at her sides. She wore a high comb in her golden curls, and from it a sheer veil, sprinkled with tiny golden stars, trailed behind her.

Lucy swept into a deep curtsy as Consuelo came up with them. "Your Highness," she said with a wide grin.

Consuelo shook her head. "You will stand," she said in a husky voice. She took Lucy's hand. "It is I who must bow to you, Miss Parnell. And ask your forgiveness."

Lucy watched in bewilderment as the Countess of Steyne sank

down in a pool of green satin before her. Her eyes never left Lucy's face. When she rose, her expression was still wary.

"She does not know, does she?" she asked Roddy.

"No," he said. "I thought it best to just let her see for herself." He reached around the countess to the freckle-faced sprite who was carrying her train.

"Charlie," he said motioning with one hand.

The boy came forward, his slim body obscured by a tunic of gauze draped with gold tissue. His wings were canted drunkenly, one up above his shoulder and one down near his hip. He was grinning at her expectantly, his dark eyes crinkled into half moons.

Lucy was totally perplexed. If there was something remarkable happening here, she was sure it was far over her head. She gave Roddy a nervous smile and whispered behind her hand. "What am I supposed to do?"

"Wait," he whispered back. "The dance is almost over."

She thought he was being metaphoric, but the band stopped playing almost immediately. Owen and the woman in the black domino came toward them through the crowd.

Lucy studied the woman who walked at Owen's side. She was tall—nearly as tall as Owen—and slender. The dark cloak she wore obscured everything else about her.

As she reached the edge of the circle that was formed by Consuelo and her train of sprites, the woman reached up to undo the strings of her mask. But before her face was revealed, a group of men thrust past Lucy, nearly jarring her to her knees.

"That's him—" one of the men muttered. The next instant Charlie Pace was snatched up and trundled off by a masked man in a black cloak. The man's two accomplices preceded him through the crowd, roughly clearing a path for him and the squirming child.

"Mother!" Charlie cried out over the sounds of the crowd. *"M-o-t-h-e-r!"*

Someone screamed, a long wavering cry. Lucy felt Roddy's hand on her arm, gripping like iron. "Stay here," he growled just before he ran off in pursuit of the three men.

Lucy didn't linger for an instant.

She knew who it was who'd carried off the child, in spite of his cloak and mask. It had been Yardley Abbott; she had recognized his heavy gold signet ring. And if Yardley was interested enough in a child to abduct it in the middle of a fete, then there was only one explanation. Charlie Pace had to be her sister's child.

She pushed and cursed her way through the crowd, following

the sound of Charlie's wails, which carried over the noise of the
revelers. She could see Roddy's hat in the distance, the red feather
bobbing as he ran.

"Please, God," she prayed. "Let Roddy catch him. Please."

Her thoughts tumbled wildly in her head as she ran. None of
this made any sense. Yardley must have gone mad—a nice irony,
considering his constant inferences against her—else why would
he have taken the child? What good would it do him?

And was the mysterious Mrs. Pace the foster parent Lucy had
been trying all week to find? Another neat irony—a woman who
lived almost in the shadow of Ballabragh. And why had Yardley
told Lucy the child was female? Or had Susanne protected her
newborn infant by lying about the baby's sex to Yardley's infor-
mants. There were no answers yet, just the urgent need to stop
Yardley from disappearing with Charlie.

The crowd thinned as she reached the first side street.

Charlie was still yelling at the top of his lungs. "Mother!" And
then his cry changed. "Samson!" he called out. "Samson, come
and save me."

Roddy was gaining on the three men, when two of them
stopped and turned. They blocked the narrow lane where Yardley
was making his escape. Roddy plowed through them, knocking
them both aside. They sprang after him and caught him in three
paces. One burly fellow held his arms, while the other smaller man
swung at his belly. Roddy kicked out and thrashed, but the smaller
man landed several punches.

Lucy plucked up a discarded orange box. She ran up behind the
man who was hitting Roddy and smashed the wooden box over his
head. He snarled and turned on her. He had lost his mask during
his flight. It was Mr. Plimpton, the lawyer. Lucy tugged off her
own mask.

"You!" he cried, reeling back as he brushed the shards of wood
from his balding head.

"Yes," she cried fiercely. "The madwoman of Peel." She raked
her fingers toward him and he backed away. "I will have your
liver." She advanced on him. "Scoundrel! Insect!"

Roddy twisted away from his captor; who was watching Lucy
with something like amazement. Roddy rounded on the man. "You
going to make me hit you again, Tom?" he asked, flexing his fists.
Tom also backed away. His nose was still tender from his last go-
round with the young gentleman. Roddy grasped Lucy by the hand
and together they flew down the lane. They skidded to a halt at the

end of the street. A black coach was racing away from them, heading south along the waterfront.

"He'll take Charlie to the Wibberlys," Lucy gasped, trying to catch her breath.

"No," said Roddy. "They may be toadies, but I doubt they'd abet him in a kidnapping. He'll make for Castleton; he can hire a boat there to take him to Liverpool." He was craning his head up and down the street. He spotted a drowsing horse tethered to a post; it was harnessed to a small market cart. As they neared the cart they saw the remains of vegetables in the back.

Roddy hoisted Lucy onto the seat, then untied the horse. "Don't fret, sweetheart," he said as he climbed up beside her. "He won't get Charlie off the island. I promise."

He whipped up the startled horse and they set off after the coach with a loud clatter.

Lucy held tight to the side of the leather seat. Roddy's urgency must have conveyed itself to the lean, swaybacked horse—he pricked his ears forward and strained against the traces. As they topped a small hill on the outskirts of Peel, they could see the dust raised by the coach ahead of them.

"We'll never catch them," Lucy muttered under her breath. The Wibberly coach was drawn by four blooded horses, while their cart boasted a lone, spindly animal. Roddy growled when he realized she was right. He could whip the poor beast into his grave and still not have a prayer of catching the coach. But still he drove on, along the winding road beside the sea. They had been traveling for about five minutes, the dust from the coach an ever-increasing distance from them, when Roddy gave a low cry and pointed to something up ahead.

Lucy stood up to see what he was pointing at and nearly tumbled from the cart. He caught her around the waist and plunked her back in her seat. "It's fog, Lucy. A bank of fog is moving in off the sea."

She strained her head up to see. Sure enough, a dense white mass was moving swiftly inland, coming up over the low cliff edge in billowing tufts. It was an unnerving sight against the dark night sky.

"Well, that's washed it," she said dismally.

"No," he said as he chucked her under the chin. "It merely evens things up. The coach can't maintain any speed in a fog like that. They may have to pull up altogether. But we can keep on . . .

we're sitting lower down than the coachman, we can see the road more clearly."

When the fog finally encircled them, Roddy handed the reins to Lucy and climbed out to lead the horse. Lucy was sure they were going to pitch over into a ravine, or topple off a cliff at any moment, but Roddy managed to keep them on the rutted road.

They were almost upon the coach before they realized it. Lucy heard Yardley's voice raised in irritation.

"I don't care about the danger to the horses. I order you to drive on."

The driver muttered something in reply.

"Don't give me your insolence, fellow. I will see that you are sacked. Now drive on."

Roddy put a finger to his mouth, motioning Lucy to silence as they climbed from the cart. Together they crept up on the hulking coach. Yardley was half out the door, one booted foot propped on the iron step, all his attention focused on the recalcitrant coachman.

Hand-in-hand, Lucy and Roddy circled around the back of the coach and went to the door on the opposite side. Roddy snicked open the door latch and stuck his head inside.

"Shhh," he said to Charlie. He scooped the child off the seat just as Yardley exited the coach from the other side, slamming the door behind him in fury. Roddy carried Charlie rapidly along the road, into the obscuring fog. He turned to grin at Lucy, but she was no longer behind him.

He stopped and set Charlie down. The child looked up at him in silent gratitude.

"Bring me the brat!" It was Yardley's voice, echoing eerily through the fog. "I know you have him. And I have Lucy. A fair trade, don't you think, Mr. Kempthorne?"

"He has a gun." Lucy said, her tone shivery and shaken. "And he's pointing it at my head."

"Are you mad, Abbott?" Roddy cried. "You'd threaten your own sister's life over this child? A child you took no interest in for seven years."

"That's changed," Yardley said evenly. "The boy should have been mine. I realize that now. Just as Susanne should have been mine."

Roddy felt the small hand slip into his. His heart clenched. "It's going to be all right," he whispered. "I promise he won't take you away."

"But he'll hurt Lucy if I don't go with him."

"I think he's bluffing," Roddy said. At least he hoped it was the truth.

The fog that separated him from Yardley danced away into two streams of white. Roddy saw that he was clutching Lucy by one arm and holding a dueling pistol canted under her chin. Roddy owned a similar pistol—it had a hair trigger and the least thing could set it off. Yardley Abbott did not have the look of a man who was used to handling firearms. Roddy began to pray.

"Abbott," he said reasonably, "this melodrama does not suit you. If you want the child so badly, go back to Peel and have your pet lawyer draw up the papers to make you Charlie's guardian—"

"I *am* the brat's guardian," he snarled. "His mother was my ward and now so is he. I'll have them both in my home, both back where they belong."

Lucy twisted her head around to gape at Yardley, setting the pistol to wavering. Roddy's heart lurched into his throat. "Keep still, Lucy!" he cried.

"You *are* mad!" she cried to her stepbrother. "Susanne is dead. Dead and buried in Parapet."

Yardley began to laugh, a low, frightening sound. "Ah, Lucy. She duped us. Every one of us. She always was a clever harlot."

"My mother is not harlot!" Charlie cried out. "You are a wicked man, and I'm glad I bit you."

Yardley glared at the child. "You'll soon learn better manners at my hands."

"You'll never again get your hands on my child."

The clear voice rang out in the fog. A figure in a black cloak stepped from the wall of wavering whiteness into the clearing. Her mask was gone and the hood of her cloak was pushed back. The fog had set her long, pale hair into deep waves that fell over both shoulders.

"Susanne!" Lucy cried out and staggered against her step-brother.

Roddy took a step toward them, his hands outstretched. "For God's sake, Lucy, keep still."

Susanne's eyes met her sister's. "This wasn't how I'd planned it, Luce." Her gaze moved to her stepbrother. "He's still coming between us, isn't he?" Susanne pushed Charlie behind her. "Stay back, sweetheart," she whispered.

With her other hand she reached into the pocket of her cloak and drew out a small pistol. "Unlike my sister, I keep mine loaded.

My husband was a crack shot," she said evenly. "He claimed I was almost as good as he was."

"Your husband?" Yardley sneered. "You told me he never wed you."

"I lied," she said with a tight smile. "Because it was easier to lie than to be forced back into your home. Home! What a misuse of a pleasant word. No, I let you think I was disgraced, let you send me off to Man. You never knew I had family here, my husband's family. I let you continue sending money, your guilt money, long after I no longer needed it."

More dark shapes had appeared out of the cloud of fog. Owen and Nonnie and the Joker drifted up beside Roddy. Lucy imagined they had brought Susanne here. Unless her sister had just wafted across the moors like a ghost—nothing Susanne did would ever again surprise her.

"This duplicity in you does not surprise me, Susanne," Yardley was saying. "You were ever a wicked, wayward child. And after you were grown, you used your beauty to ensnare men, against their will, against their good judgment . . ."

Yardley's hand on Lucy's arm was trembling as he spoke. She feared the hand that held the pistol must likewise be unsteady. Knowing Yardley, he would natter on endlessly at Susanne until the pistol discharged and meanwhile Lucy would end up with a hole in her throat. She decided it was time for a reckoning with her stepbrother.

"Yardley," she said, interrupting him, "no one here cares a fig about your prosy speeches. You are not in Oxford. This is not a classroom. Now put the pistol down; I want to kiss my sister for the first time in ten years. And if you get in the way, I shall shoot you in the belly."

She jabbed hard into his gut through her cloak. His eyes bulged as he felt the barrel of the gun against his waistcoat. "And it's loaded this time," she muttered.

He lowered his pistol with a soft curse. Roddy moved forward quickly and plucked it from his hands. He was looking at Lucy with some wonder.

"I didn't know you had your pistol with you," he murmured.

"I didn't," she said, grinning. She swept back her cloak to reveal the broken length of peppermint clutched in her hand.

Yardley snarled as Nonnie and the Joker came forward to hold him. "I haven't done anything wrong," he cried. "The boy belongs with me. I am his rightful guardian."

Charlie moved away from Owen, who had been sheltering the child behind his long highwayman's cloak. "I'm not a boy," Charlie declared. "It was only a game Mother asked me to play while Lucy was at the big house. I was in disguise."

Lucy looked at her niece with real recognition for the first time. Here at last was the lost child of her lost sister, who had sent her on this eventful journey. The child who had led her to Salvador. The child who had brought her to this island, where she had first seen the man she loved in a damp gulley.

"Oh, Charlie," Lucy breathed as she knelt down and opened her arms. The little girl ran into them. Lucy hugged her tight, fighting off her tears. "I am so very happy to meet you at last."

"It's really Carlotta," Charlie said, up against her cheek. "But I've always liked being called Charlie. It was what Mother called Papa. Her pet name for him."

Lucy stood up and took Charlie's hand. Together they approached Susanne. Lucy leaned forward and kissed her sister's cheek. "Whatever has passed between us is at an end," she said softly. "I am so happy now"

"Then you don't want an explanation?" Susanne said haltingly.

"I never said that," Lucy responded with a chuckle. "We have a deal of catching up to do."

She motioned to Nonnie and the Joker, who were still holding Yardley. "You might as well let him go. He can't get up to any further mischief."

Yardley shook them off like a dog shedding rain. He straightened his shirt cuffs and ran a hand over his thin hair. He glared at Susanne and Lucy, refusing to admit defeat. "You are wrong there. I mean to pursue this matter. I have the means to take the child from you, Susanne. You are a woman without money or power. You have no prospects. And it's clear you have let the child run wild. Just look at her . . . dressed as a boy—"

"I'm a wood sprite," Charlie protested. "A *girl* wood sprite."

"The courts will favor my petition, you know that, don't you, Susanne? They will discover I am a man of stature, of consequence—"

"You are a pompous windbag," Roddy drawled. "I expect the courts will discover that, too."

"And Mrs. Pace is not without prospects," Owen added, taking up Susanne's hand. "I intend to marry her."

"And who might you be?" Yardley asked from over his long nose.

"Owen Griffith," the Joker said. "Of Griffith Shipping. He doesn't like to talk about it, but his father supplied half the ships in the Royal Navy."

Yardley opened his mouth to make some withering comment and at that exact moment a loud *baah* resounded through the fog. Samson came thundering down the hillside, his ewes close behind him. The mealy white of the flock blended with the grayish white of the heavy mist so that the sheep appeared to be a living incarnation of some Olympian fog.

Charlie didn't hesitate a moment. She stepped forward, pointing a finger toward Yardley and cried, "Get him, Samson!"

The ram veered in his course and headed straight for the man. Nonnie and the Joker scrambled back.

Yardley laughed dryly. "Am I supposed to run away from sheep?"

"I would," Roddy said from behind his hand. "He's got a devilish temper."

When Yardley realized the ram was not slowing down, he began walking rapidly toward the Wibberlys' coach. The driver looked back over his shoulder and saw that the obnoxious, overbearing gentleman was about to take shelter in the coach. Not in his lifetime, he vowed. He whipped up his horses just as Yardley's hand reached for the door latch.

The vehicle skittered away. Yardley chased after it for several yards, and then slowed down. And sped up again when he realized the four-horned ram was nearly on his tail. He ran down the rutted road, his long legs pumping furiously as he bellowed for the coachman to stop. Samson caught him at a turning in the road. The spectators watched in awe as Yardley Abbott sailed a full ten feet over the turf and landed in a ravine.

Samson trotted back to Charlie with a smug expression on his shaggy face. Lucy gave him the remains of her peppermint stick and scratched him between the horns. That had almost been as rare as watching Roddy knock down Yardley's hired thug. Almost.

"You think he's dead?" Nonnie asked of no one in particular.

"Only if there's justice in the world," the Joker responded. "We'd best go see, though. Don't want to leave him there cluttering up the landscape."

Lucy and Susanne sat beside Roddy in the vegetable cart during the drive back to Peel. Yardley lay in the back, in a moaning stupor, among the wilted lettuce leaves and rotted mangel-wurzels. At least one of his legs was broken; Roddy had laid a large bet with the Joker that they both were. Charlie had gone along with the others in Nonnie's carriage. She'd been nearly asleep when Owen lifted her onto the seat.

However, Lucy and Susanne were wide awake. As Lucy had observed, they had a world of things to talk over. Roddy attended them with one ear, and with the other he satisfied himself by listening to Yardley s groans every time the cart jostled over a rut, which was frequently.

"Consuelo knew all along?" Lucy was saying.

Susanne nodded. "When she came here two years ago, I started sewing for her. It wasn't long before we became friends."

"You couldn't stitch a sampler without muddling it dreadfully," Lucy remarked. "I am amazed that you found someone to pay you for sewing."

"I learned while I was in Spain." She squeezed her sister's hand. "I learned many things there, Lucy. How to survive, mostly. How to endure. And I loved the people. That was what brought the countess and me together. We would spend hours talking of Spain. I even cooked for her sometimes, things that she loved."

Her voice lowered. "And then late last week, I got some disturbing news from her. A woman named Lucy Parnell was staying at the inn in Peel. And she was looking for a lost child. Consuelo wanted to bring you to Ballabragh, so she could determine what sort of person you were. She sent Roddy off to fetch you."

"I had no idea," he interjected quickly. "She just said you should not be staying at the Greene Man alone. I didn't know any of this, Lucy, I swear."

"No," Susanne said. "Mr. Kempthorne was not part of things until very recently."

"But why, Susanne?" Lucy pleaded softly. "Why didn't you just reveal yourself to me?"

Her sister squirmed on her seat. "I thought about it, at first. But then I heard that Yardley was here too. I couldn't risk coming forward then. He believed me dead, and so had no further interest in my child. But once he discovered I was alive . . . well, you saw what happened. He was going to use Charlie to coerce me to return to his home."

"But I still don't understand," Lucy said. "Surely I wouldn't have betrayed you to Yardley. You knew how I felt about him."

"Did I?" Susanne said in a hollow voice. "When he came to me in London, Lucy, he told me that you had sent him. That you wanted nothing to do with me any longer, because I had run off and upset Mama. Sent her into madness, was how he put it. How could I know that was not true? He was carrying the note I'd sent you, it seemed the only logical conclusion. That was why I cut myself off from you for all these years. I thought you detested me."

"Oh, Susanne!" Lucy clutched her shoulder. "I thought I had betrayed you inadvertently, because Yardley followed me and found your note. But I would have never given you away intentionally. I loved you. I missed you so dreadfully." Her voice broke.

This time Roddy had his handkerchief at the ready. He had learned to carry at least two when he was with Lucy. He handed it over without a word, but his mouth had quirked up into a crooked grin. She snuffled into it for a few seconds and then Susanne took it from her and wiped her own eyes.

"It was your Mr. Kempthorne who told me what really happened," Susanne continued. "How Yardley followed you that night and took the note from you. You must forgive Consuelo . . . she thought, as I did, that you had betrayed me. It bewildered her, since she sensed you were not a vengeful person. And Connie is a very good judge of people."

Lucy sighed. "She told me she saw betrayal in the Tarot cards. I thought she was rather omniscient, but she was just well-informed . . . That was you, that first night, under the black veil, wasn't it? Not Zuzu her maid."

Susanne nodded. "I wanted to have a look at you. I borrowed Zuzu's dress and veil. It shook me badly to see you again after so long. You looked so worn and sad. And then I thought, well, why shouldn't she be sad? She has wronged the only person she has left in the world. I'm sorry for thinking that, Lucy."

"I wondered why the dresses from the countess fit me so well . . . but then you and I were always the same size."

Roddy thought it was time to have his say. He leaned across Lucy to address Susanne. "Tell me one thing, Mrs. Pace—knowing as you did, how Yardley was capable of twisting the truth, why didn't you ever make an effort to reach your sister after you came here?"

Susanne bit at her lip. "I did attempt to reach you once, Lucy. I went to Manchester . . . to visit our mother. Consuelo had managed to track down where the two of you were living. But I was so upset, Mama was so far gone by then, she thought I was a friend from her days in London. I blamed myself for her condition. And so I couldn't face you, Lucy. I discovered that she died the next winter."

Lucy stared at her. "You were in Manchester . . . you went to the gatehouse at the Burbridges?"

"It was during the day, while you were with your charges. Mother never told you I was there, I gather." Her voice wavered, at the edge of tears. "Well, she didn't really know I was there."

"It's all right, Suse," Lucy said consolingly. "She wasn't unhappy. She puttered in the garden nearly every day. She could still remember the names of all the flowers, even if she forgot the names of her daughters. She thought I was Great Aunt Matilda a deal of the time. Used to ask me where Uncle William was."

Susanne tried not to chuckle, but it bubbled out. Soon both sisters were laughing, their arms around each other. Lucy tipped her head back and wiped the tears from Susanne's face with her thumb. "Little sister," she said fondly. "I didn't mind looking after her. You had Charlie to raise and I suppose in a way I had Mama. If that makes any sense."

Roddy cocked his head. "There is still something I don't quite get, Mrs. Pace. I understand why you wanted your brother to think you had died. But why not let him think the child had died, as well?"

"Mmm," Lucy said. "Why not just sever all ties with him?"

Susanne shook her head slowly. "When you have a baby of your own, Lucy, you will know why I could not do that. They are so fragile, so delicate, that you fear a puff of wind might carry them away. I could not report my child dead, not without fearing to bring a curse upon her."

"Consuelo understood that part, I bet," Roddy remarked.

"So Yardley believed I was dead," Susanne went on, "but he kept sending money to the lawyer for the child. I did need it in the beginning; I didn't want to be a burden on Carlton's family. After a few years, I began to sew for the ladies of the district. I also learned to weave from Carlton's grandmother; I started earning enough to live on and when the midwife died, I stopped collecting Yardley's money."

Susanne turned to Lucy, "And then Consuelo came to the island and as I've told you, we became friends. I did what I could to relieve her grief, but it took you, my stalwart sister, to get her out of her bed. You always were the one to get things done. I never told you how much I admired you for that, and for staying on with Papa."

"You did?" Lucy said softly.

"It's true. You were always the dutiful daughter, while I was the flyaway child. Well, you see how Charlie is . . . is she not exactly like me at that age?"

Lucy nodded. "Yes, that was the year Mama took you back to London. I felt as though I'd lost my favorite spaniel. And I mean that as a compliment."

"I left you with a great many burdens, Luce. Our mother to look after, Yardley to contend with. I've had a very pleasant life here. I do not think I can say the same for you."

Roddy plucked up Lucy's hand and kissed it quickly. "But she will, Mrs. Pace. As Consuelo's cards promised, she will be brimming over with happiness."

They had planned to reconvene in the parlor of the Greene Man. Roddy set Lucy and Susanne down at the inn's front door, where Owen was waiting, and drove on with Yardley to the doctor's home. The surgeon, who had been partaking of plum brandy during the fete, came out of his house and gaped at Yardley as though he were an oversized haddock that had somehow crawled up from the surf.

"Do what you can to mend him," Roddy told the man. "Or shoot him if he can't be mended."

Yardley, who had at last recovered consciousness, started to complain in a loud voice. Roddy looked down at him and shook his head. "And see if you can't do something about that noise he keeps making."

"What sort of noise is that?" the surgeon asked eagerly, thinking of lung congestions and influenzas.

"It's called talking," Roddy pronounced, gingerly removing a piece of rotted turnip from Yardley's hair.

He was whistling as he made his way back to the Greene Man. Everything had sorted itself out nicely. Lucy and her sister were reunited. Owen and Susanne were well along toward a happy understanding. Connie had a child to raise, Nonnie had a brother to look after. Charlie could return to being a little girl, a shepherdess instead of a shepherd. Samson had his ewes, and Roddy had Lucy, not that that was a very flattering comparison. The Joker was the only one who had not benefitted somehow from their adventures. Still, he was wealthy and quite good-looking. Roddy had actually caught him conversing with Lucy without that disdainful curl of his lip and without a lecherous gleam in his eyes. There was hope for the viscount yet.

Lucy met him in front of the inn. "It's too crowded in there," she said, as she slipped her hand into his. He led her back toward the water and they walked along, not talking for the first hundred paces. A street sweeper went by them, collecting up the debris from the fete. Roddy watched him go past, and then turned to Lucy. "I've been thinking about what sort of work I would like to do."

She nearly started back. "Work, Roddy? Whyever would you need to work?"

He shifted one shoulder. "I don't know . . . just to pass the time. I was thinking perhaps there was something we could do together."

"I can think of several things," she drawled.

"Ho," he said with a chuckle, "that was the Joker, to the life. I had really better get you away from those plaguey fellows before they corrupt you completely."

"So what was your idea?"

He tugged the lace at his throat. "It was actually more MacHeath's idea. He suggested we start a home for foundlings . . . since we proved ourselves so adept at finding babies here on this island. Not the usual sort of home, mind you. Not a dark, dreary place, but one where there is grass and open spaces. And toys to play with and animals to romp with. I expect we will need to find a teacher . . . for the older ones. Someone who knows her play-wrights and her—"

Lucy was kissing him, her hands twined in his hair, her body pressed up against him in full sight of the street cleaner and the few vendors who had not yet packed up. She was kissing him with all her strength and all her heart.

When at last she pulled back, he was the one who was breathless.

"I take it that's a yes," he said weakly.

"It's bad enough you own my heart, Roddy Kempthorne," she said crossly. "But do you have to read my mind, as well? That is exactly what I have been thinking for days now . . . that you need to do something worthwhile, something of value."

"*We* need to," he amended. "Besides having babies of our own, that is." He motioned with his head back toward the inn. "I don't suppose you'd like to start tonight."

She grinned up at him, her ramshackle boy, and then kissed him again. "Mr. Greene would surely call the bailiff then."

"Hmm, you think so?"

"We'd be making so much noise," she assured him slyly. "He'd have to call in the county militia."

He tucked her hand again under his arm and they continued down the lane. He stopped a short while later. "I have another capital idea."

"Yes, dearest?" she said and watched in satisfaction as his eyes lit up.

"I believe we must invite Yardley to our wedding . . . no, wait, hear me out. We'll be wed at Carillon and I'll tell my parents to put on their most high-in-the-instep behavior. If you think the Joker keeps his nose in the air, you should see my father when someone tries to toad-eat him."

"No," she said after some reflection. "I think we've evened the score with my stepbrother. Well, Samson did, at any rate. But speaking of your ancestral home, did I ever tell you that I went there once with my family? It was when we visited England the year before Mama moved back here with Susanne. I must have been nine or so at the time."

Roddy looked out over the water. The lights around Peel Castle had been extinguished and the castle was now a dark shadow against the velvet curtain of the night. The moon had likewise set; the party was over, the celestial lantern had been snuffed. For Roddy, however, the party was likely just getting started.

"Roddy?" Her voice was a soft sigh on the cool evening air.

He turned back and touched his brow to hers. "I was going to tell you this after we were married," he began haltingly "So you couldn't skitter away, thinking I was a bit mad myself."

"What is it?" Her hands were tight on his arms.

"When I was four years old, my brothers lured me into the boxwood maze behind our house, and left me there in the center. I was quite stouthearted as a boy, and thought nothing of it. But then the hours passed and I couldn't find my way out. I grew hungry, and then angry. Then, as the afternoon waned, I grew frightened. And I began to cry."

Lucy's heart had started missing beats. She knew where he was going with this tale.

"A very pretty young girl came across me. She'd gotten separated from her family on the grounds of the house. She picked me up from the bench, dried my tears with her jasmine-scented handkerchief and led me from the maze. Just like that."

"It was my mother's favorite scent," Lucy murmured. "I've always worn it."

"Do you remember that boy?" he asked, gazing at her from beneath his thick lashes. "Say you do, Lucy, even if you don't."

"Of course I remember," she said softly, standing on tiptoe to whisper against his ear. "He was wearing a green jacket, and had boxwood leaves in his hair, and I thought to myself, he's got the bluest eyes I've ever seen."

"Ah, you do remember, sweetheart. And you couldn't know this, because I never said it out loud, but the entire time I was lost, I just kept crying inside, 'Find me, someone please find me.'"

Lucy's eyes widened. "It was you? In my dream?" A slow smile replaced her expression of shock. "Oh, Roddy, it makes sense now. It was *you* I came here to find."

Ah, she understands at last! he mused triumphantly.

"It was all of us, sweetheart," he said aloud in a low, soothing voice. "Me and Salvador. Charlie and Susanne. I told you you make a proper little bloodhound." He touched the tip of her nose. "I told you something else once, Miss Parnell." He had twined his arms around her and was pulling her close.

"What was that, Mr. Kempthorne?"

He nudged the edge of her red satin cloak aside with his chin and then set his mouth on her throat. "I told you," he said as he felt her shiver under his hands, "that I would undress you in crimson."

"'Tis a consummation devoutly to be wished for," she murmured as her eyes closed in bliss.

"Not Shakespeare," he groaned, laughing against her hair. "No more festering playwrights."

Nonnie was wandering the streets, wishing he'd had the brains to ask the name of the pretty milkmaid he'd been dancing with. Between dances, she'd shared a lemonade with him and chattered easily about all the things that interested him—horses and dogs and the irrigation of farmland. But then he'd had to run off after that wretch Yardley Abbott, and by the time they'd returned the fete had been ending. He was tired and dispirited, though very happy for Roddy and Snowball. They'd be marrying sisters, which had a sort of rightness to it, since they were like brothers themselves. He wondered if he would ever meet a woman like Lucy, who was wise, or like Susanne, who was determined to follow her own path. A woman who would see past his rather large nose and discover he had an equally large heart.

In the lane that crossed directly ahead of him, a farm wagon creaked by, a flock of sleepy revelers crowded into the back.

"Wait, Geordie!" a young woman's voice cried. The youth at the reins pulled up his team.

"Honestly, Rena," he complained, "I've driven this wagon all over Peel looking for that fellow, and now I need to get my friends back home. We have to be in the fields tomorrow, even if you can sleep in."

But she wasn't attending him. Nonnie watched as she struggled from the back of the wagon and leapt down to the street. Her slippers pattered on the cobblestones as she came toward him.

"I'm sorry," she said breathlessly. "Sorry to be so forward. I just wanted to tell you how much I enjoyed dancing with you. And to say that you look very elegant in your uniform."

She paused then, waiting for him to make some reply. Nonnie didn't seem to be able to formulate words just then. She was so pretty, with her apple cheeks and saucy eyes. She possessed the merest snub of a nose; he was sure he wanted to kiss it. And her round, rosy mouth. But he just stood there gaping.

"Well," she said a bit awkwardly after a long moment had passed, "I'd better get back to my friends. I sneaked out tonight and there will be the devil to pay if I am caught."

She started walking away and Nonnie came out of his trance.

"It was my pleasure to dance with you," he called out. "The best birthday present I've ever had."

"Oh, was it your birthday too?" she asked artlessly. "I mean as well as the earl's. I've never met him but my parents say he is a dreadful fellow. Still, he did have a very nice fete, didn't he?"

"Very nice indeed," Nonnie said with feeling.

She was halfway to the farm wagon, when he said in a carrying voice. "I would like to call on you if I may."

She was smiling widely when she turned back to him. "I would like that above anything. I live north of Castleton. My name is Serena. Serena Wibberly."

"Oh, by George," said Nonnie in a husky, shaken whisper.

And so it was, that the longstanding feud between the Wibberlys and the Swithens of the Isle of Man came to be resolved. And in a manner that would have pleased the Bard of Avon no end.